THE EXORCISM OF SOFIA FLORES

THE MERCILESS II
THE EXORCISM OF SOFIA FLORES

DANIELLE VEGA

RAZORBILL

AN IMPRINT OF PENGUIN RANDOM HOUSE

RAZORBILL

An Imprint of Penguin Random House
Penguin.com

alloyentertainment

Produced by Alloy Entertainment
1325 Avenue of the Americas
New York, NY 10019

Copyright © 2016 Alloy Entertainment

ISBN: 978-1-59514-727-1

Printed in the United States of America

3 5 7 9 10 8 6 4

Design by Liz Dresner

THE EXORCISM OF SOFIA FLORES

CHAPTER ONE

I stand at the living room window, staring at the empty house across the street. A single strand of old Christmas lights dangles from the roof. Half the bulbs have burned out.

A woman and her son lived there until this morning. They didn't even say good-bye, just packed their things and disappeared, like everyone else in this neighborhood. I'm surprised it took them this long. After all, no one wants to live across the street from the murder house.

I exhale, fogging the glass. Rain lashes at the window and turns our yard into a swamp. A red Matchbox car floats down the driveway in a muddy river.

I stare at the churning water and try to breathe, but the air in the house feels thick. It's like inhaling sand. I cup my hands and place them over my mouth, forcing my lungs to draw in a ragged wheeze. I exhale through my fingers and choke down another gasp of air.

Breathe, I tell myself. My eyes flutter closed. *It's just a panic attack.* My chest unclenches, and I take a longer drag through my nose. The room stops spinning. I'm in control again.

I grab my phone off the coffee table. Mom is the first in my short list of favorites. The rest—Grace, Riley, and Alexis—are dead. I cast another glance out the window. Row after row of empty houses stare back at me, the tattered FOR SALE signs perched in their yards like warnings.

I hit Call and a photo of my mom, Sergeant Nina Flores, flashes across the screen. She glares at me over a bowl of cereal, a single Honey Nut Cheerio stuck to her cheek. Normally, her appearance is military-precise, but I caught her before her coffee.

The sight of Mom's face calms me a little.

"Chill, Sofia," I mutter to myself, lifting the phone to my ear.

Mom answers her phone mid-ring. "Sofia?"

"Mom?" Relief seeps through me. "Where are you?"

"I'm still at work, Sof. Is everything okay?"

I clutch the phone with both hands, shooting another look out the window. "I thought you were coming home early today."

"I told Jodi that I'd cover for everyone who took off early for Thanksgiving . . . Why? Did something happen?"

"No, I just—" I glance at the empty house across the street. It was different when I knew there was someone living there, even if she kept her curtains closed and averted her eyes whenever she saw me. "I just don't want to be alone."

Mom is silent for a beat. "Did you have another attack?" she asks, her voice gentle. When I don't answer, she sighs. "Honey, did you try the breathing exercises Dr. Keller taught you?"

I drop onto the couch and take another pull of air. Dr. Keller is the therapist who helped me realize that what happened last summer was a mental breakdown. In other words: *not real*. Because of him, I could finally accept that Brooklyn didn't make blood rain from Riley's ceiling, she didn't set fires with her mind, and she definitely didn't pull out Riley's heart with her bare hands.

He told me that I don't have evil inside of me. Just guilt.

He said that witnessing Riley's murder traumatized me, and I made up a story to cope. And I want to believe

Dr. Keller. But sometimes I can still hear the sound of Riley's heart falling to the ground. I still feel Brooklyn's lips on my cheek.

We don't kill our own was the last thing she said to me before disappearing into the woods. The police never found her.

"The exercises helped, I guess," I mumble into the phone.

Mom exhales. "See? It's like he said after your last session: the most important thing is to learn how to control your fear so it can't control you."

I pick at the skin next to my thumbnail. Brooklyn could be outside my house right now. My guilty conscience may have invented some of what happened over the summer. But Brooklyn was real, and she killed my three best friends.

Dr. Keller can prescribe all the breathing exercises he wants, but even he can't keep me from being afraid.

"How's *Abuela*?" Mom asks.

I shift my eyes to the staircase at the edge of the living room. Grandmother's rosary beads click against her table upstairs like a metronome, slowly counting the seconds. Yesterday, she woke up coughing and gasping in the middle of the night. She had a slight fever and her skin was clammy, but her temperature came down this morning, so we decided not to take her to the emergency room. "She's okay. She's breathing normally and her temp was at ninety-eight point six degrees," I say. "I checked when I got home from school."

"Good. I'm glad she's feeling better." Mom clears her throat. "And how's the rest of your day been?" she asks.

I frown and tug at a thread coming loose from my jeans. "Fine. Boring."

"What, no big Thanksgiving break party?" She's trying to be funny, but her voice sounds strained. She knows I don't have any friends left in this town. Charlie is the only person I still know in Friend, Mississippi, and he hasn't spoken to me since the night I stole his truck and tried to save Riley. I've barely said a word to another classmate since I found Grace's dead body hanging from our shed. The thread unravels, leaving a tiny hole in my jeans. I press down on the fabric, but the hole won't magically knit itself back together. None of the holes in my life will.

"Mom," I whisper, the word cracking in my mouth. "Why do we have to stay here?"

A sigh echoes through the phone. "Sofia . . ."

I blink hard to keep from crying. "Dr. Keller says this environment is toxic for me, and everyone else has already moved away. We could go back to Arizona, or—"

"I'm stationed here, in Friend. I have another sixteen months before I can apply for reassignment."

"But—"

"It's my job, Sofia. You know how the army works. There's nothing I can do."

I lay back on the couch, swallowing the rest of my argument. We've talked about this before. A lot. Silence stretches between us. Wind presses against the glass of the windows, and thunder rumbles in the distance. It reminds me of a car engine, except cars don't drive down this street anymore.

"Sweetie," Mom says, her voice a bit softer, "sometimes I wish we could leave, too. Even I get jealous of how everyone else can pack up and go. Our life is just a little more complicated than that. What's that needlepoint your grandmother has on her wall? Jealousy is cancer, or—"

"Jealousy is like cancer in your bones," I correct her. "It's from the Bible."

Mom releases a small laugh. "Right. Jealousy will eat you up inside if you let it, so let's try to look for a silver lining. Do you think you can do that?"

I shrug, even though I know Mom can't see me. "I guess."

There's a pause. "Look, I might be able to convince Jodi to let me leave a few minutes early," Mom says. "Everyone's already left for the holiday, so there's not much to take care of. How about I swing by China

Garden to pick up some takeout, and we can watch *The Wizard of Oz?*"

A small smile tugs at the corner of my lips. *The Wizard of Oz* is my favorite movie. We watch it whenever I have a bad day. "That sounds okay," I say.

"I'll call ahead and order the usual. See you soon."

"Thanks, Mom. Love you."

"Love you. Now do your homework."

"Roger that," I say, and we both hang up.

Reluctantly, I flip through my dog-eared copy of Shakespeare's *The Tempest* and open up my laptop. My last three schools have all done a unit on *The Tempest*. I could probably recite the entire play from memory. I stifle a yawn and my eye twitches.

The cover of *The Tempest* shows a girl in a blue dress staring out over a stormy sea. She has her back to me, her tangled red hair blowing in the wind. Miranda has been stranded on a deserted island with a crazy magician for twelve years but I'd still trade places with her in a second. Deserted island beats murder house any day.

Just looking at her makes my eyelids feel heavy. I'm supposed to write an essay detailing the major themes and, even though I've read the play *three* times, I can't think of a single thing to write. I stare at the blank Word document on my laptop. The cursor blinks mockingly. The sound of my grandmother's rosary beads echoes down the stairs and, after a second, the blinking and the clicking match up.

Blink. *Click.* Blink. *Click.* Blink.

I tear my eyes away from the screen and pick up *The Tempest.*

The girl on the cover stares right at me, a terrible smile on her face.

I jump up, banging my knee—*hard*—on the coffee table. I wheeze in pain at the shock. The book goes flying and hits the wall with a smack and then drops to the carpet, faceup. My heart is pounding so hard that I want to throw up.

I don't want to look. But I *have* to look. I lift my head.

The cover of *The Tempest* is normal again. Miranda stares out over the sea, her hair teased out behind her. No demon smile. I unclench my fists and stop holding my breath. The nausea has passed.

I sink back onto the couch and pull my computer onto my lap. My knee pulses with pain. I'll have an ugly purple bruise tomorrow, but I won't be able to distinguish it from the others. I've been so jumpy lately that I'm covered in welts and marks.

I lower my fingers to the keyboard and type: *Power and enslavement, the favored and the forsaken, lovers and masters. These major themes of* The Tempest—

My screen freezes. I frown and tap on the keys. Nothing.

"Shit," I mutter. I slide a finger over the trackpad, but the cursor doesn't move. It's not even blinking. I groan and close my eyes, pinching the bridge of my nose with two fingers. This is just perfect. My knee aches, my brain feels mushy, and now my computer's not working. It's like the universe doesn't actually want me to get anything done.

I open my eyes and reach for the power button to restart. A blank window pops onto the screen.

"What the hell?" I whisper. A cursor appears. Someone starts to type.

Hello, Sofia.

Fear curdles in my stomach. This isn't happening. My eyes must be playing tricks on me.

A GIF of a skinned cat opens on the desktop. Flies crawl over its limp, pink tongue, and its cloudy eyes stare out at me from a raw, bloody face. Someone painted a pentagram on the dead grass, and dripping candles form a circle around its rotting body.

Every other sound in the house goes silent. I can't hear the rain or Grandmother's rosary, but my breathing magnifies in my ears until the ragged gasps overwhelm me. I remember the smell of that cat. Milk gone sour. Fish left in the heat. I press the computer's power button, hoping to erase the image that's already seared into my brain. It won't turn off.

Another photograph appears. It's Alexis's dead body, crumpled beneath the second-story window of the abandoned house. I still don't know if she jumped or was pushed. The curve of her twisted limbs is deeply unnatural. A beautiful broken doll. She stares up at the sky, a thin line of blood dribbling from her lips. Her fingers curl toward her palms, as though she's reaching for someone.

I jerk away from the sofa and stumble to my feet, the laptop tumbling to the ground.

"Stop it," I whisper. I back up against the wall as more pictures flash across the computer screen.

A girl holding a butcher knife. Bloody handprints. Cockroaches racing across the floor.

Then a video file pops up, blocking all the other images. A train races toward the screen, headlights flashing. A horn blares, followed by a high, piercing scream. I press myself into the wall behind me, my breath fast and ragged. I'd know that scream anywhere. Karen. The girl I killed.

I squeeze my eyes shut and throw my hands over my ears. "Stop it!" I shout. "Please!"

Laughter echoes through the house.

I open my eyes and spin around, certain I'm going to see Brooklyn standing behind me smiling her terrible demon smile. But I'm alone. The laughing grows louder.

"Please," I whisper. My hands start to shake. I curl them into fists and hug them to my chest. *"Please* stop."

"So-fi-a," someone says in a singsong voice, making the hair on my arms stand up. The voice is coming from the laptop speakers.

"You're one of us, Sofia," Brooklyn says. "I'm coming for you."

"No!" I shout, and I jerk awake, gasping.

I'm lying on the couch, my computer still balanced on my lap. There's nothing on the screen except for a blank Word document and a blinking cursor. The storm beats against the windows and my grandmother's rosary beads click away upstairs. Otherwise, it's dead quiet. My chest rises and falls as I try to catch my breath. It was a nightmare. Just like all the other nightmares I've had since the day Brooklyn killed Riley and revealed my horrible secret. No one else knows that I dragged a girl onto the train tracks at my last school. Not Dr. Keller. Not even my mother.

Tears spill onto my cheeks. I try to wipe them away but they come too quickly, blurring my vision and making my breath hitch. I vowed that I would never think about that night again. It was an accident, a moment of insanity. And, after everything that happened with Brooklyn, I've more than paid for my crime.

I start to do my exercises, but my hands shake so

badly that I can't keep them cupped around my mouth. I grab my phone to call Mom again, then pause.

The time blinks at me from the home screen: 9:47. I click on my recent calls list. I talked to Mom at six fifty-two. Almost three hours ago.

"What the hell?" I murmur. I wipe the last of the tears from my eyes. "Mom?" I call, pushing myself to my feet. "Are you there?"

I listen for Mom's voice, or the sound of her footsteps. There's nothing.

The doorbell rings, making me jump.

Nerves crawl over my skin like spiders. We never get visitors. I take a step toward the door, thinking of vacant eyes and bloody footprints and tattered skin.

I don't want to answer it, but the doorbell rings again.

CHAPTER TWO

"**M**iss?" a man calls through the door. It's a deep, unfamiliar voice. I lower my hand to the knob and turn, holding my breath as I pull the door open.

A police officer in a stiff blue uniform stands on our porch, a squad car waiting at the curb. His partner sits in the passenger seat. She holds a walkie-talkie in one hand, barking orders that I can't hear.

Calling for backup, I think, and fear shoots up my spine.

"Are you Sofia Flores?" the officer asks. I nod, resisting the urge to slam the door in his face and turn the dead bolt. The last time the cops were here was the night we found Grace's body.

I listened for sirens for weeks afterward, certain Brooklyn would tell them the truth about the train accident. But the cops never found Brooklyn, and my secret remains safe. The manhunt for her continues.

I watched the rust-colored bloodstains on our driveway fade under the sun and rain until, finally, Mom scrubbed them away with a bucket of bleach and a thick, wiry brush.

That's it, I remember thinking. *It's over.*

"Miss?" The cop narrows his eyes. Rain drips from his uniform, leaving puddles on the porch. "Are you okay?"

"Fine," I say. I brace myself for the silver flash of handcuffs, for the officer to jerk my arms behind my back and tell me I have the right to remain silent. "What's wrong?"

"I'm afraid your mother, Nina Flores, was in a car accident."

The words fall flat. It takes me a long time to process what he's saying. "I . . . I don't understand."

"Sofia, your mother died in the ambulance on her way to the hospital. I'm so sorry."

I stare at the officer's mouth. His lips are chapped, and there's a tiny gap between his two front teeth. He's still speaking, but I can't hear him. The entire world has gone still. I tighten my fingers around the doorknob and focus all my attention on the way my skin feels against the brass. The sweat gathering between my fingers.

"Miss?" The officer's voice jars me back to the present. "Is there someone else here you'd like me to speak to?"

I shake my head. "I just spoke to my mother on the phone. She's fine."

Something passes through the officer's eyes. *Pity*. I curl my hand into a fist and bang it against the door. The wood rattles.

"I'm sorry—"

"You've made a mistake!" I shout. But the anger dies as soon as the words leave my mouth. I feel weak. Empty.

"Is your father home?" the officer asks.

"He died," I say in a hollow voice. "When I was little."

"What about an aunt or an uncle?" I shake my head, and the officer lifts his walkie-talkie to his mouth. "We're going to need CPS here right away," he says.

CPS—Child Protective Services.

"Roger that, over," comes crackling over the radio.

"That's okay. I'm okay, thank you." I close the door before he can say another word. I can still see his shadow through the cloudy glass panes on either side of the door. He stands on our porch for a moment; then I hear the sound of his shoes on the stairs, walking away. He'll be back. Along with a bunch of strangers who'll decide what to do with me.

I press my hand flat against the wall, steadying myself. *Your mother died in the ambulance on her way to the hospital.* I shake my head. It's not real. I just talked to her. We're going to eat Chinese food and watch *The Wizard of Oz*.

I grab my cell phone and I dial Mom's number. The silly Cheerios photo pops onto my screen. Something in my gut twists.

Mistake, I tell myself. *This is all a mistake.* Mom's fine. I lift the phone to my ear and hold my breath, waiting for her to pick up.

The phone rings. And rings. A hollow space opens inside my chest. It feels as if someone has tunneled through my internal organs, leaving a hole straight through the middle of my body. Mom always answers my calls, even when she's on duty.

I let my mind travel to the dark place. *Your mother died.* My hands start to tremble. *Car accident.*

A cruel voice echoes through my head. *And why was she in the car, Sofia?* it asks, sounding eerily like Brooklyn. I swallow, tasting something sour at the back of my throat. Mom was only driving because I begged her to come home early. Because I couldn't stand to be here alone.

The phone slips from my fingers, but I don't hear it hit the floor. The sound of static erupts in my ears.

This is my fault. And now I'm alone—an orphan.

I don't remember walking across the living room and climbing the stairs, but when I look up, I'm standing in front of Grandmother's room. Deep red light spills into the hall. It's the color of the wine they serve during communion. The color of blood. Rosary beads click against the table.

"Abuela?" I push the door all the way open. Grandmother is sitting upright in her narrow hospital bed, sliding the rosary beads through skeletally thin fingers. Several years ago, she had a stroke that left half her body paralyzed. She lost control of the muscles in her cheeks, making her face look like something melted. Skin drips from her face like candle wax, and one side of her mouth curves in a perpetual frown. I see her scalp through her wispy white hair.

I step inside the room, shifting around the cardboard boxes of Grandmother's things. Mom and I always said we'd unpack them, but we never found the time to do more than put away her clothes and lean a few of her pictures against the walls. Her favorite framed needlepoint sits on the table beside her bed.

A peaceful heart leads to a healthy body, it reads. *Jealousy is like a cancer in the bones.* Proverbs 14:30.

The pain hits all at once, like a blow to the chest.

Mom and I are never going to unpack the rest of Grandmother's room. She's never going to pick up my calls or eat Cheerios or watch that scene in *The Wizard of Oz* that she loves, the one where Dorothy falls asleep in the field of red poppies. She's gone. Forever. Because of me.

My legs crumple beneath me, and I sink to the floor, banging my hip against Grandmother's bedside table on my way down. The needlepoint falls over, sliding back behind the table. I'm shaking all over. I can't breathe. I cup my hands around my mouth and inhale, but my exhale explodes into a choked sob. I cover my face with my hands and cry.

I wish I could go back in time and tell her not to get in that car. I don't need Chinese food and movies. I'm not scared anymore. I can be brave, just like her.

Grandmother stares straight ahead, clutching the rosary to her chest. Her brittle nails curl over the tips of her fingers, all yellowed and cracked. I stare at them for a long time. Painful sobs rattle through me.

"*Abuela*," I manage to spit out. I wipe the tears from my cheeks with the back of my hand, but they refuse to stop pouring down my face. "Mom is . . . she's . . ."

Grandmother's neck muscles aren't strong enough to hold her head straight anymore, and it bobbles, slightly, as she turns. She looks at me with milky, unseeing eyes and I realize she understands. She's outlived her only daughter.

I crawl across the floor and rest my head against her mattress. Rain crashes against the window, pounding so hard that I worry the glass will shatter. I think of all the empty houses sprawled around us. Street after street of vacant rooms and overgrown lawns and muddy driveways. I'm suddenly aware that I'm about to get my wish—we can't stay in this house now that Mom isn't coming back. I'll finally get to leave this stupid town. Not that it matters anymore.

Grandmother touches my head. Her hand is nearly weightless, and her skin feels almost exactly like crumpled paper. She pats, absently, as if she's not entirely sure what she's doing.

The heavy grip on my heart loosens, just a little. I close my eyes and rest my head against her leg.

The muscles in Grandmother's hand tighten. She digs her long, cracked fingernails into my skin. Pain shoots through my neck and I jerk away, horrified.

"*Diablo!*" Grandmother says in a thin, raspy voice. She lifts a curved finger that looks like a claw and points at me.

"Don't," I whisper. "Please, *Abuela*."

"*Diablo!*" she says again. I slink away from her and sink back against the wall, shaking with sobs.

CHAPTER THREE

Two days later, I'm standing in a graveyard, staring at the flag-draped casket that holds my mother's decaying body.

A steely-gray sky stretches above me, heavy with storm clouds. The temperature has dropped below fifty degrees for the first time since I moved to Mississippi, and cool wind cuts through my dress. I shiver, clutching a bundle of poppies to my chest. A handful of petals flutter from their stems and scatter in the wind. The man who handled the flower arrangements said they're not good for bouquets, but they are—no, they *were*—my mother's favorite flowers, so I insisted he cut me a dozen. Half the petals have already blown away.

A military chaplain stands at the head of my mother's casket, white robes draped around his shoulders. His face is made up of hard lines and deep wrinkles, the collar of his jacket digging into his leathery neck.

"A reading from First Peter," he recites, starting down at a thick leather Bible. "'Dear friends, do not be surprised at the painful trial you are suffering . . .'"

I try to listen, but the wind snatches his voice before it reaches my ears. It's a small funeral, only a half-dozen soldiers from my mother's unit crowd around the coffin. Next to me Jodi Sorrenson, Mom's commanding officer, dabs her nose with a crumpled tissue.

"Your mother would have thought this was beautiful," she whispers, sniffling. A fat tear rolls down her cheek, but I don't have it in me to comfort her.

"I'm sure she would have," I say instead. Mom didn't provide specific instructions for the funeral, so Jodi did her best to guess at her wishes. The truth is, I know Mom would have hated all of this. She despised Bible quotes and graveyards. She wouldn't have wanted the military spending money and making a fuss over her. She called funerals "morbid spectacles" and always told me that, when she died, she wanted to be buried in the cheapest casket I could find and for people to donate to charity instead of buying flowers.

"Or donate my body to science," she added. "Then at least my death could help people."

She wanted everything to be quick and easy. Efficient—like she was.

I clutch the poppies in my hand. The bouquet was the one thing I chose myself. Another bright-red petal dances off into the wind. I watch the flowers scatter, and fight against the sob building in my throat. Now it's just a bundle of ugly stems.

The chaplain raises his hands. This is my signal. I'm supposed to be the first person to lay flowers on my mother's coffin. The soldiers turn to look at me, waiting, but I don't move. My feet feel as if they've frozen to the dead brown grass. Jodi nudges me with her elbow.

"Go on," she whispers.

I stare at my ruined bouquet. The stalks are skinny green things. They don't even have leaves. Tears prick my eyes but I blink, refusing to let them fall. I wanted to surround my mother with red poppies. Then, when she was underground with her tacky, overpriced coffin, she'd have at least one thing she loved to make her feel less alone.

I can't give her these ugly stems.

Jodi steps forward, placing a white rose on my mother's coffin. The others follow. Some leave flowers, others just bow their heads and move on. I stay rooted in place as the few guests pay their respects. The honor guards meticulously fold the flag draped over my mother's casket, and present it to me. I barely hear the words they say as I take the stiff fabric in my hands. Jodi glances at me when the guests start to leave, but I refuse to meet her eyes. She nods and pats me on the shoulder.

"I'll wait by the car," she says. "Take as much time as you need."

I listen to her heels crunch against the dead grass. When I'm sure she's gone, I step forward and sink to the ground next to my mother's coffin, the flag nestled on my lap. I lean my head against the shiny wood, a tear crawling down my cheek. I don't have the strength to wipe it away.

"Maybe this is just a dream," I say. I trace the whirls of wood with my finger. "Like in *The Wizard of Oz*. Maybe we just have to click our heels."

Mom used to joke that Dorothy's trick of clicking her heels together and saying, "There's no place like home," wouldn't have worked for us. We've had so many homes that the shoes wouldn't know where to send us. I always giggled with her when she said that but, secretly, I didn't agree. Home doesn't have to be a place. It can be a person. I'd always known where my home was. Until now.

"There's no place like home," I whisper. I wipe the

tears from my cheeks, and set the flower stems on the ground next to the coffin. The wind blows, spreading red petals over the dead grass. I shiver and wrap my arms around my chest, watching the petals dance across the crumbling stone angels and moss-covered tombstones. Almost like droplets of blood.

Almost like someone's trying to warn me.

* * *

Jodi drives me home after the service. She offers to come in but Wanda Garrity, my social worker, is supposed to be waiting for me, so I tell her she doesn't have to. I climb out of the car and head to the house. Jodi waves and then her car disappears down the street, taillights flashing red. I lift my hand, a second too late.

Jodi gave me her phone number and told me to call if I needed anything. The stiff paper presses through the pocket of my coat, the corners digging through the fabric.

The house feels different. I notice it as soon as I step through the front door. The air hangs heavier on my shoulders. It seems to vibrate.

"Wanda?" I call out, but no one responds. She must be running late.

I close the door behind me, and the walls inch closer. This is exactly where I was standing when I found out my mother was dead. I close my eyes and that moment replays on a loop, like a nightmare that won't end.

Wanda showed up about an hour after the police left. I was still in Grandmother's room, shaking and sobbing, when she found me. She told me to pack a bag, and she took me to a group home for the night. I'm not eighteen yet, so the state won't let me stay in the house alone.

No one knows what to do with me, but everyone seems to agree that I can't live here. Wanda offered to call family, but Mom didn't have any siblings or close friends. She and my dad never married, and besides, he died when I was little. Our only other family lives in Mexico, and they couldn't even afford plane tickets up for the funeral. They wouldn't be able to take me in.

"Wanda?" I shout again. My voice bounces off the walls, echoing back to me. Wanda told me she'd meet me here after the funeral so I could pack the rest of my things and we could "discuss my options." None of it sounded good.

A few key words repeat in my mind: *Foster care. Group Home. Adoption.*

I hurry up to my room. Jodi arranged for my grandmother to be sent to a nursing home, so there's no one else here. It's the first time I've been alone in days.

I pull a suitcase out of my closet and place it on my bed. Then I open the top drawer of my dresser and remove underwear and socks and my neatly folded T-shirts. The rest of the house has already been packed up, my mom's things either in storage or sold off. Jodi and her friends swept through here and, before I knew it, everything was gone. At least they let me do my room myself. The house is supposed to be rented again after I leave, but I can't imagine anyone wanting to live here. Our story was all over the news. Everyone in Friend knows about the "murder house."

I focus on the stitching unraveling from the hems of my favorite jeans, and the way my Converse sneakers fit perfectly into the shoe pouch in my suitcase. I've packed my things to move dozens of times before. The motions are methodical and familiar. I can almost pretend Mom is downstairs in the kitchen, covering dishes in Bubble Wrap and humming along with the radio. I start to hum but my voice sounds shaky, so I stop.

That's when I hear it. Whispering.

The hair rises on my arms. I stop folding, a flannel shirt still clutched in my hands. I drop the shirt and turn toward the sound. The window above my desk is open. The screen broke over the summer, leaving a space just large enough to climb through.

A chill curls around my spine. I stare at the window, trying to remember the last time I undid the latch and pushed it open. Wind makes the curtains dance. The whispering drones on.

I swallow. I'm being stupid. Someone probably left

their TV on, or started playing music. But no—nobody lives in this neighborhood anymore. The entire block is empty.

I take a step toward the window and the sound grows louder. It sounds like cicadas.

"Brooklyn?" I whisper. I picture her crouched on the roof just below my window, her hair spiked, smudged black liner circling her bloodshot eyes. She smiles, and dozens of black bugs scurry over her teeth and cling to her lips and cheeks, wings twitching.

I'm coming for you . . .

I slide a biology textbook off my desk. It's heavy, the faded cover slick beneath my fingers. I take one step toward the window, cringing as the floorboard creaks beneath my feet.

The whispering drills into my brain. I can't quite make out the words, but it sounds like someone saying my name.

Sofia. Sofia.

I take another step toward the open window and, this time, the floorboards stay silent. I lift the biology textbook over my head.

Sofia . . .

I take a deep breath, and then leap toward the window, heart hammering. I search the roof frantically, my muscles tightening, preparing to swing.

The roof is empty.

I glance across the street and notice a sprinkler jutting up from the lawn, squirting a steady stream of water over the muddy grass. It makes a buzzing sound. Like a whisper. Fear drains from my chest, leaving me deflated.

I lower the book and release a short, unamused laugh. The neighbors had an automatic system installed a few weeks before Mom and I moved here. I *knew* that. They must've forgotten to disable it before they left.

A knock comes from the other side of my bedroom door.

I scream and whirl around so fast that my textbook flies out of my hands. It hits the floor with a thud.

"Sofia?" a woman calls from the hall. The voice isn't Brooklyn's.

"Um, just a second," I say. I let my breathing steady, and then I cross the room and pull my bedroom door open.

A short, dark-haired woman stands in the hall. She wears a navy-colored suit and low heels. It's just Wanda, my caseworker.

"Is everything okay?" Wanda asks, blinking her insanely long lashes. Her huge doe eyes and downturned mouth always leave her looking depressed.

"Sorry, you scared me," I say.

"The door was unlocked. Didn't you hear me knocking?"

I shake my head and Wanda gives me a small, polite, smile. "It's nice to see you again, Sofia," she says. "Do you mind if I come in?"

I move aside and Wanda steps into my bedroom. She sits in the chair next to my desk while I perch at the edge of my bed, nervously tapping my foot.

"I'm sorry to do this today," she says. "I know you just got back from your mother's funeral."

I pick at a piece of dry skin next to my thumbnail, suddenly aware of the way my tights make the backs of my knees itch.

"Have you decided where you want to go? I know it's a big decision," she continues, trying to sound positive.

"Can't I just stay here?" I ask, even though I already know the answer. "I'm graduating next year, and then I'll go away to college . . ."

Wanda shakes her head. "You know we can't allow that. You're still under eighteen." She pauses. "I've done some digging, and I think I've found a loophole we can work with. In her will, your mother stipulated that you were to be left in your grandmother's care. Your grandmother isn't fit to be your legal guardian but, since she's been officially appointed, the state's at liberty to default to the arrangements she made in her own will."

"Did my grandmother even have a will?"

"She did. Unfortunately, it's a bit outdated. She wanted her daughter—or legal dependent, in this case—sent to a school run by the Catholic church."

"Catholic school?" I ask. The words sound strange to me, like I'm talking about someone else's life. I'm an army brat, not a Catholic schoolgirl.

"I went ahead and made some calls to schools in the area. Have you heard of St. Mary's Prep?" Wanda asks.

There's something off in her voice as she asks the question, like what she wants to say is, *Have you heard* what happened *at St. Mary's Prep?*

I shake my head. "Should I have?"

Wanda clasps her hands in front of her, considering me with those giant, sad eyes. "It's a Catholic boarding school in Hope Springs, Mississippi," she explains. "It's a few towns over, but it's the closest one and is very well regarded. There wouldn't usually be any openings, but I was informed that a student left very suddenly last week. You have a spot there, if you'd like it."

I don't know what to say. Everything is happening so fast.

"I know it's not a perfect solution," Wanda continues. "But St. Mary's has a scholarship program for students of . . . lesser means. It would cover tuition and board, as long as you kept up your grades and obeyed the school's morality code. Plus, there's a nursing home less than twenty minutes away by car. I called them this morning and they have space if you'd like to transfer your grandmother."

I stare at Wanda, unsure how to respond. Catholic school. I picture plaid skirts and stained glass and nuns in long black habits. And it's a *boarding* school, which means I wouldn't get to leave the mean girls behind at the end of the day. I'd have to live with them.

"If you decide to go with St. Mary's, you'd officially be a ward of the school," Wanda continues. "That means you wouldn't qualify for a more traditional adoption. I understand if you want to try your luck at that. I'm told that the group home in Friend fills up pretty fast, especially with the holidays coming up in just a few weeks. There aren't a lot of beds available, so we'll need to get you moved in as soon as possible, if you want to stay around here."

I swallow. *Group home.* I think of the stained mattress I slept on for two nights, the cold concrete floors, and girls with cruel smiles. I imagine eating Christmas dinner in that sterile cafeteria.

I push away my concerns about St. Mary's. I'm being stupid—just like a minute ago, with the sprinkler. I'm inventing things to be scared of.

"I'll go to the school," I say. Wanda smiles.

"Oh, Sofia, that's great. I really think it's the right choice. Listen, I have some brochures and things in my car. Let me grab them for you."

She slips out of my room, giving me one last grin before she pulls my bedroom door shut behind her. I stare at the door for a moment, listening to the sound of her footsteps on our stairs.

A strange emotion rushes through my body, and it takes me a long moment to recognize what it is. *Hope.* Since my mother died, I thought I'd never feel hopeful again, but there's no mistaking the fragile, feathery feeling in my stomach. St. Mary's Prep School. Maybe this is the sign I'd been hoping for.

Movement flickers at the corner of my eye. I jerk around, my hands groping for a weapon.

But it's just a cicada. The black bug crawls across my wall and disappears behind my dresser, wings twitching.

CHAPTER FOUR

Everything I own fits inside two olive-green military duffels and an oversized rolling suitcase covered in burgundy flowers. I packed the rest into cardboard boxes and sent them to our storage unit just outside Hope Springs. I'm giving the house one last walk-through when I spot my grandmother's needlepoint leaning against the wall in her now-empty room. *Jealousy is like a cancer,* it reads. Jodi and the others must not have seen it when they packed the rest of her things. I kneel on the floor and pick it up. The frame is smooth in my hands, the painted wood starting to chip. I think of my mom saying those words during our last phone call, and my chest twists.

I slide the picture into my suitcase. It fits perfectly in the front pocket.

A silver minivan pulls up as I'm lugging my bags to the side of the road. The words ST. MARY'S PREP stare out from the side door. A woman with a shaggy brown bob rolls down her window and sticks out her head.

"Sofia Flores, I hope?" she calls.

"That's me," I say, struggling to drag my bags across the muddy yard.

"Let me help you." The woman starts to open her door, but I pull my duffel over my shoulder, and shake my head. First rule of being the new girl—never show weakness.

"Nah. I got 'em."

The woman hops out of the van anyway. The top of her head barely clears my chin, but she tugs my over-stuffed duffel off my shoulder and hauls it to the back of the van. She unlatches the rear door with one hand and tosses the bag inside.

"I'm Sister Lauren," she says, reaching for my suitcase.

"Sister?" I glance down at her navy-blue St. Mary's sweatshirt and white sneakers. "You're a nun?"

She tosses her hair out of her eyes and shoots me a smile that wrinkles her nose. "Surprised?"

I shake my head—then cringe, wondering if God will smite me for lying to a nun. Sister Lauren just laughs.

"It's the clothes," she explains. "Usually, when people think of nuns, they think of the penguin suit and funny hat."

"You don't wear that?"

"Only during class and Mass." Sister Lauren brushes her hair behind one ear, a strand of chunky brown beads dangling from her wrist. She catches me looking at them and thrusts her arm forward.

"They're prayer beads. From Uganda," she explains. "I was a missionary there for a few years after divinity school."

"They're beautiful." I push the beads around her wrist, admiring the way the sunlight gleams against the wood.

"The women who made them were so inspiring. If you're interested in missionary work, let me know. We have some outstanding volunteer programs at St. Mary's."

I've never considered missionary work before, but I try to picture it. Flying to some faraway place with all my possessions packed away in a single suitcase. Helping out at an orphanage or school. I smile at the thought. It's the kind of thing that would have made my mother proud.

"I'll definitely think about it."

Sister Lauren loads my last duffel into the back of the van and slams the door closed. Her eyes flick to the house behind me. "Is there anyone you want to say good-bye to before we head out?"

I look over my shoulder at the last place I ever lived with my mother. The windows are dark and a FOR RENT sign stands in the yard, swaying in the wind.

I square my shoulders and take a deep breath.

"Nope," I say, blinking a tear away. "It's just me."

* * *

The minivan crawls through the streets toward West 72, the only highway that leads out of Friend. We're traveling at ten miles below the speed limit and stopping at every light. At this rate, it's going to take three hours to get to Hope Springs. Pastel-colored houses and depressing strip malls creep past my window, then slowly give way to stretches of flat, dusty land and spindly trees. A headache pounds at the back of my skull. My eyes droop . . .

I must have fallen asleep because, a second later, I'm blinking my eyes open and wiping the drool from my chin. We're not in Friend anymore. Tangled tree branches drip over the road above us, blocking out the sky. A thick layer of moss covers their trunks and knotted roots creep up from the ground like huge, muscular snakes. It's like we've driven into a Gothic fairy tale.

Sister Lauren has the radio turned to some Christian rock station and she's singing along under her breath. She turns the volume down when she notices me stir.

"You awake?" she asks.

"Yeah." I groan and roll my head, trying to stretch my sore muscles. The road has changed from paved cement to packed dirt, making the minivan rock. "How long was I out?"

"About an hour. We're getting close."

I nod and peer out the window. Sunlight trickles through the trees like gold dust. It feels different than the sun in Friend. Softer. Like someone's found the dimmer switch. Wind moves through the trees, making the branches sway lazily.

We roll past massive houses with peeling painted and shuttered windows, and weave through a small business district. It's the middle of the week, but most of the shops are dark, and CLOSED signs hang in their windows. I frown and glance behind us. No cars on the street and no people on the sidewalks. The whole town has a dreamy, unreal quality to it. It makes me think of *Sleeping Beauty*. Not the Disney movie, but this older fairy tale my mom used to read to me before bed. In that version, the whole town fell asleep when Beauty pricked her finger. They'd slept for a hundred years before the Prince rode in to rescue her.

"It's pretty here," I say. We pull off the main street and down another dirt road that's lined with twisted, dripping trees.

"Isn't it?" Sister Lauren says. "I'm still getting used to all the moss and weeping willows."

"You aren't from the South?"

"Nope. I'm a new girl, just like you. I started at St. Mary's this year, actually. I almost missed the deadline to get my resume in for the job, but I guess the Big Guy was on my side, because I made it in just under the wire."

Sister Lauren smiles and touches the tiny silver cross hanging from her neck.

"What do you teach?" I ask.

"English lit."

I twist toward her in my seat. "That's my favorite subject. Or it was at my old school."

"Yeah? What were you reading?"

"Lots of Shakespeare and Dickens. And we just finished a unit on *The Great Gatsby*."

Sister Lauren places a hand over her heart. "Oh, *Gatsby*," she says in a swoony voice, like she's talking about an ex-boyfriend. "That's one of my favorites. You're a junior, right? You're probably in Period 1 English with me on Mondays. I'll see you bright and early at seven thirty."

"Seven thirty in the *morning*?"

Sister Lauren laughs. "Intense, right? Father Marcus runs a tight ship."

"Sounds like it." I study Sister Lauren's face. She has big eyes, and the kind of friendly smile that's almost familiar. "Is Father Marcus the principal?"

"He's the dean," Sister Lauren explains. "He's been with St. Mary's longer than any other teacher. You'll meet him today."

I knot my hands in my lap, trying not to show my nerves. Sister Lauren pulls up to a stop sign and glances over at me.

"Don't look so terrified," she says. "None of the teachers at St. Mary's bite."

An anxious laugh escapes my lips, and the sound is so unexpected that I flinch. I haven't laughed since Mom died. Heat rises in my cheeks. I'm not sure if I should feel guilty or relieved. It feels wrong to laugh now that she's gone—but also good. Like taking a drink of water after a long, punishing run.

Sister Lauren slows the minivan to a crawl and turns onto a wide, tree-lined road. A black iron sign arches above us. It reads: ST. MARY'S PREP.

"Home sweet home," Sister Lauren says. My heart climbs into my throat. We crawl forward, and I scoot to the edge of my seat. Red brick and stained glass peek through the moss-covered trees. I spot circular windows that look like eyes, and tall stone pillars. An elaborate iron gate circles the school grounds.

To keep us from getting out. I bite my lip, pushing that thought out of my head. If Dr. Keller were here, he'd say I was letting paranoia control me, and he'd make me do my breathing exercises. But I don't want to seem like a freak in front of Sister Lauren, so I just stare straight ahead, studying my new home.

St. Mary's Preparatory Institute is three stories high, and shaped like a giant U. The bricks are discolored from years of exposure to the sun and wind, and a white cross peers down from the school's highest tower. Fear prickles along my spine as we drive beneath the dark shadow it casts over the road.

"It's . . . old," I say. A statue of the Virgin Mary stands in the courtyard between the school's two wings. Mary bows her head, her arms open and welcoming. Rust stains the white stone of her dress. It looks like blood winding down her legs and pooling at her feet.

"I know it's a bit spooky," Sister Lauren says, "but you'll get used to it. That's our chapel over there." She points to a small, whitewashed building to the left of the main school. "It's the only one on campus, which means the boys use it, too. But you go to Mass at different times, so you won't see them."

I nod. Ivy snakes over the chapel's white walls and stained glass, practically obscuring the colorful images of Jesus and the saints. A window on the highest floor is boarded up. It's like the building has turned wild. Like the woods are trying to reclaim it.

Sister Lauren pulls the minivan to a stop next to the tall iron fence surrounding the school. A priest in black robes waits at the front entrance. He climbs down the steps, his hem trailing in the dirt behind him. Metal clinks against metal as he unlocks the padlock and drags the gates open.

"Listen, Father Marcus can be . . . intense," Sister Lauren says. The quality of her voice has changed. She sounds younger, less sure of herself.

"Intense how?" I ask. Sister Lauren flashes a stiff smile.

"You'll see."

We drive through the gates and park the van near the steps. As I get out of the car, I study Father Marcus's deeply lined face and hooded eyes. He doesn't look mean, exactly. But he's not someone I'd want to cross.

"Thank you for your trouble, Sister." Father Marcus's voice is strong and deep, made for leading prayers and reciting announcements at the front of a packed auditorium. Wispy, dandelion puffs of hair form a halo around his bald head. "If you'll take the van back to the garage, I can handle Miss Flores from here."

"But the bags—"

Father Marcus raises a hand, cutting Sister Lauren

off. His eyes fall on me. The effect is similar to being hit with a spotlight. I feel exposed. Naked. I glance at my shoes, my cheeks growing hot.

"Miss Flores looks perfectly able-bodied. I'm certain she can manage them. You'll meet us at the entrance to the girls' dormitories so you can show Sofia to her room."

"Of course," Sister Lauren says. She climbs into the van while I wrestle my bags out of the back. The grounds are strangely silent. I can't even hear the distant drone of insects that I've grown accustomed to since moving to the South. I strain my ears, listening for voices, or a car engine, or wind rustling through the tree branches. There's nothing.

Sister Lauren whispers "good luck" as I walk past her window. She winks and drives away, the van's tires spitting up rocks and clouds of dirt behind her.

"I'm Father Marcus," the priest says once we're alone.

"Sofia," I say. I pull a duffel bag over my shoulder, trying not to grimace at its weight. "But I guess you knew that already."

"I'm the dean of St. Mary's Preparatory Institute," Father Marcus continues, as though I hadn't said anything. "Please, follow me."

He turns and starts down the path toward the school at a steady clip. I hurry to keep up with him, tugging my suitcase along behind me. One of the wheels gets caught on a rock and the duffle topples over, spilling its contents onto the ground. Father Marcus stops walking and waits for me to gather my things, but he doesn't offer to help.

"The boys' dormitories are located in the East Wing," he explains once I pull my suitcase upright. "You'll find the girls' dormitories located in the West. Girls are not allowed anywhere near the East Wing and vice versa."

I balance the duffel bag back on top of my rolling suitcase. "Yes, sir."

Father Marcus cocks an eyebrow, nose wrinkled in distaste. "The main building holds all classrooms, the school's auditorium, as well as my offices and your teachers' sleeping quarters. It also acts as a buffer between the two wings to prevent any . . . fraternization. You are not allowed in the main building outside of school hours without written permission from an instructor. Is that clear?"

Heat gathers in my face. "Yes, sir."

Father Marcus narrows his hooded eyes. "In this institution, we believe that unnecessary contact between the sexes prevents students from realizing their full relationship with the Lord." He pauses and presses his dry lips together. Then he turns, black robes billowing behind him. "This way, please."

I struggle up the stairs, following Father Marcus through heavy double doors that open onto a dimly lit hall. I stop in my tracks as soon as the door slams shut behind me. My other duffel bag slips from my shoulder.

An arched ceiling soars overhead, crisscrossed with ancient wooden beams. Chipped frames line the walls, each holding a faded oil painting of some long-dead saint. Their eyes stare out at me. Watching. Sunlight streams through the stained glass, painting the creaky wooden floorboards red and blue and gold. The school is somehow beautiful and terrible at the same time. Like an extravagant mansion left to decay.

"Sofia?" Father Marcus stands at the foot of a twisting staircase, one gnarled hand resting on the ornately carved handrail. A ring glitters from his index finger, a silver cross set against a shield.

"Sorry," I murmur, hurrying to catch up. I try not to groan as I hoist my luggage up the stairs.

"St. Mary's is one of the oldest Catholic schools in the country," Father Marcus explains as we climb. "We're second only to Ursuline Academy in New Orleans."

I stop on the second-floor landing, next to a marble statue of Jesus, to catch my breath. "I think I read that on your website," I say. Father Marcus curls his lip at the mention of their website, like the Internet is something unpleasant that he wishes would return to the hell it came from.

"Many of our works of art and furnishings date

back over two hundred years," he continues, "so we'd appreciate if you'd refrain from carving your initials into our walls, or sticking gum on the bottom of your bed."

"I wouldn't, I mean—"

"The grounds are off-limits after nine in the evening and before six," Father Marcus says, talking over me. "Anyone caught outdoors during those periods will be . . . punished."

The way he says "punished" sets my teeth on edge. We reach the top of the stairs and stop beside a thick wooden door. A smudged plaque next to the door reads LADIES' DORMITORIES.

"We are here to help save your soul, Miss Flores," Father Marcus continues. "I make that promise to every young person who walks through our gates. But it must be understood, we do not suffer"—his upper lip curls—"*defiance*. You will respect your instructors, and you will show up *daily* for Mass services. I expect to see you at confession."

He wets his lips, leaving beads of saliva in the corners of his mouth. "You are here on scholarship, are you not?"

I nod, not sure I trust myself to speak.

"Understand that your scholarship is contingent upon you keeping up your grades, participating in school activities, and respecting our morality code." Father Marcus lifts a thin, crooked finger. "One misstep and your scholarship privileges will be revoked. Is that clear, Miss Flores?"

I knew my scholarship could be revoked, but hearing Father Marcus say it makes it actually seem possible. My chest tightens. If St. Mary's doesn't work out, that leaves me back in a group home in Friend.

I swallow. "Yes, sir."

Footsteps thud on the steps below me. I flinch, but it's just Sister Lauren. She hurries up the staircase, her face slightly red.

"How was the tour?" she asks.

"Informative," Father Marcus says. He studies me for another long moment. "Sister Lauren will show you to your room from here. Good luck, Miss Flores."

He nods at me and then heads back to the first floor. Sister Lauren peers down the staircase after him.

"I think he likes you," she says when she's certain he's out of earshot. She takes my duffel bag off my shoulder.

I stare at her, incredulous. "Why would you think that?"

"I've never heard him wish anyone luck before."

"Maybe he just thinks I'll need it."

Sister Lauren flashes me a kind smile. She pulls a heavy brass key out of her pocket and unlocks the door to the dormitories.

"You'll feel better once you've met your new roomies,"

she says, leading me down a much more modern-looking hallway. Wipe boards and photographs hang from the doors, and I hear the faint sound of talking and giggling behind the walls. Everything seems so normal, so nice, but I've been the new girl more times than I can count and I'm not fooled. High school is hell. It doesn't matter how many cute photos these girls tape to their doors, or goofy messages they write. They're screwed-up underneath. Just like we all are.

But this time, Mom's not waiting at home to ask me about my day. I'm all on my own here. It suddenly feels as if someone's wrapped a meaty hand around my windpipe.

"Breathe," I mutter to myself.

"Did you say something?" Sister Lauren asks, glancing over her shoulder. I shake my head.

"No, I . . . I'm fine."

Sister Lauren stops at a door marked 23 and knocks twice before pushing it open.

"Ladies, I'd like you all to meet your new roommate," she says. I take one last deep breath, and tug my bags through the door.

"Hi—" My suitcase handle slips from my fingers and slams to the floor.

Brooklyn lies on her stomach on the floor, playing with a pair of oversized black glasses. Bright-red lipstick stains her mouth. Riley leans against the far window, her tanned arms crossed over her chest. She cocks one eyebrow, a grin twisting her lips.

"Sofia?" Sister Lauren touches my arm. A shiver skips over my skin. The room comes into focus, and I realize I'm mistaken. The girl I'd thought was Riley is actually Asian. Freckles cover her round face and big cheeks, and there's a cherry-red knit hat topped with a silver pom-pom pulled low over her glossy black hair. Riley wouldn't be caught dead in that hat.

The other girl sits up, the black glasses still dangling from her fingers. Her red lipstick reminds me of Brooklyn, but otherwise she looks completely different. She's tiny, for one thing. I'd mistake her for a little girl if I saw her from behind. Tangled blonde hair hangs almost to her hips. She smiles at me, and I notice a gap between her two front teeth.

I crouch to pick up my suitcase, worried that I've already killed my reputation.

"Hi," I say, straightening. "I'm Sofia."

The Asian girl steps forward. The pom-pom on her hat bobbles as she walks. Her smile gets wider. It's so genuine and sincere that it catches me off guard.

"I'm Leena," she says, sticking out a hand to help me with my suitcase. "Welcome to St. Mary's."

CHAPTER FIVE

As soon as Sister Lauren pulls the door closed, Leena pushes the fuzzy red hat off her forehead and presses an ear to the door, screwing up her freckled face in concentration. "You think she suspected anything?" she whispers.

"Not a chance in hell," my other roommate drawls from her spot on the floor. She pulls down the front of her T-shirt to reveal a candy necklace that stains the skin on her neck pink and green.

"They don't allow candy here," she explains, tossing the oversized glasses she'd been playing with onto a pillow next to her knee. "Pretend they're . . . vitamins."

"Um, sure," I say. That's another new-girl rule—agree with everything, even if you don't mean it. I drop my duffel bags at the foot of the only unoccupied bed and look around. The dorm is tiny. Twin-sized beds crowd three of its four walls, two narrow dressers wedged between them. I guess we're supposed to share. Bedspreads and pillows spill onto the floor, and bookshelves stuffed with paperbacks and framed photographs of baby animals line the walls.

"What didn't Sister Lauren suspect?" I ask, glancing up at the ceiling. Someone started to paint a mural of the moon and stars across it but stopped midway through, leaving the rest of the space white.

"Our secret," Leena says in a conspiratorial voice. The word *secret* turns my stomach. Secrets only lead to trouble.

Leena plucks the black-framed glasses off the pillow and pushes them up her nose. She blinks, like she's seeing my face clearly for the first time. "What do you think, Sutton?" she asks the other girl. "Should we tell?"

Sutton has gotten up from the floor to study her reflection in the mirror on the back of the closet door, but she turns at the sound of Leena's voice. She flips her long, messy hair over her shoulder. "I don't know, Leenie-bean. You think we can trust her?"

"Look," I cut in, "whatever it is, I don't—"

But Leena is already crossing the room. She yanks a yellow-and-pink-striped pillow off her bed and tosses it to the floor.

"Ta-da!" she announces, motioning to a shivering ball of white fluff with bloodshot eyes.

"It's a bunny." I drop onto my bed, staring. The fluff ball looks at me, its pink nose twitching. It hops forward and sniffs Leena's pillow. Sutton releases a peal of laughter as Leena scoops the bunny off the bed.

"Ooh, he's the *best* bunny," Leena coos, making a kissy face. "Aren't you just the best bun-bun?"

"You look surprised," Sutton adds, nodding at me. She digs under her bed, and produces a warm can of Diet Dr Pepper. "Did you think we were gonna pull out a baggie of cocaine?"

"No," I say, but the doubt in my voice gives me away.

Sutton grins and hands me the soda. "Soda is against the rules, too," she says when I take the can from her. "Pretend it's . . . mineral water."

"Thanks," I say. I crack open the can and take a long drink. So far, this place doesn't seem terrible. I'm not sleeping on a concrete floor, and the girls are actually talking to me like they want to be friends.

"No problem," Sutton says. "And just so you know, neither of us is in here for drugs. No judgment if that's your deal. Pot just turns me into a space cadet."

"The boys giving you the pot turn you into a space cadet," Leena says. Sutton smirks.

"That, too." She sticks her candy necklace into her mouth and chews off one of the beads.

"I don't do drugs," I say, wiping a drop of Dr Pepper off my lower lip. Leena sits down next to me on the bed, and plops her bunny in my lap. I flinch, nearly dropping my soda.

"Meet Heathcliff. He's our fourth roomie."

"He lives in our closet," Sutton explains. "Don't worry, you won't even know he's here."

I stare down at the bunny, trying not to let my distaste show on my face. I've never been an animal person. When I was eight years old, I accidentally sat on my pet hamster, Mr. Whiskers (I wasn't a very creative child). Poor Mr. Whiskers barely survived. After that, Mom decided he'd be safer with our neighbors across the street.

Secretly, I was glad. I hated the way his cage smelled, and the twitchy, ratlike look of his little face. I could always hear him moving around in the dark while I slept. It gave me the creeps.

Leena frowns. "He isn't bothering you, is he?"

"Of course not! He's . . . sweet," I say, absently stroking Heathcliff's fur. I expect her to take him back, but she just leaves him in my lap, letting him gnaw on the edge of my jeans.

"Can you believe I found this cutie outside the chapel?" Leena asks, wrinkling her nose at Heathcliff. "His poor little leg was broken and he could barely hop."

"Leena made him a cast out of toothpicks and Band-Aids." Sutton rolls her eyes, but she leans forward and scratches Heathcliff behind his ears. The bunny hops toward the end of my bed and pushes his wet pink nose into her hand like he's looking for a treat. I try not to seem too relieved. That rabbit was starting to smell.

"Okay, time to spill," Sutton says. She pushes Heathcliff away and wipes her hand on her jean shorts. As she leans back against the bedframe, her skinny legs stretch out across the floor. "What are you in for?"

I frown and take another sip of soda. "What do you mean?"

"What horrible thing did you do to get sent here?" Leena asks. "It's already December and St. Mary's doesn't usually take new students midyear, so Sutton and I figured it had to be really bad."

"Stealing?" Sutton guesses. She pulls her legs to her chest and wraps her arms around them, resting her chin on her knees. "Drinking? Sleeping with your high school guidance counselor? If it's the last one, I'm going to need pics."

"Gross, Sutton," Leena cuts in, giggling. Sutton makes a face at her. Her front teeth are stained pink from the candy necklace.

"Wait." I hold up my hands to get them to stop talking. "What do you mean what did I do to get *sent* here?"

Leena stares at me. Her glasses magnify her dark eyes, making them look a little unsettling. "Didn't you know? This is where they send bad kids."

"Everyone here has gotten caught shooting heroin or sexting her English teacher or painting lewd graffiti on playground equipment," Sutton adds.

"Or, if you're me, your super-strict mother caught you trying a beer *for the first time ever* and flipped out," Leena mutters.

Sutton turns to her and smirks. "When you told me that story it was *four* beers, and you were sneaking into your bio classroom to set all the frogs free."

"They were going to dissect them!" Leena says. She throws a pillow at Sutton, but Sutton catches it before it hits her in the face. "It's not my fault there was an *alarm* on the freaking door." Leena shakes her head, exasperated, and turns back to me. "My mom completely freaked out at me. I have to call her every single day just to check in and, I swear, she thinks she'll be able to smell the beer on my breath through the phone. She's the worst—you have no idea."

Mom. Mother. She. I try to count how many times Leena has casually mentioned her mom already. My mom's cell phone photo flashes into my head: hair sticking out of her short ponytail, the Cheerio stuck to her cheek. I feel a needle prick of pain just below my left eye and blink until it goes away. I never realized how lucky I was to be annoyed by my mom.

"So, being sent here is, like, a punishment?" I ask, trying to keep my voice casual.

Sutton flashes me a sympathetic look. "No one told you, huh?"

I shake my head, remembering the way Wanda studied my face when she asked me whether I'd ever heard of St. Mary's. She had to have known the truth and she sent me here, anyway.

Does that mean she thinks I'm a bad kid? She's a social worker. Maybe she can tell that I'm rotten just by looking at me.

"So what did you do?" Leena scoots to the end of my bed and leans back against my pillow. "Was it really bad?"

My chest tightens, and I consider making something up. I could say I got sent here for shoplifting. I could even pretend to call my mom every day to check in, just like Leena.

The lie sounds so good that I want it to be true. But I have to keep telling myself that Mom is never going to pick up her phone again.

"My, um, mom was in an accident," I say. The words

feel strange in my mouth. I don't think I'll ever get used to saying them. "She died."

The color drains from Sutton's tanned face. "Shit, Sofia," she says. "That's awful."

"I'm so sorry we asked," Leena adds. She scoots closer to me and squeezes my arm. "It's got to be so awful to lose a parent. Sutton's dad—"

"He died, too," Sutton finishes, cutting Leena off. "It happened when I was really little, though, so I barely remember him. It's not the same."

I nod, and stare down at the bunny hopping around my bed. His white fur clings to my jeans and sheets. "My caseworker found this place," I say. "She thought it would be a good option since I don't have any family nearby. She didn't mention the part about it being a punishment."

"It's really not so bad. Promise," Sutton says. "Sure, St. Mary's can be strict. But there are perks, too. I mean, the eye candy can't be beat."

Leena grins and nods at the window behind her. "She means that the boys' dorms are just across the courtyard. Father Marcus makes them run sprints from the courtyard to the creek every morning at six o'clock sharp."

"I don't think he realizes we can see them from our window," Sutton adds.

I smile, grateful to think about anything other than Mom. I roll the empty soda can between my fingers. "Better than an alarm clock, I guess?"

"All girls at St. Mary's wake to the sounds of grunting, sweaty young men," Sutton says.

"At least it gives me something to say at confession each week." Leena folds her hands together, pretending to pray. "Dear Father, forgive me for I have sinned. I've had impure thoughts about a boy. *Again*."

"You've got a thing for a St. Mary's boy?" I ask.

"She's got a thing for *Julian Sellito*." Sutton's tongue curls around the name, making it sound dirty. Leena groans and puts her head in her lap.

"He's my one weakness," she admits, hiding her face, her voice muffled. "He makes me want to do very bad things."

"But he barely knows she exists, because Leenie-bean is a total prude." Sutton flicks the pom-pom on Leena's fuzzy red hat, making it bob in place. Leena shoots her a look, then leans forward and scoops up Heathcliff.

"I'm not a prude." Leena strokes Heathcliff's back, blushing so hard that her freckles turn red. "Jude and I have just never had a chance to talk before. Now that we're both in the play, I'll finally get a shot."

"Maybe lose the hat first," Sutton suggests.

Leena's lips part in a wide grin. "You haven't even seen the best part." She pinches the folded edge of the hat, and tinny music echoes through the room.

"Rocking around, the Christmas tree, have a happy holiday . . ."

Leena wiggles her hips and bounces in place. I laugh at her ridiculous dance.

"It comes with Velcro antlers, too," she says, collapsing back onto my bunk. "You can stick 'em on the sides and pretend to be a reindeer."

Sutton scrunches up her face, laughing. "Stop! Put it out of its misery!"

"Fine." Leena pulls the hat off. Her hair sticks straight up from her head. "Better?"

"Perfect," Sutton says. "He'll definitely fall in love with you now."

"Maybe." Leena shrugs, turning a little red. "Unless some other girl gets him first."

"Don't be crazy. Only a total bitch would go after Jude." Sutton's eyes flick over to me. "Leena's been in love with this guy since freshman year," she explains. "Everyone knows that."

"Right," I say, picking a piece of white fluff off my jeans. "What about you? Are you swooning over a St. Mary's boy, too?"

"Nah, my guy's a townie," Sutton says. She scrunches

her hair with one hand, making it look even more tousled. "I sneak out to see him sometimes, but, you know. It's tricky. St. Mary's has rules about dating."

I frown. "What kind of rules?"

"Don't," Leena says, and Sutton snickers. "That's their entire policy. Don't date, ever. It's evil. The Lord will smite you. Not that my mom would ever let me be alone with a guy anyway. I'm pretty sure she's hoping I'll let her pick the guy I marry."

I wince. There it is again—*mom.* I never realized before how often people mention their mothers.

Leena looks at me and her face falls. "Oh God, I didn't even think . . ." she says. "I shouldn't be complaining about my mom when . . ."

"She didn't mean anything by it, Sofia, really," Sutton adds.

"No—I know. I'm sorry, I didn't mean to react like that." If I don't get it together, I'm going to be known as the girl with the dead mom all year. I force my lips into a smile and try to think of something to change the subject. "So they're pretty strict here?"

Leena's shoulders unclench. Crisis averted. "It's not so bad. Kind of like going to school in the fifties," she explains.

Sutton snorts. "Yeah, the eighteen fifties," she says. She digs another can of soda out from under her bed, and cracks it open. I must have a worried expression on my face because she tilts her head, sympathetically. "Don't worry, Sofia," she says. "There are ways around all the rules. We'll help you navigate."

"I don't know. I'm here on scholarship," I say. "If I get expelled—"

"You won't get expelled," Leena cuts in. "They haven't expelled anyone in years."

"That's right," Sutton adds, flashing me a wolfish grin. She lowers her voice, making it sound creepy. "Once you're at St. Mary's, you *never* escape."

"Really?" I laugh nervously. Wind creeps in through the open window, raising goose bumps on my arms. I shiver and Sutton's smile softens.

"Sofia, I'm kidding," she says. "Seriously, don't look so freaked. This place is totally normal. No worse than any other crappy school I've been to."

"Of course." I force my lips into a smile, and push myself out of bed. "It's getting a little cold. Do you mind if I close this?"

I nod at the window. Sutton and Leena both shrug, so I cross the room and push aside the curtains. Something catches my eye.

Three long gouges claw across the windowsill. I frown and run a finger over them, feeling the grooves' sharp edges, the tiny splinters sticking out of the wood. They look like they were made by fingernails. Like someone tried to claw her way out of this place.

* * *

I lay awake that night, Sutton's words running through my head.

Once you're at St. Mary's, you never escape.

Goose bumps crawl up my skin. The claw marks on the windowsill flash through my head, and I roll onto my side, mattress springs creaking beneath me. If Mom were here, she'd tell me to stop obsessing. Sutton was joking. I'm letting fear control me.

A tear crawls down my cheek. I find my thumb in the dark and tug at a piece of skin near the nail. I can't keep doing this. I'll never fit in if my roommates wake up and hear me crying about my dead mom.

"Go to sleep," I whisper to myself. Heathcliff hops back and forth, paws crunching on the shredded newspaper lining the bottom of his cage. I pull my pillow over my head to block him out. The faint scent of rabbit piss hangs in the air, making me feel sick.

Leena shifts in bed. Sutton releases a light snore and mutters something under her breath. They've both been asleep for hours. It's like they don't hear the bunny rustling around in its cage. They don't see the way its red eyes seem to glow in the dark.

I stare at the back of Leena's head. If anyone should

be kept awake by the bunny, it should be her. He's her little bun-bun, after all. But Leena fell asleep almost as soon as she crawled into bed. Right after her nightly phone call with her mom.

Jealousy is like a cancer in your bones, I remind myself. I squeeze my eyes shut. Mom would tell me to find the silver lining. Don't let jealousy consume me.

A minute passes. Heathcliff starts drinking from his water dispenser. There's a tiny silver ball lodged in the spigot to keep the water from rushing out all at once. When Heathcliff licks it, the metal ball hits the side of the spigot, making a kind of wet, clicking sound.

Click click click. Pause. *Click click click.*

It reminds me, strangely, of my grandmother's rosary beads clicking against her table. I think of her sunken face, her bloodshot eyes, and raspy voice. *Diablo,* she called me. *Devil.* But I'm not evil. Dr. Keller told me I'm not. Brooklyn was wrong.

Click click click.

The sound haunts my dreams long after I drift off to sleep.

CHAPTER SIX

I wake the next morning to the sounds of someone shuffling around the room.

"Get up, sleepy," Leena says. I roll over, groaning. Heathcliff kept me up most of the night. I'd be surprised if I got more than an hour of sleep.

Leena's piled her black hair on top of her head in a messy bun. She pulls on a fuzzy robe covered in giant yellow lemons. I stare at it and instantly hear my mother's voice. *When life gives you lemons, make lemonade.* I smile sadly. I always hated when she said that, but I'd give anything to hear her say it again.

"Mass is in a half an hour," Leena says, filling Heathcliff's food bowl with tiny brown pellets.

"What time is it?" I mutter, pushing myself up. I didn't bother unpacking last night. I reach for the duffel bag and dig around for my toiletry case. Leena loads bottles of shampoo and body wash into a plastic shower caddy.

"Just after six," she says. She picks up a can of raspberry-scented shaving cream, shakes it, then tosses it into the trash can next to her dresser. "Sutton's already in line for the shower. I told her we'd meet her. Hurry, hurry!"

Make lemonade, I tell myself. I slip on a pair of brand-new flip-flops that I bought for the showers, grab my towel, and follow Leena out of our room. The line for the bathroom stretches all the way down the hall.

"You've got to get up early to get in a good shower," Leena says as we take our place next to Sutton at the end of the line. "But Sutton was too busy sexting her boyfriend this morning and forgot to wake me up." She shoots Sutton an annoyed look.

Sutton giggles. "What can I say? I've got to keep things interesting."

"You have a cell phone?" I ask. Wanda told me that they weren't allowed and made me put mine in storage. Sutton presses a finger to her lips.

"A *secret* cell phone," she whispers. "Shhh."

I glance around, but the other girls aren't paying attention to us. I expected to hear talking and giggling as we wait in line, but the St. Mary's girls seem different. Strange, even. They're quiet, and the circles under their eyes tell me I'm not the only one who didn't get much sleep last night.

Father Marcus's voice echoes through my head. *We do not suffer defiance.*

I turn back to Sutton, careful to keep my voice low. "What did you send him?" I ask.

Sutton tightens the belt on her bathrobe. "Nothing crazy," she says, eyes wide and innocent. "Just a shot of me and my two besties."

I frown. "Are you talking about us?" I ask. Leena groans and pulls me closer.

"She's talking about her *boobs*," she whispers into my ear.

Sutton bursts into laughter. "You're just jealous," she says, pushing her cleavage together.

We're running late by the time we finally leave the dormitories and head through the wooded grounds to the chapel. Every girl in St. Mary's has on the same uniform: blue jacket, plaid skirt, white polo, and stiff saddle shoes. Leena dresses her outfit up with dangly beaded earrings, and Sutton folds her waistband over twice, leaving two inches of skin between the bottom of her skirt and the top of her knees. As she races to the chapel, her skirt twists in the cool autumn wind and I notice that she has deep scratches crisscrossing her knees and thighs.

"It's not some crazy sex thing," she says when she catches me looking. "I'm on the varsity field hockey team this year." She winks. "Don't look so scandalized."

Leena and Sutton hurry ahead of me, easily picking their way past rocks and gnarled tree roots. I move slower, stumbling over twigs and catching my heavy skirt on the bushes and branches that line the path. The grounds are beautiful but overgrown, the dirt paths crowded with weeds and pebbles. St. Mary's girls flit through the trees around me like strange exotic birds. I see them from the corners of my eyes—a bare leg, a lock of blonde hair, or a spot of blue plaid—but they're gone by the time I turn my head.

Sutton grabs my arm and tugs. She's strong for someone so tiny, and I stumble forward a few feet. "Come *on*. If we're late, we miss the altar boys and they're the best part."

"You don't want to be late to your first Mass," Leena adds ominously. She shakes her head for emphasis, and her dangly earrings knock against the sides of her face.

I force my feet to move faster, ignoring the sharp pebbles piercing the soles of my shoes, and the whip-thin sticks slicing at my bare ankles. The chapel sits just ahead, its whitewashed walls slightly yellow in the early morning light. Church bells peal through the air. A crow leaps from a nearby tree, cawing.

Sutton, Leena, and I slip through the heavy doors. A second later, a cute guy wearing a white robe pulls the doors shut with a thud.

"Just made it," Sutton whispers, smiling at the altar boy. Leena pushes her forward.

"You have a boyfriend," she reminds her in a loud whisper.

"I might not be planning to buy, but that doesn't mean I can't check out the merchandise," Sutton says, glancing over her shoulder. The boy keeps his gaze focused dead ahead, like he's some handsome Roman statue.

Most of the pews are already full, so we head to the front of the chapel. Sutton and Leena kneel next to the very first pew, cross themselves, and then slide down the row to make room for me. I copy their movements, even though it feels strange to cross myself. I can't shake the feeling that everyone's watching me, waiting for me to mess up.

Leena and Sutton kneel on the floor of the pew, resting their clenched hands on the back of the row in front of us. They close their eyes and bow their heads. I mimic them, but I keep my eyes open a slit so I can see what's happening. I've never been to a service like this before—my mom hated church.

The room is small and bare. Wooden pews stretch across the floor, surrounded by empty white walls. A small oil painting of the Virgin Mary hangs from the wall behind the altar. The stained glass windows are the only other decorations.

An altar boy pulls the heavy curtains behind the altar open and ties them to the side with thick rope. Another boy wearing white robes walks into the chapel. He carries an ornate golden cross. Two more file in behind him, each holding a single lit candle. I study them until I notice that everyone else still has their eyes closed. I snap mine shut and clench my hands tighter.

I hear more movement at the front of the chapel, but I resist the urge to open my eyes. A heavy smell floats through the air, clouding my head with strange spices, vanilla, and smoke.

Silence fills the room. There must be a hundred other students in the chapel with us, but no one coughs or whispers or laughs. Beside me, Leena seems to be holding her breath.

"Peace be with you," Father Marcus says in a deep, gravelly voice.

"And also with you," the students around me recite, their voices merging into one.

Leena touches me on the shoulder and my eyes flicker open. Everyone else has already opened their eyes and taken their seats. Even Leena and Sutton have slid, silently, back into the pew. I'm the only one in the entire chapel still kneeling.

My palms sweaty, I take my seat on the pew next to Leena. It's like I'm in the middle of a complicated dance, only no one taught me the steps.

Father Marcus stands at the front of the room, surrounded by a small army of altar boys in white robes. Father Marcus wears a wine-colored robe, gold thread glinting from the hems of his sleeves. Another altar boy stands beside him, clutching a heavy, leather-bound Bible in his hands.

"And now, a reading," Father Marcus announces. The altar boy hands Father Marcus the Bible. He's taller than the priest and he has to bend over to hand him the Bible. I wonder if he's a student from the boys' school. Or maybe he's Father Marcus's apprentice—like a priest in training?

"Please turn your Bibles to John, chapter two, verse fifteen," Father Marcus says.

Everyone around me reaches for the Bibles hanging from the shelves on the back of the rows in front of us, but I'm distracted by the altar boy. He hovers just behind Father Marcus, his face all hard lines and sharp angles.

He looks like he was carved from stone. Shadows pool in the dips and curves of his skin, elongating his nose and chin, and making his eyes look deeper than they should. A small wooden cross hangs from a leather cord around his neck. He rubs it with his thumb while Father Marcus speaks.

"Sofia," Leena whispers, poking me in the ribs. She has her Bible spread out between us, offering to share. I tear my eyes away from the altar boy and try to follow along.

"For everything in the world, the lust of the flesh, the lust of the eyes, and the pride of life," Father Marcus reads, *"comes not from the Father, but from the world."*

Father Marcus looks up from his Bible and stares over our heads with a glassy, unfocused look. He lets the silence hang. Then he licks his thin lips and turns the page, the sound echoing off the walls.

"The lust of the eyes comes *not* from the Father, but from the *world*," he repeats, louder this time. "Here, John is warning you about beauty and lust and *sex*—"

Sutton giggles. She tries to cover it with a cough, but she's too late. Father Marcus fixes his gaze on her, fury etched across his ancient face. Sutton stares at her knees, her face going pale. The energy in the room changes. Students shift in their pews. No one dares to make a noise.

Father Marcus clears his throat and tears his eyes away from Sutton. "John is warning you that these things were created not by God, but by the world. To *tempt* you. Desire is a temptation. Want of any kind is a temptation. *Do not love the world, or anything in the world*, John writes. *If anyone loves the world, love for the Father is not in them*."

I glance away from Father Marcus at the same moment that the altar boy turns toward the audience. His eyes lock on mine.

Shaggy black hair hangs over his forehead and ears, just past needing a haircut. Two thick eyebrows arc over his eyes, giving him the look of someone who's always on the verge of laughing.

I don't realize I've stopped breathing until the air around me turns hazy. Sutton was right. The altar boys here are *hot*. The boy cocks one of his amazing eyebrows. It changes his entire face. Now he looks boy-next-door cute. The kind of guy who teases you when he likes you.

"Leena," I whisper. She glances up from her Bible. I nod at the altar boy. "Who's that?"

"Oh." Leena reddens and glances down at her lap, a smile twisting her lips. "That's Jude, the guy I was telling you about. I think I just caught him looking at me. Did you see?"

CHAPTER SEVEN

*O*nly a total bitch would go after Jude.

Sutton's warning echoes in my head. I didn't even know who he was, I remind myself. I didn't mean to stare at him.

I make my way alone to my first class of the day. St. Mary's is a maze. The hallways twist around one another and dead-end at strange places. Stairways seem to appear out of nowhere, and the light is so dim that I can barely see two feet in front of me. I get the feeling that whoever built this school wanted the students to get lost.

Once you're at St. Mary's, you never escape . . .

"Stop it," I mutter to myself, pushing Sutton's creepy warning out of my head. A crow flies past the window, its shadow stretching long across the hall. A shrieking laugh booms from inside a classroom and then cuts off as a door slams.

I wander down wrong hallways twice before finally digging out the map Leena sketched for me. She went over my schedule after Mass and drew little stars on all my classes. I have a strange thought as I stare down at the paper—what if Leena intentionally drew the stars in the wrong places? What if she wanted me to get lost?

I shake my head, pushing the thought aside. I have no reason to mistrust Leena—she's been nothing but nice to me. I stop in the middle of the hallway and squint down at my map.

A girl rushes past me, knocking into my arm. My map and notebooks go flying.

"Sorry," she calls over her shoulder.

"Wait!" I yell after her. "Do you know where Sister Lauren's—"

But the girl disappears around the corner before I finish my question. I drop to my knees and gather my notebooks.

"Hey—" The voice sounds like a hiss, and it comes from right next to me. I jerk my head up, but there's no one there. I hug my books to my chest, and push myself to my feet.

"Hello?" I call.

Someone giggles. The sound rises, and then fades just as quickly. I hurry to the end of the hallway and peer around the corner just in time to see a door swing shut. The hallways are now completely empty. It's my first day and I'm late.

"Creepiest school ever," I mutter, glancing at Leena's map as I retrace my steps. My English class is room 108. It's just two hallways down, which is strange. I could've sworn I was just there. I follow the map and find room 108 hiding at the end of a hallway. Finally. I hover near the doorway, listening to the students talk and laugh and greet their friends. No one looks at me, but I still feel awkward.

"All right, everyone, settle down," Sister Lauren says, standing behind an old wooden desk. I didn't recognize her in her full nun's habit. Black robes rustle around her legs and a white headpiece obscures her short brown hair. A long gold cross hangs from her neck. I clear my throat to get her attention.

"Sofia! I didn't see you there," she says, smiling. "Welcome to Junior English. Let's see, there's a free desk in the corner, next to Mr. Sellito. Go ahead and take a seat."

Mr. Sellito. I turn and see Jude crouched over a desk near the wall. He glances up at the sound of his name, but doesn't look at me. He's dressed like all the other boys now, in creased navy pants and a stiff white shirt, a plaid tie knotted around his neck. A dark lock of hair falls over his forehead, blocking most of his face. I replay the moment where our eyes locked in the chapel, and heat rushes to my face.

Only a total bitch . . .

I grit my teeth, forcing the words out of my head. I *didn't* go after Jude, so I have no reason to feel guilty. Still, Sutton's warning is stuck in my head. She seems very protective of Leena, and I don't want to ruin the only two friendships I have at St. Mary's. I try to ask Sister Lauren if there's another desk, but she's already turned to write something on the chalkboard.

People are looking at me. Someone giggles in the back row. I stare down at my notebooks and hurry to my desk.

"Let's all turn to page thirteen," Sister Lauren says, dusting the chalk off her hands. She opens the top drawer of her desk and pulls out a paperback book. "Sofia, you're welcome to use my copy until we get you one of your own."

She drops the book onto my desk. I blink down at it and, for a second, I think I'm seeing things.

The Tempest. Of course that's what we're reading.

Sister Lauren's copy looks exactly like the one I have back in my dorm. A woman with wild red hair gazes out over an angry sea. I stare at the woman's back for a long moment, daring her to turn and look at me. To smile her horrible smile. All teeth and hair.

Jude shifts in the seat next to me. He still smells like the smoky vanilla incense that was burning in the chapel. I tilt my head to the side, pretending to stare at the crack running across the wall behind his shoulder so that I can study him from the corner of my eye. He's scribbling something in a battered notebook, but it doesn't look like notes. His handwriting is small and slanted and half the words are scribbled out.

He pushes his sleeves up to his elbows. He's wearing the same wooden cross he had on in the chapel, only he's knotted the leather around his wrist, like a bracelet. The cross is worn and shiny, as though it's been rubbed smooth by his hands.

"In this scene, Prospero and Miranda have just witnessed the shipwreck," Sister Lauren begins. I tear my eyes away from Jude and stare down at my book.

The class drags. I've read *The Tempest* so many times that it's hard to pay attention as Sister Lauren talks about themes and imagery. My eyes glaze over, and my stiff new shoes dig into the backs of my feet. I can practically feel the blisters forming on my skin.

"Sofia?" Sister Lauren says.

The sound of my name snaps me back to attention. I blink. "Um, yeah?"

"Can you tell me why you think this passage was so compelling?"

My palms are immediately sweaty as I start flipping through the yellowed pages. The words blur together. "Um . . ."

A second ticks past. I narrow my eyes, pretending to study a line of text. I have this play practically memorized, but I have no idea which passage she's talking about.

"Come *on* . . ." the girl behind me mutters. Another student laughs under his breath. I curl my fingers around the edges of the book. I want to sink down through the floor and disappear.

"*The isle is full of noises,*" Jude whispers. He tilts his head toward me, pretending to study the cross knotted at his wrist. "Caliban's speech. Act 3, scene 2."

I feel an instant gut punch of relief. I wrote a paper on Caliban's speech last year. "This passage is compelling because it's so different from anything Caliban has said before. It changes the way the audience views him. They know he's a tortured soul."

"Very good, Sofia," Sister Lauren says. She writes Caliban's name on the blackboard, the chalk sending a high-pitched screech through the room. "Now if you'll all—"

The bell rings, cutting her off. Students around me stand and gather their things. I twist around, hoping to catch Jude and thank him. But he's already hurrying toward the door.

"Sofia?" Sister Lauren calls from the front of the classroom. "Could I speak to you for a moment?"

I grab my notebooks and walk up to Sister Lauren's desk as she erases the chalkboard. "Listen, if this is about how I need to follow along better, I know—"

"What are you talking about?" Sister Lauren leans against the chalkboard. "I think you did a great job today."

"Oh. Thank you."

"I wanted to talk to you about the school play. I'm directing this year and I thought you might be interested in helping out. We're doing *The Tempest*," she says, nodding at the paperback in my hands.

I hesitate. Leena said she and Jude were in the play. I don't want her to think I'm interfering.

"I know it sounds like a lot of extra work, and you're probably already overwhelmed, but you should consider it. First impressions are important at St. Mary's, and Father Marcus looks more"—Sister Lauren hesitates, searching for the right word—"*favorably* on students who get involved in school activities. He thinks it keeps them from getting into trouble."

Sister Lauren smiles, but there's an edge to her voice. I don't want to ask what kind of trouble she's talking about.

"What would I have to do?" I ask.

"Well, the roles are cast, but you could help with set design. You look like you'd be good with a nail gun."

The blood drains from my face. The sound of metal shooting through skin and bone echoes in my head.

"Sofia?" The voice makes me flinch. Sister Lauren is staring at me, confused. "Are you okay?" she asks. "I'm sorry, I was joking."

"I'll do the play," I say, swallowing and trying to dig up a smile. "But only if I don't have to use a nail gun."

* * *

After classes are over, Sister Lauren puts me to work painting sets. I kneel next to a cardboard tree, adding some painted texture to the bark. Spotlights shine down from the rafters, their glare so hot that a tiny bead of sweat rolls down my neck and disappears beneath the collar of my school uniform.

A senior boy named Connor saws a two-by-four in half backstage, and two girls talk in low voices while sorting through a trunk of plastic props. One of the girls is named Alice—I recognize her from my history class—but I haven't met the other girl. Someone practices the cello in the music room next door. Haunting snatches of music drift through the walls.

"Try to find the rhythm of the language," Sister Lauren says to the crowd of actors gathered in a semicircle around her. Leena catches my eye and waves. During lunch, I told her I'd be doing set design and she squealed so loud that half the cafeteria turned and looked at us.

I lift my hand to wave back just as Father Marcus pushes through the heavy stage curtains, his dark robes nearly blending into the shadows. He fixes me with his pale blue eyes and frowns. The wrinkles in his forehead deepen.

I lower my hand, feeling as if I've just flashed a symbol of the Antichrist instead of waving to a friend. Leena mentioned that Father Marcus comes to every practice, probably to make sure that no one accidentally touches a member of the opposite sex.

"Careful. You're dripping."

I flinch and whirl around, practically flinging my paintbrush across the stage. Jude leans against the wall behind me. The top few buttons of his uniform hang open, revealing the white T-shirt beneath. His plaid tie dangles, undone, around his neck.

"Oh—hi," I say.

"You sit next to me in English, right?" he asks, his mouth twisting into a grin.

"Yes," I say, looking away from his full lips. "About that, I wanted to thank you for—"

Jude shakes his head. "Hey, it's no big deal." He snaps his fingers. "Didn't I see you during Mass, too? You were with Leena?"

Leena's name jars me out of my stupor. *Off-limits.* "Yup." I turn back around and dunk my brush into the can of green paint. "And you're Jude, right? Leena's mentioned you."

I put a little something extra into the word *mentioned* but if Jude notices, he doesn't show it.

"Hold up." He leans forward, swiping his thumb across my knee. I flinch, but he holds up his hand, showing me a smear of green on his fingertip. "Gotta be more careful with that thing," he says, nodding at my paintbrush.

The skin along my leg prickles. I adjust my plaid skirt over my knee, feeling suddenly exposed.

"Mr. Sellito!" Father Marcus's sharp voice cuts through the auditorium. He steps away from the curtain, the heavy cross swinging around his neck like a pendulum. Jude looks up and Father Marcus glares, pointedly, at Jude's undone tie. "Make yourself *presentable.*"

Jude's lips curl into a smile. He pulls his tie into a clumsy knot and buttons the top of his shirt. One of the girls behind me starts to giggle, but Jude doesn't seem to notice.

"Of course, sir," Jude says, crossing the stage to where the other actors are standing. "Sorry, sir."

Sister Lauren clears her throat. "Now that Jude's here, let's start at the top of act 3."

The actors shuffle around to grab their scripts and move into place. Jude slides his own rolled-up pages from his back pocket. I turn back to my task, anxious to drown them out. I've seen more than my fair share of teenagers butchering Shakespeare.

"Jude, begin with 'Admired Miranda,' whenever you're ready," Sister Lauren says.

There's a beat of silence. And then, "Admired Miranda. Indeed the top of admiration, worth what's dearest to the world . . ."

Jude's voice rumbles across the stage and sends a shiver dancing up my spine. I tilt my head—just a little—so I can watch him from the corner of my eye.

"Full many a lady I have eyed with best regard . . ."

He even *looks* different. There's something about the way he squares his shoulders and thrusts his jaw forward. There's no mischievous tilt to his lips now. He gazes at Leena like she's something precious. My breath catches. Another drop of paint hits my knee, pulling me out of the moment.

I flinch and wipe at the paint splotch with my thumb, smearing it across my leg. I turn to see if anyone's caught me, but Jude has entranced everyone. Even I find it hard to look away.

Jude's eyes lock on mine, and he angles his body ever so slightly in my direction. I glance over my shoulder, convinced there's some other, prettier girl behind me. But there's no one. He's looking at *me*.

"The harmony of their tongues hath into bondage brought my too diligent ear," he says in that deep voice. Another drop of paint hits my leg. This time, I don't even look down. I've read this play three times, but this is the first time I've ever heard it performed out loud. It's beautiful. Like a love poem. I find myself wishing I'd gotten here early enough to audition for a part. I imagine myself standing across from Jude instead of Leena.

Jude smiles slightly—just a quirk of his lips—and something inside my chest flips. "O you, so perfect and so peerless," he says, "are created of every creature's best."

When he finishes, the whole theater is still, as if under a spell. I feel as if I've just woken from a deep sleep.

I glance around the room, only to see that Leena's also looking directly at me, frowning. Guilt twists my stomach, but I push it away. It's not my fault Jude was looking at me. Leena already has the lead role in the play—what more does she want?

"Leena?" Sister Lauren says. "It's your line."

"Right." Leena turns back to her script. "If you'll . . . um . . . sit down." She hesitates, then motions to a stool at the corner of the stage a beat too late. "I'll bear your logs a . . . logs? Is that right?"

"We're actually on the next page." Jude shifts forward to point at her script, and Leena flinches. The script slips from her fingers.

"Sorry," she mumbles, bending to pick it up. Her face has turned a deep shade of red.

I should feel sorry for her but, instead, I feel a tiny prick of victory. I'd have been a much better Miranda. I know the play by heart.

"Um, I am a fool?" Leena says. "To weep for—" She flips to the next page, frowning.

"Leena, I think you turned one page too far," Sister Lauren says, cutting her off. "Start with 'I do not know one of my sex.'"

"I do not know one of my sex," Leena repeats, her voice low. She swallows and glances at her script, flipping quickly through the pages. "As . . . as well as it does . . . ?"

The victory I felt a second ago fades. Leena looks miserable. I shift toward her, my head bowed.

"No woman's face remember," I whisper, just low enough for her to hear. "Save, from my glass, mine own."

Leena exhales, and some of the red fades from her cheeks. "No woman's face . . ." she repeats, louder.

"Thank you," she whispers a moment later, while Jude's reading his line.

"Anytime," I whisper back. The back of my head prickles, as if someone's watching me. I glance up.

Father Marcus stares out from the shadows of the stage curtains, a deep line creasing the skin between his eyes. The corners of his mouth curve into a permanent frown.

My skin buzzes under the intensity of his gaze. I'm suddenly filled with the urge to cover my face, worried he'll see my horrible thoughts reflected in my eyes. He'll know I wanted Leena to do badly. That I enjoyed watching her squirm.

Father Marcus touches the cross hanging from his neck, his lips moving silently.

It feels, strangely, as though he's praying for me.

CHAPTER EIGHT

I leave the auditorium hours later, long after the sun has set and the last bits of warmth have drained from the air. I shiver, tugging my coat tighter around my shoulders. It's not usually so cold this far south. Maybe we'll get a snowy Christmas.

I hurry across the grounds, anxious to be back in my dorm. The other actors and crew members had already left, and even Sister Lauren took off about half an hour ago, saying she had a stack of papers to grade. I thought about leaving, but Father Marcus's face flashed through my head every time I started packing up my things. I'd remember how he watched me from the shadows, lips moving silently, as though in prayer. *One misstep and your scholarship privileges will be revoked,* he warned me that first day. That was enough to keep me gluing ivy vines to cardboard tree trunks, and arranging tree branches around the edges of the stage. Maybe if I work hard enough, he'll decide I'm good enough to stay.

Dead grass crunches beneath my shoes and gas lamps flicker, casting eerie shadows across the frosted sidewalk. Sutton told me St. Mary's is a historic site, so the school has to keep the campus the same as it was in 1893. Tonight, the lamps seem fainter than usual. But maybe it's just my imagination.

A twig snaps behind me. I freeze, nerves crawling up my spine. I spin around, peering into the gloom of the lawn.

"Hello?" I call.

No one answers.

I listen for another sound—footsteps or breathing— but the harsh wind hides all other noises. My eyes start to separate the shapes from the darkness and the world pieces itself together again. I take a deep breath, trying to slow my rapidly beating heart. I'm being paranoid. There's no one else out here.

Someone grabs my arm.

I bite back a scream and whirl around.

Father Marcus stands behind me, a grave expression

on his face. He looks much more creased and wrinkled up close. He reminds me of the portraits of the dead saints in the main hall, cracks spiderwebbing across their painted faces.

"Miss Flores," he says in a voice like gravel on sandpaper. "What are you doing out so late?"

"I was, um, setting up for the play." Even though I was just doing schoolwork, I feel like I've done something wrong. "I must've lost track of time."

"I see." Father Marcus fixes his icy blue eyes on me, making me feel even colder than when I first stepped outside. I shift in place, unsure whether I should keep walking toward my dorm or wait to be dismissed.

"I'm concerned, Miss Flores," Father Marcus says after a long silence. "You didn't stay for confession after Mass this morning."

I knot my hands together. "I didn't know I was supposed to."

Father Marcus holds my gaze. I'm hit, again, with the fear that he knows what I'm thinking. I find a dry piece of skin next to my thumbnail and tug, focusing on the bright stab of pain. I fight the urge to keep walking back to my dorm.

"When I was a young man, I was sent to a small village in Colombia to act as a missionary," he says. He gestures toward the girls' dorm and we begin to walk down the path together. A strange scent clings to his robes—mothballs and incense. I try not to wrinkle my nose as I follow him. "The village was called La Cumbra. It was a superstitious place. The locals performed witchcraft and voodoo. Wicked things."

Father Marcus is quiet for a moment, his eyes unfocused. He presses his lips together, and then separates them with a soft smack, the cracks lining his mouth glistening with saliva.

"The people of La Cumbra were desperate for a relationship with God," he continues. "Can you imagine that, Miss Flores? To feel *desperate* to connect with the Lord?"

I don't realize that he expects me to answer until he stops speaking, and fixes me with those cold eyes. I clear my throat.

"Yes, Father," I say.

Father Marcus nods and slows his steps. "The people of the village would cover their bodies with black mud. They'd lie in the dirt, surrounded by a ring of fire, and they would pray to the Lord to make them clean. These rituals would take days sometimes. Weeks. I used to marvel at them. These people wanted nothing more than to know our God. This country doesn't seem to share that same devotion. They would never cover themselves with mud. They would never lie in the dirt."

Father Marcus stops walking and his eyes bore into me, waiting to see my reaction. I shift my eyes to the ground.

"What about you, Miss Flores?" Father Marcus asks. "Are you . . . devoted?"

"Yes, Father," I murmur.

"And yet . . . you do not feel the need to confess your sins. You are not willing to remain behind after Mass, your first Mass at this institution, and work on strengthening your relationship with the Lord."

Heat rises in my cheeks. *One misstep,* I think. It would be so easy for him to send me away.

"Sin never leaves us, child," Father Marcus continues. "It is only through asking the Lord for His forgiveness that we might hope for absolution."

"Of course, Father."

"Would you like to confess now?" he asks.

My voice freezes in my throat. "Here?" I manage to squeak out.

"*The Most High does not dwell in houses made by human hands.* Acts 7:48. The Lord sees us wherever we are, child. You may kneel."

What the hell? I think. But I'm too afraid to say no. I kneel in the grass, trying to ignore the way the rocks dig into my bare knees. Cold air creeps up my legs, making my plaid skirt flutter.

Father Marcus places a hand on my forehead. His skin is rough and damp. Wind howls through the trees around us, rattling the branches and blowing through the last of the dead leaves.

I've never confessed before. "I don't know the words," I say.

Father Marcus presses his palm against my forehead, tilting my head up toward his face.

"Now you say, *forgive me, Father, for I have sinned*," he says. "And you tell me how long it's been since your last confession."

"Forgive me, Father," I repeat in a voice that sounds nothing like my own, "for I have sinned. It's been . . . this is my first confession."

He nods, his hand sweaty against my forehead. "May God, the Father of all mercies, help you make a good confession," he replies.

Silence stretches between us and I realize it's my turn again. I'm supposed to confess something. I open my mouth.

The train flashes into my head, its headlight flashing white in the trees. The horn blares, making me flinch under Father Marcus's hand.

Not that. I think. *Anything but that*. My chest tightens, but I force myself to breathe. I imagine Brooklyn holding my wrist, her fingernails cutting into my skin, her eyes glowing red. I can still hear her voice. *We don't kill our own.*

I grit my teeth. I made that up, I remind myself. Dr. Keller said it never happened. There's no evil in me. I have to concentrate. There has to be something I can tell Father Marcus. My brain flashes forward, to the police officer standing on my porch. *Your mother's been in an accident.*

I push the memory aside, tears stinging my eyes. I can't tell him that.

Father Marcus's hand feels heavy. Like it's pushing me into the ground. I close my eyes and think of . . . *Jude.* Jude watching me during Mass this morning, a slight curl to his lips. Jude seeming to recite his lines to me during the play. I think of the hurt expression etched across Leena's face, and how good it felt when she messed up her lines. Heat burns through my chest. I barely feel the wind whipping against my legs.

"I . . . covet," I say, repeating a word my grandmother once used. *Codiciar* in Spanish.

Father Marcus shifts, black robes swaying around his feet. "And what do you covet, child?"

The thought of describing my romantic fantasies to Father Marcus makes something in my stomach clench. But Jude's not the only thing I covet. My mouth feels suddenly dry.

"I'm jealous of my roommate," I explain. "She has this great life. She's the star of the play, and she has a family and friends. Sometimes I wish it was mine."

Father Marcus's hand curls. The edges of his long, yellow fingernails press into my scalp.

"In First Peter 2:1, the Lord commands us to rid ourselves of all malice and all deceit, hypocrisy, envy, and slander of every kind."

Father Marcus falls silent, his words still hanging in the air between us. A rock lodges itself painfully against my leg, but I don't squirm. Pain cuts into my knee and I feel something sudden and warm trickle down my shin. Blood. Still, I don't move. The muscles in my neck strain against the weight of Father Marcus's hand.

"As penance, you'll perform three Hail Marys and an act of contrition," Father Marcus says.

"Yes, Father," I say, automatically. Maybe Leena can tell me what that means.

"Very well. I absolve you from this sin, my child. In the name of the Father, the Son, and the Holy Spirit. Amen."

"Amen," I whisper.

Father Marcus removes his hand. I stumble to my feet, feeling strangely cold and achy. Father Marcus grabs my arm before I can take a single step away from him. His fingers tighten around my wrist.

I turn slowly. "What is it, Father?"

Father Marcus reaches for my face without a word. His breath smells sour, and it takes all my willpower not to recoil. He drags his thumb over my forehead, tracing a cross into my skin. It burns, even after he lowers his hand.

"Blessed be the name of the Lord," he says.

CHAPTER NINE

I take the stairs to my dorm two at a time. My forehead still feels branded with the cross Father Marcus traced on my skin with his sweaty, papery finger. I touch it lightly, wondering if it'll actually help. Maybe my sins will disappear, like magic.

Sutton's too-loud, too-sharp laugh booms down the hall as soon as I turn the corner. I pause, the laugh triggering something in my memory. It sounds wild. Unhinged. I frown and push open the door to our room.

"Hey, Sofia," Leena calls. She sits cross-legged on the floor, leaning back against our mirrored closet door. Heathcliff lies in her lap, leaving little white bunny hairs on her dark-wash jeans. Some pop song I don't recognize blares from the speakers on her bookshelf.

Sutton peels off her sweater and tosses it onto her bed. "I need the white one with the lacy things at the edges," she says, her voice half whine. She yanks a drawer open, pulling so hard it nearly falls out of the dresser. "He hasn't seen that one yet."

Leena picks up Heathcliff, and makes kissy faces at his little pink nose. "I think you wore it last week. It's dirty."

"Damn, you're right," Sutton mutters, pulling open another drawer.

I drop my bag next to my bed and shrug off my coat. "What's up?"

Sutton glances over her shoulder at me as she digs around for a top. She's wearing more makeup than usual. Thick eyeliner coats her lids, and rosy patches of blush cover her cheeks. She looks older, her eyes dark, her face thin and angular.

"Just getting ready to meet my man," she says, shoving the drawer back. The bottles on top of her dresser rock in place.

I glance at Leena. She cuts her eyes toward Sutton, and mimes taking a drink.

As though on cue, Sutton plucks a tiny bottle of Jim Beam off her dresser and pours it into a can of Diet Dr

Pepper. The pop song comes to an end. Sutton touches a button on her iPhone, and it starts over at the beginning. She hums along with the opening chords.

"Maybe I should just wear this?" she says, motioning to her bra. It's yellow and lacy, with tiny white daisies lining the straps. Sutton's heart-shaped silver locket hangs down between her breasts.

"You'll be cold if you go topless," Leena says, giggling. She leans forward and grabs a light-pink top from a pile on the floor. "What about this one?"

Sutton takes the top from Leena and tugs it over her head. "You're so smart, Leenie-bean," she says, her voice muffled by the fabric.

I collapse onto my bed, throwing an arm over my eyes. "You're sneaking out?" I ask.

"Shh!" Sutton pulls her head through the top's opening and brings a finger to her lips. She tries to keep her face serious, but a giggle escapes. "I'm meeting Dean."

"Sutton, come on, you've got to be cool." Leena plops Heathcliff onto the ground and stands, helping Sutton fix her top. "Remember what we talked about? If you get caught, we all get into trouble. You have to be sneaky."

"I know, I know. I'll be good." Sutton applies a thick layer of pink to her lips and smacks them together.

"Don't stay out too late," Leena adds. "We have that physics test tomorrow, remember?"

"Physics is easy, Leenie," Sutton says. "Sometimes objects move, and sometimes they don't."

"You're going to have to be more technical on the test," Leena says.

Sutton rolls her eyes. "I gotta go. I'm gonna be late."

She slips the lipstick into her jeans pocket and unlatches the window. Our room is on the second floor, but the grounds slope up at the edge of the courtyard, so our window is actually only a few feet above the grass. I'm still lying in bed, and I push myself up onto one elbow so I can see outside.

A guy who looks like he's about twenty hovers near the edge of the woods, leaning against a tree with his arms crossed over his chest. Fog creeps over his feet, making him look like he's standing in silver ankle-deep water. He has swimming-pool blue eyes and golden hair that sweeps away from his forehead.

I wave, but his eyes slide over me, as though I'm not even there.

"Don't be offended," Sutton says, pulling her purse strap over one shoulder. "He just got off work at the bar. He's probably still stressed from all the frat guys trying to get him to take their fake IDs."

She wiggles her fingers at Dean. He jerks his chin up in an almost nod.

"You guys are so cute," I deadpan. Leena snickers, then pretends to cough when Sutton glares at her.

"I'll see you guys later," Sutton says. She hoists herself through the window and drops, easily, onto the ground outside. I push the window shut. Sutton leans forward and presses her lips against the glass, leaving behind a smudged kiss mark. I watch her race off into the trees, and I'm hit, again, with the same déjà vu feeling I got when I heard her wild laughter from down the hall. She reminds me of someone.

I shiver and yank the curtains closed. "Isn't she worried she's going to get in trouble?"

"Sutton doesn't worry about that when Dean's involved," Leena says. "They're in *love*. You know she's been with him for almost a year?"

"That's a long time." I lean over the side of my bed and grab my schoolbag. I have a physics quiz tomorrow, too, and I'm not as confident as Sutton that I understand force and motion. I pull my textbook out and quickly flip to chapter three. "How'd they meet?" I ask.

Leena is quiet for a beat. I look up from my book and see her frowning down at Heathcliff.

"You're going to think it's weird," she says, finally.

"What? Was he her teacher or something?"

Leena shakes her head. "Worse."

"Well, now you *have* to tell me."

Leena's cheeks redden. "Dean is, um, Sutton's aunt's . . . son."

I look up from my book too quickly, and a tiny flare of pain shoots down my neck. "Her . . . cousin? Sutton is dating her *cousin?*"

"It's not as weird as it sounds! Sutton's dad has been in jail since she was five years old, and—"

"Wait," I cut in. "Her dad's in jail? I thought he'd died."

"Oh, shit—I wasn't supposed to tell you that." Leena bunches her hand in a fist and presses it against her mouth. "Sutton tells everyone he died because she thinks it makes her sound less trashy. You can't tell her I told you. She'll be *so* pissed."

"I won't," I promise. "So, her cousin?"

"She met Dean for the first time a couple of years ago. I guess they kind of . . . hit it off."

I press my lips together to keep from making a face. Leena looks up at me and sighs.

"Look, I know it's gross, okay! But they say they're in love." She shrugs and scratches Heathcliff between his ears. "Anyway, that's why Sutton got sent here. Her mom thought it'd be good for her to get away from Dean. But then Dean got a job at a bar in town and moved to Hope Springs. Sutton says he's saving for a ring."

"Wow," I murmur. Cousin or not, I've never heard of

a guy planning to propose so young. "I guess that's kind of sweet?"

Leena drops to her knees and peers under Sutton's bed. She digs around for a second, then grabs a box of S'mores Pop-Tarts and sits back up. "Want one?" she asks, leaning against the bed frame.

I nod, and Leena tosses me a foil-wrapped package. "Sutton always has the best junk food," she explains.

"And booze, apparently," I say, thinking of the bottle of Jim Beam.

"She keeps more in her dresser if you want some," Leena says.

I shake my head. "I don't drink anymore."

"Me either." Leena pops a piece of Pop-Tart into her mouth. "Don't you hate the way it makes you act? I'm not myself at all. After that thing with the frogs, I was like *no, thank you*. Never again."

"I know how you feel," I say, staring down at my Pop-Tart.

"Anyway, Dean buys all this stuff for her. If you want something, just tell her and she'll ask him to get it for you." Leena nods at the Pop-Tart box. "These were Abby's favorite."

I bite into the Pop-Tart. Gooey marshmallow and melted chocolate oozes onto my tongue. "Abby was your old roommate, right?"

Leena nods. "She was cool. She was, like, one of those girls all the guys fell in love with. She was going to help me come up with a plan to talk to Jude. But then she took off." Leena pushes her glasses up her nose, accidentally smearing chocolate across her lip.

I think of Jude's dark eyes and velvety voice. The Pop-Tart suddenly tastes stale. "Where'd she go?"

"Dunno. We've been texting her from Sutton's phone but she hasn't responded yet. We think she went to New York. Her sister lives there. She probably wants to settle in before letting us know what's up." Leena shrugs. "Or maybe she thinks we'll tell someone."

"I don't get it. Was she expelled?"

"Not exactly. She used to sneak out with Sutton sometimes and, about a month ago, I guess she hooked up with one of Dean's friends. Sutton thinks maybe she's, um, *pregnant*." Leena whispers the word, then glances around the room as if she's worried someone will overhear her. "We think she didn't want Father Marcus to find out and expel her, so she went to stay with her sister while she figured out how to deal with it."

I break off another piece of Pop-Tart. Graham cracker bits crumble from my fingers and settle between the pages of my physics book. "She'd get expelled just for getting pregnant?"

Leena nods. "Dating is against the morality code. You

could get expelled just for being alone in the same room with a boy."

I tilt my textbook, pouring the crumbs into a little pile on my bed. "That's *insane*."

"Tell me about it." Leena glances at the window. I follow her gaze, and notice that I can still see Sutton's pink lipstick smeared across the glass behind the gauzy curtains. "Do you think it's completely crazy to go after Jude when I *know* I'll get in trouble if I actually try to date him?"

Guilt curdles in my stomach like food gone rotten. I fold the wrapper over the rest of my Pop-Tart. I don't feel hungry anymore.

"I don't know," I say carefully. "I guess it depends on how much you like him."

Leena looks right into my eyes. I should tell her about the chocolate on her face. I don't, and I'm instantly hit with a dark, satisfied feeling. Apparently, confession didn't work after all.

Silence stretches between us and, suddenly, I know she's going to ask me about play practice. She's going to accuse me of flirting with Jude.

"I used to think it was just a stupid crush," Leena says, "But it's different now. I think I felt something during practice. It was like he was reciting his lines directly to me, not to my character. Did you notice?"

I wait for her to say something else, but she just tilts her head to the side and smiles at me innocently. She really didn't notice him flirting with me. Or maybe she just didn't want to notice.

"Yeah," I say, clearing my throat. "I think I know what you're talking about."

Leena smiles so wide it looks as if her face might split in half. She glances at the alarm clock on her bedside table and her smile fades. "Crap, is that what time it is? I completely forgot to call my mom."

I twist around to look at the clock. The red numbers read eight forty-five. "It's not even nine yet. She's probably still awake."

"Yeah, but she'll be pissed. She expects me to call every day at the exact same time and, if I'm even a few minutes late, there's hell to pay." Leena pushes herself to her feet, Heathcliff still nestled in the crook of her arm. She shoves her feet into her slippers. "She's a nightmare. You have no idea."

I press my lips together and stare down at my hands. My mom was like that, too. I used to get chewed out if I came home even a minute after curfew.

I smile at the bittersweet memory. Leena pauses next to Heathcliff's cage.

"I'm such an idiot!" she says, smacking herself on the forehead. "I keep complaining about my mom and you . . ."

"It's fine," I say quickly. "Go call your mom."

"Are you sure?" Leena looks down at Heathcliff, who's gnawing at the edge of her shirt. "I could stick around if you want to talk or something."

I shake my head. "That's okay. I don't really like to think about the past."

"Here, take Heathcliff. He'll cheer you up."

Leena dumps the bunny into my hands before I can say another word. His fur feels greasy. Like he needs to be washed. He stares up at me with one beady red eye.

I force the word "thanks" out of my mouth. Leena watches me for a moment.

"You're not really into animals, are you?" she asks. I stroke Heathcliff's dirty back with two fingers, trying to keep the disgust from my face.

"No, I am," I say. "He's . . . cute."

Leena grins and heads into the hall, leaving me alone with the bunny.

I stare at the door, wishing we could switch places. I want to be the one hurrying down the hall to call my mom. I wouldn't even care if she was mad, or if she yelled. Just that she picked up the phone.

Heathcliff smells even more like piss than he did the last time I held him. I try to breathe through my mouth. Leena's copy of *The Tempest* lies next to her bed, the pages dog-eared. I shift Heathcliff to one hand and reach for it. A piece of notebook paper flutters from the pages. I unfold it, and see that it's an essay Leena wrote comparing the character traits of Prospero and Caliban. She got an A.

I open the book to a love scene between Miranda and Ferdinand. All of Leena's lines are highlighted in yellow marker.

"Do you love me?" I whisper, reading Miranda's first line out loud. I imagine standing onstage across from Jude, and jealousy pierces my heart like a blade. Leena gets a mom, and Leena gets Jude, and Leena gets to be the lead in the play. Heathcliff squirms in my hand.

"Stop moving," I mutter, holding him tighter. Leena even gets a stupid bunny that she makes everyone else take care of.

Two tiny, sharp teeth drive into my finger. I curse loudly. The door swings open and Leena steps back into the dorm.

"I forgot my—" Leena starts. I stumble to my feet, and Heathcliff rolls out of my lap and onto my bed, then hops to the floor.

"Careful!" Leena says, scooping a shivering Heathcliff into her arms. She looks up and her expression softens. "Oh, Sof, are you okay? He didn't bite you, did he?"

"Yeah, he did," I say, staring down at my hand. Two crescent-shaped marks cut across the pad of my thumb.

Blood oozes up and spills over onto my finger. It comes fast and hot, winding into the cracks of my knuckles and trickling into the spaces between my skin and fingernail. I curl my thumb into my palm to control the bleeding. So much blood for such a tiny cut.

"He's never bitten anyone before," Leena says. She sets Heathcliff down on the floor and pushes herself to her feet. "Let me get you a Band-Aid."

"I'm sorry I dropped him." But even as I'm apologizing, I imagine grabbing that fluffy white head with one hand and twisting. I can practically feel his skinny bones breaking beneath my fingers.

I cringe at the image, disgusted with myself. That stupid needlepoint was right—jealousy is like a cancer. I need to get it under control before it turns me into someone I'm not.

I stick my thumb into my mouth while Leena digs around in her closet for a Band-Aid. The blood tastes metallic against my tongue.

CHAPTER TEN

I open my eyes, and I'm standing in the woods. Barefoot. I don't know how much time has passed, or how I got here. Dead grass crunches beneath my feet. My toes look almost blue, but I don't feel cold. I don't feel anything. Moonlight illuminates the trees, casting shadows across the ground. The shadows look like they're moving, reaching for me. I look up, but the trees are still. There's no wind.

A choked whimper breaks the quiet. It sounds like an injured animal. Goose bumps climb my legs. I cross my arms over my chest, and something warm and wet seeps through my nightgown. I look down.

Blood coats my arms. I jerk backward, horrified. It soaks into my nightgown, staining the lacy fabric red. It winds around my wrists and drips from my elbows. It feels warm. Sticky. I try to wipe it away, but there's too much. I smear it across my hands. It oozes between my fingers.

I hear the noise again. A small sound, barely a breath. I stare at my bloody arms, and I start to shake. This blood isn't mine.

What did I do?

I turn around. A pebble stabs my toe. An animal scurries through the brush, rustling the leaves before going still.

Leena kneels in the dirt, her hands tied behind her back, a piece of duct tape covering her mouth. Blood leaks from her nose and from the torn, ragged skin near her scalp. Sweaty strands of hair frame her face, and a purple bruise blooms beneath one swollen, bloodshot eye. Deep red slashes climb her thighs. A bloody butcher knife lies in the grass, inches from my toes.

Mine. I pick up the butcher knife. The wooden handle feels warm beneath my fingers. Like it belongs there. I step toward Leena, and she flinches, releasing a muffled sob. She is the animal—the prey.

I pull my arm back and slash—

I wake up, gasping. Sweat plasters my pajamas to my body. I can't move. The room slowly comes into focus.

Sutton snoring from the bunk across from me. Heathcliff licking his water dispenser. Dawn creeping through the window.

I roll onto my side and stare at Leena's bunk. Leena lies on her back, her eyes closed. There's no blood on her face, no swollen eye or torn skin. Her eyelids twitch as she dreams. I force myself to inhale and then breathe out again, slow. I didn't hurt anyone. It was a nightmare. Leena's safe.

I check the clock on my bedside table. It's five thirty-eight in the morning. My alarm isn't set to go off for another twenty minutes, but the nightmare is still fresh in my head. I feel blood coating my fingers, anger pounding at my skull.

I didn't just want to hurt Leena. I wanted to kill her.

I crawl out of bed and pull on a pair of jeans and sneakers. My fingers shake so badly I can barely tie the laces. Leena murmurs something in her sleep and rolls over. Her blankets rustle and the mattress springs creak.

I freeze. I don't want her to catch me. I remove my jacket from its hook on the back of the closet door and creep out of the dorm. Leena stays still.

I hurry down the stairs and out the dorm without thinking about where I'm going. I just want to put space between Leena and me. That nightmare felt so *real*. I could smell her blood. I could feel her fear.

My chest tightens and, for a long moment, I can't

manage to inhale. Leena's my friend. I would never hurt her. *Never*. The ground seems to lurch beneath me. I lean against the wall just outside the building and cup my hands around my mouth.

Breathe. I choke down a lungful of air. Cold nips at my nose and lips. I exhale, and a misty cloud of breath leaks through the cracks in my fingers.

The old chapel sits just ahead, half hidden by trees. Tangled ivy snakes over the walls, twisting into thick knots around the double doors and stained glass windows. The vaulted roof pierces the sky like a dagger. I'm not supposed to be out of my room before six am, but it's just the chapel. They can't expel me for praying.

I walk across the grounds, dry grass crunching beneath my sneakers. The chapel looks silver in the early morning light, and darkness obscures the stained glass windows. I push open the door. The hinges creak and echo off the walls of the empty room.

A heavy wooden cross stands at the front of the aisle. Votive candles cover the altar, half melted in red glass candleholders. They flicker in the gloom, sending shadows dancing across the marble floor. I frown, wondering if the altar boys have to keep them lit all the time.

I slide into a pew and pick up a Bible with a broken spine. I let it flop open on my lap, and read the first line that I see.

Lord, if you are willing, you can make me clean. The words ring through my head like a bell. That's all I want. For someone to wipe away my pettiness and jealousy. For someone to take away my nightmares. I want this so badly that it beats in my chest like a second heart.

"Sofia?"

I jerk around. Jude stands behind me, a faded leather jacket slung over his gym shorts and long-sleeved T-shirt. His hair's all rumpled, as if he just got out of bed.

My chest rises and falls rapidly. It takes me a moment to catch my breath. "What are you doing here?" I ask.

"The guys all run sprints at six am," he explains. "I like to come here first and say a quick prayer. The chapel's usually empty."

I start to stand. "I'm sorry, I'll—"

"No, don't go." Jude slides into the pew beside me, close enough that our shoulders almost brush against each other. He smiles, then ducks his head, embarrassed. "It's kind of nice to have company."

"Yeah," I say. A thin layer of stubble shadows the bottom of his face. I imagine running my fingers over it.

"What're you doing here?" Jude asks, shrugging off his jacket. He's rolled his shirtsleeves past his elbows, and I notice a strange mark in the crook of his arm. Almost like a burn.

"Did you hurt yourself?" I ask, nodding.

Jude slides his sleeve down over his arm. He's not smiling anymore. "No, it's nothing."

I frown, but then Jude turns so that his body faces me on the pew, and my curiosity slips away. Dark hair curls around his neck, and the candlelight makes his skin glow gold. He stares at me for a long moment without saying anything.

I blush and look down at my hands. "You keep doing that," I say.

"Doing what?"

"*Looking* at me. You did it during play rehearsal, too."

Jude blinks. "Wow. I'm sorry. I swear I'm not a total creep—you just remind me of this picture Father Marcus has in his office, that's all."

"What's it a picture of?"

Jude glances up at me, sheepish. "Um, the Virgin Mary?"

I glance at a painting of the Virgin on the wall behind the altar. She has pale skin and dark blue eyes. "But she's white."

Jude follows my gaze. "Well, yeah, in that painting she is. The picture in Father Marcus's office is actually of Our Lady of Guadalupe. It's from a basilica in Mexico City where he did some missionary work after divinity school. She's Latina, like you."

Our Lady of Guadalupe. The name tugs at something in

my head. I think of the religious postcards and pictures gathering dust in Grandmother's room. "It sounds familiar."

Jude frowns. "You're not Catholic, are you? How'd you end up at St. Mary's?"

"No, I'm not Catholic." I look back at the painting of the Virgin Mary, my neck stiff. I swallow and say, "Actually, my mom died a week ago. St. Mary's was the only place that would take me."

There's a beat of silence, and then Jude puts a hand on my shoulder. His touch vibrates through me. "I'm really sorry, Sofia. That's awful."

"Yeah." I feel a familiar sting at the corner of my eye and blink to keep myself from crying. "It's still pretty hard to talk about."

"Have you thought about praying?" he asks. "God can be a great help at times like this."

His eyes are like sparks in the candlelight, absorbing every flicker.

"I don't know," I say. "I've never prayed before."

"It's easy. I'll show you." Jude slides his hand from my shoulder to my wrist. He wraps his other arm around me, pressing his body against my back.

I hold my breath. I feel his heart beating against my spine. He exhales, and his chest rises and falls against me.

"Is this okay?" he asks. His voice sounds different. Huskier. I nod.

Jude lowers his chin to my shoulder, and his breath tickles the hair on the back of my neck. He folds his hands over mine. His palms are warm.

"I always start by saying *Dear Holy Father*," he says.

"Dear Holy Father," I repeat. Jude laughs. It vibrates through his body, and into mine.

"You don't have to speak out loud to pray," he says. "Just think it. Think of God, and all the things you want to say to Him or ask Him or thank Him for. God will hear you, but He may not answer right away. He'll answer in His own way, in His own time. Go ahead. Try it."

I close my eyes, but I don't think about God. I think about how I can feel the heat of Jude's body through my T-shirt, and how his skin smells like soap and leather. The rise and fall of his chest as it presses against my back.

"Amen," Jude whispers, moving his fingers away from mine.

"Amen," I repeat.

CHAPTER ELEVEN

I see Jude again at play rehearsal. He and Leena run lines onstage while Sister Lauren watches from the front row. I try not to stare as I walk backstage.

"Wherefore weep you?" Jude says. His deep voice resonates throughout the theater, sending a tremor through my stomach. My hands still tingle where Jude touched them.

I hesitate near the curtain. Jude catches my eye, and my heart leaps into my throat. I sneak a glance at Leena. She's frowning over her script.

"At mine unworthiness," she says. She clears her throat, and shifts her weight to her other foot. "That dare not offer . . . um . . ."

Feeling reckless, I lift my fingers in a small wave. Jude flashes me a half smile and turns back to his script. I can't help the warmth that spreads through my chest. "That dare not offer . . ." Leena repeats. She trips over the words, making me wince.

Only a total bitch would go after Jude, I say to myself. Sutton's warning is the verbal equivalent of a cold shower. I am not that kind of girl. I will not go after my friend's crush.

I slip backstage, where Alice Merle is ripping up old sheets to look like sails and Dale Buford is lugging buckets of sand to create a makeshift beach. No one's looking at me. I drop my bag next to my feet and slip off the Band-Aid wrapped around my thumb, exposing the spot where Heathcliff bit me. It's just a tiny, crescent-shaped cut. Barely even there.

Jealousy is like a cancer, I think, and I drive my sharpest fingernail into the cut. Pain flares through my skin. I gasp, and tears spring to the corners of my eyes. But I don't move my fingernail. The pain is good. I focus on it, letting it wash over me.

I will not go after Jude.

Blood oozes around the edges of my fingernail. It feels sticky and hot against my skin. I move my fingernail and the pain dulls. I take a deep breath and reposition the bandage over my reopened scab.

The curtain behind me twitches. I jerk away as Sister Lauren yanks it back.

"There you are!" she says, stepping backstage. "Didn't you hear me call your name?"

I shake my head, trying to hide my bleeding thumb in the folds of my skirt. "Sorry. I was distracted."

Sister Lauren adjusts her white headpiece. *She saw my fingernail,* I think. I curl my fingers around my bloody thumb. She won't understand why I had to do that. I search my head for an excuse.

"No worries—I appreciate your focus, Sofia. Speaking of which, would now be a good time to take a look at our trapdoor?" she asks.

I blink. "Excuse me?"

"Remember? We were having a problem with the mechanism and you told me your old school had one just like it." Sister Lauren pinches the bridge of her nose between two fingers. "I could've sworn we talked about this after class this morning."

"Oh, right!" My cheeks flare as the conversation comes rushing back to me. "Yeah, of course, I'll take a look."

"Great!" Sister Lauren turns, her black robes swishing around her ankles. She leads me onto the main stage, and motions for Leena and Jude to stop rehearsing.

"Would you all mind shifting stage left?" she calls.

The actors move out of my way. I crouch beside the trapdoor, careful not to look at Jude. My Band-Aid is already stained with blood.

Leena kneels next to me. "You missed it!" she whispers, glancing over her shoulder. Her eyes linger on Jude. "There was this part in the script where Ferdinand was supposed to kiss Miranda's hand. I thought we'd just skip it, but Jude actually took my hand and . . . and he kissed me! A *real* kiss."

Leena touches her hand as she says this. She can't stop smiling.

"That's . . . great, Leena," I say. My response sounds stilted, but Leena doesn't seem to notice. Anger curls around me. The air in the auditorium seems hotter all of a sudden. The moment in the chapel—the moment I'd been replaying over and over—seems stupid, and childish. I press my injured thumb into my forefinger. *I will not go after Jude.*

"I think they're waiting for you," I say, proud that I manage to keep my voice steady. I nod at the actors gathered on the other side of the stage. Leena pushes herself to her feet.

"I'll tell you all about it later," she says. I stare at her back as she walks away. Her long black hair. Her swinging plaid skirt. Today, she's rolled the waistband to make it shorter.

A drop of blood hits the scarred wooden floor next to my knee. I look down and realize I'm still pressing my fingers together. My Band-Aid's a bloody mess.

I swear under my breath and turn my attention to the trapdoor. My thumb is bleeding freely now. I'll need to fix the door quickly so I can run to the nurse's office for a new bandage. Sister Lauren said the door latch has been sticking during Caliban's entrance. I fumble with it, but my Band-Aid slips around on my thumb while I work, and I have to stop to shift it back into place. I grit my teeth and try the latch again, trying to tune out the actors on the other side of the stage. This time I leave a thick red smear of blood across the floor. It glistens under the bright stage lights.

I wrinkle my nose and try to wipe the blood away with my hand. Gross. I really need a new Band-Aid. I slide the trapdoor closed and hurry backstage. I might have an extra floating around the bottom of my bag.

Jude's deep voice booms through the stage curtain, followed by Leena's halting, nervous lines. I crouch next to my bag and fumble through homework assignments and broken pens, holding my injured thumb so I don't bleed anywhere.

I can't believe Jude kissed her, I think, pushing aside my English notebook. *I can't believe I'm not even allowed to flirt with him because she liked him first.* I yank my physics textbook out of the bag and drop it on the floor with a little more force than necessary. The angry, jealous thoughts keep popping into my head. I tell myself I don't mean them, but I can't stop thinking about how unfair this all is. Leena already has everything. She should know what it feels like to have something bad happen for once in her life.

My lips curve into a smile at the thought. I catch myself a second later, and force them back into a tight line. It's not as though I want something really bad to happen to Leena. Just a little setback, to balance out the scales.

A sharp crack, like wood slapping against wood, bangs through the auditorium. There's a scream, and then something heavy slams into the floor, cutting the scream short.

A sour taste hits the back of my throat. I drop my bag, and I'm instantly on my feet, racing across the stage.

"Call an ambulance," someone yells. Footsteps pound down the aisle and a door slams open. I push back the heavy curtain, my heart hammering in my chest.

No, I think. *Just don't let it be . . .*

All the actors have gathered around the trapdoor. The actor who plays Prospero has climbed inside, and is speaking in hushed tones to someone I can't see. Sister Lauren's face has gone white. Everyone's here.

Everyone except Leena.

"What happened?" I ask. Jude is kneeling next to the trapdoor, but he looks up at the sound of my voice. There's something dark and frightened reflected in his eyes.

"Leena fell," he says, but he sounds far away. I stare past him, down into the darkness beyond the edge of the trapdoor. It seems to pulse. I inch forward until I can see Leena's tangled hair spread across the ground below and, in the second before horror washes over me, a thought echoes through the back of my head:

She deserved it.

* * *

Sister Lauren insists that we all head back to our dorms but no one leaves the theater. We linger on the front steps until an ambulance speeds through campus, red and blue lights flashing through the trees. It slams to a stop in front of the auditorium, and two men in dark jumpsuits leap from the back, a stretcher balanced between them.

Sutton races across the grounds, but I can't face her. Disgust floods my stomach. I step into the woods, pressing my back against the cold, rough tree bark and letting the shadows hide me. Tears stream down Sutton's face. She looks around, maybe for me. Sister Lauren approaches and they talk in low voices that I can't overhear. The men hurry back down the steps, and this time there's a body on the stretcher: Leena's body.

She isn't moving. I curl my hand into a fist and bunch it near my mouth. *Oh God.* She isn't moving. No one speaks as they load her into the ambulance. A sob claws at my throat, but I can't let it out or people might see me. If they see me, they might ask questions.

Like, *Weren't you working on the trapdoor?*

And, *Why wasn't it locked? What did you do?*

I close my eyes. I hear the sharp crack of the trapdoor slamming open. Leena's scream rings through my ears—cut off, abruptly, when her body hit the floor. I wanted something bad to happen to her. Didn't I think that, seconds before she fell? Didn't I think that she *deserved* it? I was jealous, and I wanted Jude for myself. And then she fell through the trapdoor I'd been working on. What a nice coincidence.

Nausea curls inside of me. It rises in my throat like the tide. I turn and double over, vomiting on the packed dirt ground. I wipe my mouth with the back of my hand and force myself to walk away. My shoes smack against the ground, every step sounding like an accusation.

My fault, my fault, my fault.

I pull open the dormitory door and walk straight into a wall of people. My body feels as if it's on fire. I duck my head, trying not to meet anyone's eye. Voices buzz around me, high and jittery. Nervous. I pick out bits and pieces of conversations as I weave through the girls of St. Mary's.

"Did she . . . ?"

". . . accident?"

"But who . . . ?"

They know, I think. Somehow, they all know about the trapdoor. They know this was my fault. I walk faster. Eyes follow me down the hall and up the stairs. I feel them on my back, like pinpricks of heat burning through my skin.

"Sofia! Wait!"

Sutton's voice stops me cold. I hesitate outside our room, feeling unmoored, like someone snipped clean through the strings that kept me tied to the ground. Sutton races up behind me, panting.

"What are you doing? Leena was asking where you went."

"She's awake?" I swallow. It feels like there's something stuck in my throat. "Is she . . ."

"She's going to be okay," Sutton says before I can finish my sentence. "The ambulance guy said she hurt her leg pretty bad, but they can fix it. She'll need a cast."

I collapse against our door, relieved. "Thank God."

"Alice is giving me a ride to the hospital," Sutton says. "Do you want to come?"

I press my lips together. I don't want to tell her, but she's going to hear it from someone else, anyway. "*I'm* the one who was working on the trapdoor, Sutton. I must've left it unlocked. It's my fault Leena fell."

Sutton nods but, otherwise, her expression remains unchanged. She already knew, I realize. Someone already told her. It's my third day at this school and I already have a reputation. That's got to be some kind of record. "Leena doesn't blame you," Sutton says.

I shake my head, not sure I believe her. "You should go. Leena will want to see a friendly face."

For a second, it looks as if Sutton might say something else. But she turns and hurries down the hall without me.

I push our door open and step into the dorm, my eyes traveling over the room. Sutton's hairbrush and bobby pins tucked away in a wicker basket next to her bed. A stack of Leena's books on the floor, ragged notebook edges peeking out between the pages. A squeaky carrot toy forgotten in the corner.

I lift my hands to my mouth and start my breathing exercises. In and out, in and out. The whispers and stares fade away. My breathing steadies.

"Leena will be okay," I say out loud, testing the words. I wait for the lump to leave my throat. But it just sits there, like food I can't swallow. Leena might be okay, but that's just luck. I still hurt her.

We don't kill our own. The words float into my head. I trusted Dr. Keller when he told me I wasn't evil. But he wasn't with Brooklyn that night. *I* was. I remember the flash of red in her eyes, the evil moving inside of me when she grabbed my hand.

Brooklyn's voice whispers to me. *You're one of us, Sofia. I'm coming for you.*

I lift a hand to my chest and only then do I notice that my Band-Aid has fallen off my thumb. My fingers are sticky and wet. Blood coats my palm.

A shiny drop winds around my wrist and falls to the floor.

CHAPTER TWELVE

The rest of the day passes in a blur. All anyone can talk about is Leena and the accident.

I spot Sister Lauren waiting in front of the main building on my way to the dorms after dinner, the St. Mary's van parked at the curb behind her.

"Hey, Sofia, why don't you hop in?" she calls to me. She's dressed in her St. Mary's sweatshirt and jeans again, her hair a little flat from the habit she wore during classes.

"Are you going to the hospital?" I ask. Sister Lauren nods.

"I'm dropping off some extra clothes for Leena. The

doctor says she has to stay overnight. Want to come along?"

I open my mouth, an excuse already forming, when Brooklyn's voice floats through my head. *You're one of us.* I snap my mouth shut, shame warming my face. Only a terrible person wouldn't visit a friend in the hospital.

"Perfect," I say.

Leena's asleep when we get to her room, a thin blanket pulled up to her chest. I can't see her new cast, but there's a large lump under her blanket. The lights are off and the fluorescents in the hallway leave a green tint on her skin.

"Let's ask the nurse if it's okay to wake her up," Sister Lauren says.

I stop her before she gets to the door. "No, don't," I say. It's easier this way. I'm not quite ready to look Leena in the eyes. "She probably needs her rest."

"If that's what you want." Sister Lauren takes a stack of clothes out of a St. Mary's tote and places them on Leena's bedside table. "Are you feeling okay, Sofia? You seem a little off."

I shrug, staring down at Leena's sleeping form so I don't have to meet Sister Lauren's eyes. Leena moans in her sleep, a look of pain flashing over her face. I hug my arms to my chest, trying to come up with a reason to get the hell out of here. This is too much. Leena's my friend and she's in pain and it's because of me. Because I was jealous. Because I'm evil.

I squeeze my eyes shut, the old argument playing on a loop in my brain: *I'm not evil. Dr. Keller said it was guilt. What happened with Brooklyn didn't really happen.* For the first time, I realize how meaningless these words are. *Karen. Alexis. Grace. Riley. My mom.* They're all dead because they knew me. Because there's something wrong with me.

The low blare of a train's horn sounds in my ears. I flinch, my eyes shoot open. It takes a long moment for me to realize that the sound isn't a real train—just an alarm somewhere else in the hospital. It drones on for a moment, then dies.

"Sofia?" Sister Lauren touches my shoulder and I whirl around.

"Sorry," I say. I squeeze my hands into fists, forcing the train out of my mind. "The alarm surprised me."

"Are you feeling guilty about Leena? Because I promise you, it wasn't your fault. I'm the teacher," she says. "I should have been paying closer attention."

I nod, but I'm not really listening. My palms feel sweaty, even as the air-conditioning coaxes goose bumps from my arms. I glance back at Leena. The pain has faded from her face. She looks peaceful.

"Do you believe in demonic possession?" I ask, my

voice barely above a whisper. Sister Lauren tilts her head to the side, a frown twisting her mouth.

"Have you been watching too many scary movies?"

"So you don't think it's real?"

"I didn't say that." Sister Lauren sinks into a chair next to the hospital bed, studying Leena's pale face. "It's kind of a complicated question." She pauses, weighing her words. "I think it happens, but not like in the movies. Demons can't take over your body and make you do whatever they want. I think it's more like getting sick, if that makes sense."

"Like catching a cold?"

"Well, I don't think it's as easy as catching a cold. I believe that when someone does something unforgiveable, a demon . . . attaches itself to them."

The train's headlights flash in my head. I feel Karen's cold fingers wrapping around my wrist, her skin sticky with beer. She screams.

Sofia, get off the tracks!

I wrap my hands around my arms, shivering. I have done something unforgiveable. I've tried my best to forget about it, but Brooklyn knows my secret. And now she's never going to let me go.

"So that's it?" I ask. "You make one mistake and you have to live with the demon for the rest of your life?"

"Well, no, not exactly. I think that's just the first step.

The unforgiveable act allows the demon to find you, like sending a flare up into the sky. But true possession can only happen to a weak soul. The Devil can only take you if you give in to the evil."

"What do you mean give in to—" I stop, my grandmother's needlepoint flashing in my head. *Jealousy is a cancer.*

That's it. I lower myself into a chair, my knees trembling. I'm letting jealousy control me and it's making my soul weak. That's how Brooklyn is getting in.

Sister Lauren leans forward, taking Leena's hand in her own. I stare at the back of her head. "How do I make my soul strong?" I ask.

You're one of us.

"How do you get rid of the demon?" I ask.

"I'm not as much of an expert as Father Marcus," she says, "but anyone can save their soul if they develop a relationship with God. You have to free yourself of distractions and focus on Him. Don't let yourself be made weak with desire."

Free yourself. Distractions. Desire.

I think of Jude's hands on mine, and his hair and the smoky smell of his skin. My cheeks grow warm. "You make it sound easy."

"It's not. It's a lifelong journey." Sister Lauren twists around in her chair, her face drawn in concern. "I know sometimes it can feel like there's something wrong with you, Sofia, but the truth is we all have evil inside of us. It's only through seeking the Lord that we're made pure. You should come to Bible study sometime. We can work this through with prayer."

I smile halfheartedly, wanting to believe that's true.

"What if prayer doesn't work?" I ask, my voice cracking. I clear my throat. "What if I can't form a relationship with God?"

The frown on Sister Lauren's face deepens. A line appears between her eyebrows. "Then I guess the demons win," she says.

* * *

I head straight to the chapel after I get back from the hospital. It's after dark and cool moonlight streams in through the windows, the stained glass turning it red and gold and green. My footsteps echo off the marble floor, the sound magnified by the arched ceilings and stone walls.

Jude sits in the first pew. I freeze, all of the oxygen whooshing out of my body. I should come back later. Jude is a temptation. He's making me weak.

But I take one step forward, and then another. I can't seem to control myself. It's as though my feet aren't connected to my brain.

Jude's hunched over in prayer, the collar of his

St. Mary's uniform all rumpled and creased, the hair on the back of his neck coming to a familiar point.

I'm suddenly aware of a million tiny things. My skirt is too heavy, and my ankle itches, and the curls around my neck have started to frizz—the stray hairs tickle my ears. But it's too late to turn back now. I stop next to his pew, and clear my throat.

Jude flinches and his eyes widen.

"Hey," he says. His voice sounds thick, as if there's something caught in his throat. "I didn't hear you come in."

"Sorry," I say. "I can sit in the back if you want to be alone."

"No, please." Jude slides over to make room for me on his pew. *Leave,* my brain whispers, but I perch at the edge of the wooden seat, too nervous to move any closer.

"I was hoping to see you again," Jude says, staring down at his clenched fists. I bite back a smile.

"About that, I . . ."

Jude lets his hands fall open and I trail off. His wooden cross lies in his palm, the leather cord dangling between his fingers. "I was praying for Leena," he explains.

I shift uncomfortably. It feels hot in here even though the chapel is barely heated. It's stifling.

"That's nice of you," I say. Jude shakes his head and bends back over his cross, a lock of hair falling into his eyes.

"It's not *nice*," he spits out, squeezing his fingers around the cross. The muscles in his shoulders tighten. "This whole thing was my fault. I was right there when she fell. It was just like—"

Jude stops talking abruptly and slams his fist against the pew. The wood shudders beneath my legs. He clenches his eyes shut and a vein throbs near his temple.

But I stare at Jude without saying a word. How have I never noticed the pain on his face before? It's etched into every curve, every angle. Dark circles shadow the skin beneath his eyes and deep lines crease his forehead. Leena's voice echoes in my ear: *This is where they send the bad kids.*

For the first time, I wonder what Jude did to earn his spot at St. Mary's. What secret is he hiding?

Jude swallows and the muscles in his face relax. He rubs a hand over his chin and, just like that, the lines and shadows vanish. There's no pain anymore, no darkness. He's just Jude again.

"Sorry," he chokes out. "I've been working with Father Marcus to control my anger. I guess I'm still learning that I can't fix everything that goes wrong in the world."

I think of my mother's face, a Cheerio stuck to her cheek. "Me, too."

"Father Marcus says I need to learn to trust God. He says this is all part of His plan." Jude turns to me, his eyes narrowing. "Do you believe that?"

"No," I say without thinking. "This was the Devil's plan, not God's."

Jude nods, but I'm not sure he really heard me. He stares off at a spot in the distance, his eyes losing focus. "I think that, too, sometimes," he says, almost to himself. "I've been taking all these extra classes with Father Marcus, really pushing myself to get closer to God, but then something like this happens and it all seems meaningless."

Jude clenches his eyes shut and lowers his head to his hands. "I keep having doubts . . . about myself, about God. About everything."

I scoot closer to Jude, even as my brain screams at me to leave. But I can't go now. I can't let Jude blame himself when I know Leena fell because of me. Because I'm weak.

"This wasn't your fault," I say. "It's—" *mine*, I think but Jude shakes his head before I can get the word out.

"You don't know the whole story." Jude cuts his eyes toward me. "I was distracted today. If I'd been paying attention, Leena never would have gotten hurt."

Jude shifts his body closer and lowers his hand to mine. The temperature in the chapel seems to rise another ten degrees. My hair sticks to the back of my neck and sweat gathers between my thighs.

I close my eyes and for a long moment all I think

about is his skin pressed against my own. I feel the rough calluses on his fingers, his heart beating in his palm. I imagine turning my hand over and weaving my fingers through his.

Free yourself.

"I can't," I say, my eyes flickering open. Jude jerks his hand away from mine, as if he's been burned.

"I'm sorry," he murmurs. "I thought—"

"I like you," I say. "It's not that."

Jude searches my face, but I keep my eyes focused on the pew in front of me. I'm not strong. If I look at him, even for a second, I know I'll cave. "Then what is it?" he asks.

"I made a promise to a friend," I explain. "I've already hurt her a lot, and I'm trying to make up for it."

Jude is quiet for a long moment. I study the huge wooden cross looming over us, my eyes traveling over every crack in the ancient wood. I'm still not entirely sure how to pray, but I find myself making a wish, like when I toss a coin into a fountain, or find a stray eyelash on my cheek.

Please, I think. *Help me do the right thing.*

"This friend," Jude says finally. "She means a lot to you?"

"Yes."

"Then you shouldn't do anything to hurt her."

Jude stands. I shift my eyes down to my lap and pick at the skin around my thumbnail. The sudden burst of pain feels refreshing. Like taking a deep breath. Jude slips out of the pew, his legs brushing against my knees as he moves past me. He walks out of the chapel without another word, his footsteps echoing off the walls.

* * *

Sutton finds me after classes the next day. She's dressed in her blue-and-white field hockey uniform, hair pulled back in a tight ponytail. She tears the wrapper off a Snickers bar with her teeth.

"You're going to get in trouble," I say, glancing down the hallway.

"It's medicinal," Sutton says, eating half the bar in one bite. "I have a migraine. Did you hear? Leena's back."

"Really?" I stop in the middle of the hallway and some girl I don't recognize walks right into my back.

"Campaigning for class klutz, Ally?" Sutton shouts. The girl turns and sneers at us.

"Is Leena okay?" I ask. "How's her leg?"

Sutton crumples up her candy bar wrapper and shoves it in her backpack. "Her leg is fine. Her cast is covered in more dirty jokes than a toilet stall."

"*Leena* wrote dirty jokes on her cast?"

Sutton wrinkles her nose. "Okay, fine, the jokes were mine. You should sign it while there's still space."

She cocks an eyebrow and I hear what she's really saying. *Go talk to Leena.*

"Are you sure she—" I start.

Sutton shakes her head. "Stop. I'm not going to be your go-between. We've got that game tonight, and if I don't hurry, I'm going to miss the bus. Talk to Leena!" She slips past me before I can say another word. Tonight's game is in Jackson, which is three hours away, so the entire team will be staying at a motel. Leena and I have the dorm to ourselves until morning.

It's the perfect time to talk, but every time I imagine facing her, I see Jude's smile. Smell his shampoo. Feel the weight of his hand on mine.

I can't avoid our dorm forever. I take a deep breath and head down the hallway.

Leena lies on her bed, a tangle of yarn balanced on her lap. A white cast covered in stickers stretches from below her knee to down around her toes. She wears an oversized sweater, her glossy black hair hanging around her shoulders. She's piled blankets and pillows beneath her knee to keep her leg elevated.

"Oh my God," I murmur, pushing the door shut behind me. Leena straightens, and the yarn rolls off her lap and hits the floor.

"Crap," she mutters, watching the yarn roll across the floor. I lean down and pick it up.

"I'm sorry," I say, staring at the yarn. Saying that out loud is like opening a floodgate. Words pour from my mouth so fast I barely realize what I'm saying. "I'm so sorry, Leena. I've been a terrible friend. All of this is my fault."

"Your fault?" A blush creeps over Leena's cheeks. "Sister Lauren told everyone in the auditorium that the trapdoor was busted, but I was the only one dumb enough to fall through it." Leena stares at a spot on her leg. I follow her gaze and see Jude's name scrawled across her ankle.

"If you want the truth, I was too busy staring at Jude to look where I was going," she says. "Stupid, huh?"

I swallow, thinking of the gold glint in Jude's eyes. The way he always seems to smell like incense. "That's not stupid," I murmur.

Leena presses her hand flat against the cast, covering Jude's signature. "Anyway, that's why I got hurt. You didn't do anything wrong."

I turn the words around in my head. Dr. Keller said the same thing over and over during our first session. I'd been a wreck after my friends' deaths. I thought there was evil inside me, controlling me, but Dr. Keller convinced me it was just guilt. He told me that, if I wasn't careful, my mind would keep going back down that path. That I'd drive myself crazy thinking the Devil's out to get me.

I release a breath, realization dawning on me. That's exactly what happened. There was a terrible accident and I convinced myself it was my fault. But maybe this isn't a sign that I'm possessed. Maybe it really was just a freak thing.

For the first time since Leena fell, I actually allow myself to believe that's true.

Leena leans over and pulls open a drawer in her bedside table. She shuffles around for a moment before removing an orange Sharpie. "Sign my cast?" she asks.

I take the marker and uncap the top. "What should I write? Sutton told me you like dirty jokes."

"No more! Please!" Leena cringes, staring down at the stickers plastered over her cast. "I had to use all my stickers to cover them up before Sister Lauren saw."

"Okay, fine." I lean over her leg and sketch two floppy ears and a twitchy little nose.

"Is that Heathcliff?" Leena asks.

"Yup." I add a fluffy tail and two big feet.

"Wow, Sofia. It actually looks like him. You're good."

"I used to draw a lot," I explain. I sketch a little bubble coming out of the bunny's mouth and write *Get Well Soon* before capping the marker. "There. You're all done."

"You're so much more artistic than I am," Leena says. "Did Sutton tell you I started knitting? I'm making a scarf."

She pulls a tangled red-and-green yarn rectangle out of the basket next to her bed, the cast making her movements stiff and clumsy. She straightens with a grunt. "Ta-da!"

Only the very kindest person would call the thing she's holding a scarf. One end is nearly six inches narrower than the other, and it's way too short to wrap around her neck. Lumps of yarn jut out at weird angles, and the pattern—some sort of snowman wearing a top hat—stops in the middle of the scarf, as though she got tired of doing it.

"It's . . . good," I say.

"You're such a liar." Leena smirks at me and flips the scarf around, examining it through narrowed eyes. "This is the worst scarf ever knitted."

"You might want to stick to acting."

Leena drops the scarf in her lap. "Speaking of acting, this broken leg might be a blessing in disguise. Sister Lauren's worried I won't be ready for opening night, so she's making me do an extra rehearsal tonight." Leena's eyes flash. "A *private* rehearsal. With Jude."

"Just the two of you?" I ask.

Leena uncaps her marker and draws a tiny orange heart on her cast, not far from Jude's signature. "Sister Lauren's going to chaperone, but otherwise, yeah. Just the two of us."

CHAPTER THIRTEEN

Leena leaves for rehearsal a few minutes later, and Sutton's not going to be back from her hockey game until tomorrow morning, so I grab my history textbook and huddle down in bed, desperate to catch up on my reading from the past few days. I never realized how hard it would be to study when you share a room with two other girls.

I flip a page of my book and uncap a highlighter. For an hour or two, I lose myself in my homework. I haven't done a unit on the post Civil War era at any of my other schools and most of the names and dates are unfamiliar. If I still want to take the final at the end of the semester, I have a lot of catching up to do.

I raid Sutton's junk food stash for dinner and read until my eyes go blurry. My head pounds with new information. When I finally check the clock, it takes my brain a moment to make sense of the numbers. 7:45.

I rub my eyes with my palms and check the clock again, but the time stays the same. It's been three hours since Leena left for rehearsal. What could they be doing for three hours?

An image pops into my head: Leena and Jude standing shoulder to shoulder in an empty theater. Jude brushing Leena's hair aside, whispering something in her ear. Jude raising Leena's hand to his lips and . . .

I turn a page so hard that it rips away from the binding.

"Calm down," I say to myself. Jude likes *me*. He wouldn't kiss another girl.

But you rejected him, a little voice whispers at the back of my head.

I turn back to my book, desperate to focus on anything else. Heathcliff moves around in his cage. He gnaws at his carrot toy, making it squeak. And squeak. I flinch every time the noise splits the room's silence.

An hour passes. *Squeak squeak.*

"Stupid bunny," I mutter, shoving my book aside. I climb out of bed and grab the carrot from Heathcliff's cage. I'm surprised nobody's thrown the damn thing away. I toss the carrot into the corner and climb back into bed.

Silence. I roll onto my stomach and pull my book closer.

Heathcliff hops across his cage. His paws make a soft *thwomp thwomp thwomp* on the sawdust. I grit my teeth together, but it's fine. Much better than the damn carrot.

A minute passes. Heathcliff starts drinking from his water dispenser.

Click click click click. Pause. *Click click click click.*

I curl my toes into my bedspread. *It's fine,* I tell myself. But it's not fine. We're not even supposed to have pets in this place. Why did Leena have to rescue a damn bunny? It's stinky and loud and it's not even cute, for Christ's sake. It has these bright-red eyes that look like tiny drops of blood in the middle of all that white fur.

Click click click click.

I turn another page. Why would anyone name a damn rabbit "Heathcliff" in the first place? I mean, how pretentious can you get? If Jude knew, he'd probably laugh.

Click click click click.

Another hour or so passes this way until, finally, I groan, and check the clock on my side table. It's almost ten. Leena's been hanging out with Jude for five hours.

I roll onto my side and stare at the bunny's cage.

Heathcliff glares back at me with those beady little bloodshot eyes. I can't believe I have to hang out in a room reeking of rabbit piss while Leena gets to be with Jude. Heathcliff is *her* pet. She should have to deal with him.

Click click—

I throw my pillow at Heathcliff's cage. It hits the glass with a soft *thwack*. Heathcliff bounces to the far corner, shivering. I have a sudden, horrible thought: *Why couldn't he have just died when Leena tried to fix his stupid leg?*

It's a terrible thing to think. I push it to the very back of my head, but I can't help the tiny spark of glee I feel at the idea. Leena's little "bun-bun" is a menace. I'm sure Sutton kind of wishes he'd have a little accident, too.

Frustrated, I switch off the overhead light and climb into bed. It's officially time for this day to be over.

Heathcliff finds his water dispenser again. His tongue sends the metal ball spinning and clicking. I pull a pillow over my head to block out the sound, but I can't fall asleep. My mind plays images of Leena and Jude on a loop. Jude touching Leena's arm. Jude leaning toward her face. Jude lowering his lips to hers . . . Heathcliff returns to his water bottle and the clicking starts again. *Click click click.* *Click click click.* It reminds me of Grandmother's rosary beads hitting her hospital bed. I can't stop clenching my shoulders. Grinding my teeth. I lie like that for hours, begging my brain to calm down. Fall asleep.

Then the darkness around me moves, taking on mass and shape. Jude crouches in front of my bed. The smoky, vanilla smell of incense clings to his hair. I smile at him, groggily. I must've fallen asleep at some point because my eyes are heavy and fuzzy. The room loses focus at the edges, like in an old photograph. Jude lifts a finger to his lips.

"Quiet enough?" he whispers.

A scream rips through the stillness. Jude breaks apart, his body nothing more than shadows that flit to the corners of the room like bats. I jerk awake.

Leena flicks on the lights. The bright fluorescent glow assaults my eyes. I cringe, blinking.

"What's going on?"

"Where's Heathcliff?" Leena hobbles across the room, her crutches creaking beneath her weight. "Did you let him out of his cage?"

"What are you talking about?" I murmur, still half asleep. "He's in the closet."

"He's *not* in the closet."

"Maybe Sutton took him out?" I say, rubbing my eyes with my palms.

"Sutton's in Jackson for that stupid game. Remember?" There's an edge to Leena's voice that sends something jittery and cold shooting up my spine. I blink, and my eyes start to adjust to the light.

"We'll look for him, okay?" I say, crawling out of bed. Leena nods. A tear slides out from the corner of her eye and rolls down her cheek but she brushes it away, hard. I open the closet, checking behind boots and coats. "I swear, he was in the cage when I—"

Someone knocks on the door, then eases it open without waiting for an answer. Sister Lauren sticks her head into our dorm.

"I heard a scream." She tucks a short brown lock of hair behind one ear. "Is everything okay?"

"We lost—" I start, but Leena jerks her head to the side to shoot me an angry look. *Shit*. The bunny's a secret. My head spins, trying to come up with a good lie. "I mean, Leena lost her favorite earrings, and . . ."

"Could the thing you lost have anything to do with this room smelling like a zoo?" Sister Lauren asks, wrinkling her nose. I press my lips together, not sure what to say. I knew it reeked of piss in here.

Leena opens her mouth to answer, but her face crumples. She lowers her head to her hands, her shoulders shaking. Sister Lauren kneels next to her and slides an arm around her shoulder.

"I'm not going to bust you, okay? Now, what was it? A hamster?"

Leena lifts her face from her hands. "A bunny."

"Let's check the hall," Sister Lauren says, squeezing

Leena's shoulder. "Sofia, you want to give the dorm another look before you head to bed?"

"Of course. I'm sure he's around here somewhere, Leena."

Leena nods again. Sister Lauren helps her to her feet and leads her into the hall. Our dorm is tiny, and it doesn't take me very long to search every inch of carpet. Heathcliff isn't in the closet or hiding behind the dressers. He isn't under either bed. He's just *gone*.

I know the bunny isn't here, but I check the entire room again, and then a third time after that. Sister Lauren and Leena haven't come back yet, so I look inside dresser drawers, and behind the books in our bookcase, and on the higher shelves in the back of our wardrobe. I don't get it. Heathcliff was in a cage, on a table in the closet. He couldn't have just escaped.

Finally, I collapse back onto my bed, frustrated. The sheets are pleasantly cool to the touch. My eyes droop. According to my alarm clock, it's past midnight. I can't believe Sister Lauren and Leena are still out looking. They must be searching every inch of the school. I'm going to be a zombie tomorrow if I don't get some sleep, so I stretch out across the cold sheets, yawning.

My fingers brush against something soft. My entire body stiffens. I reach a little farther, fingers grasping. It feels like hair, or . . .

I jerk my hand out from under the pillow and sit up. Not hair.

Fur.

I half leap, half fall out of my bed. Blankets tangle around my legs, and I lose my balance, slamming to the floor. Dull pain spreads through my shoulder and down my arm, but I barely notice.

I reach forward, and I curl my fingers around the pale pink pillowcase. My hands tremble.

I rip the pillow away before I can change my mind, letting it drop to the floor next to me. Heathcliff lies on the white sheets, his red eyes staring up at the ceiling. Blood blossoms across his fur like roses. I curl my hand into a fist and press it against my mouth to keep from screaming out loud. I *smell* him, all sharp and metallic. Like pennies.

That bunny cannot be lying there. Someone would have had to sneak into my locked room, silently kill it, and slip it under my pillow without making any sound. It's not *possible*. It's another Brooklyn nightmare. I pinch myself on the shoulder and a bright burst of pain flutters through my skin.

Or . . . could *I* have done this?

I wished for something bad to happen to Leena. And then she fell through a trapdoor and broke her leg. And tonight, just before I went to sleep, I wished that

Heathcliff was dead. Sister Lauren said demons could attach themselves to you. She said it was just like getting sick . . .

My mind slams closed on that line of thinking. *No*. This wasn't me. I'm not possessed. I would have remembered killing a bunny.

Footsteps sound in the hall outside my dorm. I go rigid, waiting for the door to fly open. For Leena to burst inside and see what I've done. But the girl moves past my room, the sound of footsteps fading as she makes her way down the hall. I exhale, my chest tight with worry. It doesn't matter how this happened. I have to get rid of it.

I work quickly. I rip the sheets off my mattress, and wrap them around the bunny, so I don't have to look into the creature's dull red eyes. I ball the sheets together, tight, and then I tug the case off my pillow and shove them inside. There. It looks innocent now. Like laundry. I tug my comforter over my bed, then shove a pillow underneath at the last second. Leena will think I'm sleeping. I throw a coat over my nightgown and creep across the room, easing the door open , the pillowcase heavy in my hands.

Hallway's empty. Dozens of doors stretch between the stairs and me, each one closed, hiding God knows what behind its polished surface. I creep forward until I reach the staircase. Then I run.

Icy rain pounds at the ground outside, creating rivers

of mud through the grass. I slosh through it, cringing at the sudden cold on my feet. Sleet slithers under my collar and cuts down my back, instantly soaking my thin nightgown. Mud oozes through my toes and climbs up around my feet and ankles. I hobble toward a thick grove of trees near the front fence. I drop to my knees and thrust my hands into the mud.

No one can find this bag. *Ever.*

I dig. Mud creeps in between my fingers and gushes up past my elbows. It's slick and cold, and soon my skin's gone numb and I can barely move my fingers. The muscles in my arms scream with pain but still, I dig. Pebbles and twigs bite my fingers, and a sharp rock peels away the skin along my knuckles. Blood appears, dark as oil against my skin. I grit my teeth, working through the pain.

Thunder rumbles in the distance, and a flash of lightning cuts across the sky, illuminating my shallow hole and bloody pillowcase. I sit back on my feet, gasping. This will have to do. I shove the pillowcase into the hole, then cup my hands and shovel dirt and mud on top of it. Something inside of me loosens when the last bit of pink cloth disappears below the ground.

It's over. The bunny's gone for good. Beneath the panic and the horror, I actually feel sort of . . . *good.* Heathcliff's dead, but it's okay. I fixed it. No one will ever know what happened.

I catch my reflection in the front door as I limp back to the dormitory. Mud covers my body. It's caked in my hair and in the creases on my knees and elbows. Long brown fingers streak along my calves. My nightgown is ruined. It's plastered to my legs, the hem ragged and torn. A hole has opened up just below my hip and a tiny glimpse of brown skin peeks through.

I lift my eyes to my face and, for a second, I don't recognize myself. I'm *smiling*. The expression is grotesque, like someone else has arranged my features into what they think a human smile should look like. My eyes are wide and manic, my lips stretched tight over my small white teeth.

My expression instantly changes into one of horror. What is wrong with me?

I lift a hand to push the door open and my fingers are raw. Bloody.

I hurry into the hall, a plan forming in the back of my head. I can't go to my dorm like this. Leena will know something's up. They keep fresh towels in the laundry room. I'll just sneak down and steal one, then hit the shared bathrooms on our floor. There's nothing suspicious about needing a shower. I'll shove my nightgown into my laundry bag before Leena can see it and change into—

"Sofia?" Sister Lauren's voice cuts through my

thoughts. I freeze. Water drips from my coat, forming a puddle on the floor.

Footsteps pound against the hall behind me. I'm too terrified to turn. I rack my brain, trying to come up with some excuse for why I was outside. Why I'm bloody and muddy and wet. My head goes blank. I have the sudden, foolish urge to run.

"Sofia?" Sister Lauren says, again. She's right behind me now. I release the breath I'd been holding, and turn.

Sister Lauren's eyes widen at the sight of me. She frowns, and a crease wrinkles the skin between her eyebrows. She opens her mouth, and then closes it again. She tilts her head to the side and understanding crosses her face.

"Oh, Sofia. Were you outside looking for Leena's bunny?"

Her words fall into my hands. The perfect lie, fully formed and waiting. All I have to do is take it.

"Yes," I say, surprised by the confidence in my voice. Like this was planned.

Sister Lauren smiles and shakes her head. "You're such a good friend," she says. "Leena's lucky to have you. Now go back upstairs and get cleaned up before anyone else sees you."

She nods at the staircase behind me, winking.

CHAPTER FOURTEEN

I don't sleep for the rest of the night. I lie on my back in bed, staring at the twisted crack running across the ceiling. I didn't have time to find new sheets, and the rough fabric of the mattress chafes my skin. I roll onto my side. A tiny spider clings to the glass outside our window. He casts a shadow over my bedside table as he scurries away.

The red numbers on my alarm clock tick past.

3:01. 4:15. 5:07.

I close my eyes, but the numbers are seared into my lids. Only now they look like eyes. Heathcliff's beady red eyes.

At five forty-seven, I crawl out of bed and dress silently. Leena fell asleep crying hours ago, but I still check her face to make sure her eyes are tightly shut. A strand of hair sticks to her cheek, fluttering when she breathes.

I creep past her and ease the door open, holding the knob to close it without catching the latch. Then I hurry down the staircase, out the main door, and across the grounds to the chapel.

It's empty this time. Silent. I head to the first pew, cross myself, and kneel. First the trapdoor, then Leena's bunny. And what's worse—I *liked* it. Both times I felt a spark of happiness that something horrible had happened. Brooklyn said there was evil inside me. She said I was just like her. I close my eyes and clasp my hands in front of my chest, but I'm not quite sure how to form a prayer. One question circles my head, instead.

Is the evil taking over my soul?

I dig my teeth into my lower lip, focusing on the pain until the question fades to the back of my mind. I'm nothing like Brooklyn. An evil girl wouldn't be kneeling inside a chapel at six in the morning. Possessed girls would never try to pray.

I stay kneeling, my back and shoulders stiff, but it's not the Lord I think about. It's my mother. I can practically smell the soapy scent of her skin and hear her

soothing me in her calm voice. She would know exactly
what to say if she were here.

"Mom," I whisper. "Please tell me what to do."

Pain pounds through my knees. I clench my hands
together so tightly that my fingernails leave tiny,
crescent-shaped marks on the backs of my hands. But
nothing happens. My mother doesn't speak to me.

Thwap!

The sound breaks the silence of the chapel. Chills
dance up the backs of my arms. My eyes shoot open and
I jerk around, expecting to see someone standing at the
chapel door.

But there's no one. The door stays shut.

I take a deep breath and twist around, still balanced
on my knees. Tiny white candles flicker from the altar at
the front of the room, sending a kaleidoscope of light and
shadow across the chapel's floor. Leena told me they're
called prayer candles. Apparently, they stay lit day and
night, until their tiny wicks finally burn out. I never
found them creepy before but now I can't help noticing
how the tiny spots of brightness leave the corners even
darker. Anyone could be hiding there.

Thwap!

I stumble to my feet, hugging my arms to my chest.
The darkness seems to pulse. I can practically see it

pressing in against the tiny spots of light. Threatening to extinguish them.

Thwap!

Heavy velvet curtains cover the wall behind the altar. I can just make out their edges in the light of the prayer candles. I open my mouth to call out, but something stops me. Maybe it's the silence. The chapel is so quiet that I hear the flames flickering, the wind rubbing up against the glass in the windows. I move forward, my footsteps soundless on the marble.

Thwap!

The noise echoes from the other side of the curtains, making the velvet flutter. It sounds like something wet and heavy slapping against the floor. I lower my hand and push the curtains open. Just an inch.

Thwap!

Candlelight spills past the curtains, bathing my feet in gold. It takes a moment for my eyes to adjust to the sudden glow.

Jude kneels on the floor inside the small room. Naked. Sweat clings to his bare skin, and deep red welts crisscross his shoulders. Tangled flesh bubbles up around his spine and twists down his back and around his waist. Fresh cuts overlap the old ones, the skin raw and angry. He stares at the floor, his wooden cross clenched in his fist.

A shadow moves behind him. I recognize Father Marcus's dark robes and the silver ring glinting from his gnarled finger. A length of leather rope dangles from his hand. He raises it over his head and, for a second, he just holds it there, the tapered end hanging between his shoulders.

The muscles in Jude's jaw tighten. He squeezes his eyes shut.

Father Marcus lowers his arm in a smooth, quick arc, bringing the whip down across Jude's back.

Thwap!

Something wet hits my cheek. *Blood.* My mouth falls open and I want to scream, but my voice gets trapped in my throat. I take a step backward and the sole of my sneaker squeaks against the marble.

Jude's head jerks up. His eyes lock on mine. A hundred emotions flicker across his face, all of them ugly.

Jude says something but I don't stick around long enough to find out what it.

I just run.

* * *

Leena hobbles around backstage, leaning into the crutches wedged beneath her arms. She stumbles, her crutch snagging on the edge of her costume.

"This is a disaster," she mumbles, untangling her skirt. "I'm going to fall flat on my face."

It's the opening night of *The Tempest*, a week after I witnessed the unsettling scene with Jude. I've been avoiding him, trying to keep a low profile and comforting Leena over Heathcliff's disappearance. Thankfully, I've convinced her to give up the search and told her that I'd even help her sneak a new pet into our room. She wants a mouse named Rochester.

The air around us buzzes with voices and the occasional nervous giggle. Actors flit across the stage dressed in stiff costumes, their faces caked with makeup. I'm helping glue the last tattered sails into place while Sutton crouches on an overturned milk crate, studying an ugly cut that twists across her thigh.

"You'll be fine, Leenie-bean," she drawls, picking at the scab.

"You're going to make it bleed," I warn, watching her dig her nails around the edges of her skin.

"Ugh, I know." Sutton makes a face. "It's *so* gross. But I want it gone before I see Dean." She starts picking at the scab again. "Stupid field hockey."

Leena balances on her good leg and waves her crutch between us. "Guys, focus. This is an emergency. I'm supposed to be onstage in like ten minutes."

"Can't you go without the crutch?" Sutton asks.

"Not if I want to walk."

A wicked smile crosses Sutton's face. "All the more reason to lean on Jude's big, strong arms."

Hearing Jude's name makes me flinch. I absently wipe my cheek with the back of my hand. I can still feel his blood on my face.

"I'm going to see if there's something I can use in the prop closet," Leena says, pushing through the stage curtain.

Sutton waits until Leena's gone and then leans forward, the milk crate creaking beneath her weight. "What's up with you?"

I turn my attention back to the sails I'm supposed to be working on, my heart beating so loudly I'm sure Sutton can hear it. I haven't told anyone what I saw in the chapel. I'm not sure they would believe me. "What do you mean?"

"Every time someone says Jude's name, you make the same face my mom makes when I bring up my dad." Sutton screws her face up, demonstrating. "It's like someone walked across your grave."

I laugh but it sounds hollow, even to me. I keep seeing Father Marcus's silver ring glint in the darkness, blood arcing through the air. I tell myself there must be some reason, but what explanation could there be for *that*? It was sick. Twisted.

My hands start to tremble. I curl them tighter around the glue gun so I don't drop it.

"Damn, Sofia," Sutton says, touching my shoulder.

"You look like you're about to lose it. Are you still thinking about that bunny? I'm telling you, Leena must've forgotten to close his cage. He used to get out once a week."

If only—Heathcliff feels like the least of my problems now. "I think it's just stage fright," I manage.

"You're not even in the play," Sutton says.

The hall door slams open before I can answer. The sudden thud makes Sutton and me jump. Sister Lauren pokes her head backstage.

"Five minutes to curtain!" she calls. She glances at Sutton and raises an eyebrow. "Funny, Sutton, I don't remember casting you."

"I'm calming your crew with my witty commentary," Sutton says.

"Thanks for that. Now it's time to take your seat."

Sutton squeezes my arm and stands. "We'll talk later," she says. I nod and she follows Sister Lauren back into the hallway.

Band members tune their instruments in the pit below. The air fills with strings screeching and horns honking. I hear muffled footsteps on the other side of the curtain as the audience takes their seats. I shake my hand out to stop the trembling and put the final touches on the sail. It's almost showtime.

The stage curtain rustles. "Hey."

The muscles in my shoulders tighten at the sound of Jude's voice. I fumble with the glue gun, accidentally dropping a hot bead on my finger.

"Crap," I mutter. Jude kneels next to me. He's already dressed as Ferdinand, with an emerald-green tunic buttoned up to his chin and a gold sash knotted at his waist. His wooden cross hangs from a leather cord around his neck. It looks as though the makeup crew loaded his hair with some product to make it look windblown, and a few days' worth of stubble covers his cheeks and chin. Sister Lauren must've wanted him to look disheveled. His character has been shipwrecked, after all.

"Are you okay?" He reaches for my hand, but I jerk it back. Hurt flashes across his face.

"I'm fine," I say. Jude leans back on his heels, hands folded in his lap. He was sitting in the same position that morning in the chapel. I think of the sweat glistening from his bare skin. I hear the crack of the whip hitting his back.

"Sofia," he says. "I was hoping we could talk."

I squeeze my eyes shut, forcing the horrible memory away. "I'm sorry," I say. "I have a lot of stuff to get ready before you—"

Jude grabs my wrist. *"Listen,"* he says in a low, urgent voice. "There are things about me that you don't know. Things about my past, and what I did to . . . it's complicated."

"Complicated?" I repeat. What I saw wasn't complicated. It was disturbing.

"Father Marcus is helping me work through some stuff," Jude explains. "What you saw . . . it's a really old Catholic tradition. It's supposed to bring you closer to God. We thought it might help."

"Help with *what*?" I ask.

Sister Lauren's voice blares over the loudspeaker. "Five minutes to curtain! Take your places."

Actors shuffle across the stage and duck into the wings. The stage manager hisses at me to get off the stage.

"I told you," Jude says, his voice low. "I have trouble sometimes, with anger and self-control. Father Marcus says I have a 'hero complex,' whatever that is. Like wanting to help people is supposed to be wrong. He thought this might help me give in to God."

Jude's eyes flicker over my face, concern etched into his features. For a second, I forget about what I saw in the chapel. I stare at the curls lying against his neck. The freckle next to his upper lip. A familiar mix of anxiety and want flares to life in my chest.

"Can I ask you a favor?" Jude stands, offering his hand to help me up. This time, I take it without flinching.

"What is it?"

Jude drops my hand to untie the wooden cross from his neck. "This was my father's," he explains. "I wear it every day, but Sister Lauren says it doesn't go with my costume. I was wondering . . . could you hold on to it for me?"

"Of course." My voice sounds thicker than usual. Like it belongs to someone else. The corner of Jude's mouth curls into a smile. He leans in close, lifting the leather cord to my neck. His fingers brush my skin, leaving trails of heat along my collarbone.

He finishes knotting the necklace, but he doesn't move his hand away. My throat goes dry.

"Sofia," he murmurs. His breath tickles the side of my face. He curls his hands around my shoulders, pulling me to his chest. "I can't stop thinking about you."

"We shouldn't." I feel his heart beating through the fabric of his tunic. He's close enough to kiss. All I have to do is lift my face. I lean in closer. "Jude . . ."

"Jude?" The curtains rustle, and Leena hobbles backstage, plastic vines wrapped around her crutches. "I thought I saw you . . ."

I jerk away from Jude, but it's too late. Leena freezes. Her eyes move from Jude to the wooden cross hanging around my neck.

She blinks, and in that instant it's like something in her breaks. Her mouth goes slack and all the color drains from her face. Her stage makeup looks heavy and garish against her pale skin.

"Leena," I start, but she stumbles away from me. She grips her crutches so tightly that her knuckles turn white.

"We're needed onstage, Jude," she mutters before pushing through the curtains. "We're starting."

CHAPTER FIFTEEN

I don't stick around to watch the play. I duck into one of the dressing rooms and hunch down on a stool at the makeup table, hiding like a coward. My reflection stares out from the mirror. I shift my eyes to my knees. I can't stand to look at myself.

Speakers hang from the ceiling, broadcasting the play to the empty room. Leena's staticky voice bounces off the walls around me. She recites every line perfectly.

I hide there until the play is over, and then I busy myself backstage, sweeping sand and gathering props until I'm sure Leena has headed back to the dorm. I've practiced my apology a dozen times by then, but it still sounds wrong. Forced. Leena will never forgive me.

Our dorm is empty when I get back, but there's a note waiting on my bed.

We're meeting up with Dean and his friend at the chapel to toast Leena's AMAZING performance. Come meet us (use the back door)!!! —Sutton

ps—destroy this message after you've read it. xoxoxo

Leena snuck out? I swear under my breath, crumpling the piece of paper in one hand. She'd never risk getting in trouble if she hadn't seen Jude and me backstage. I push myself to my feet and grab my coat.

* * *

Moonlight paints the chapel's whitewashed siding silver. It glints off the stained glass windows, making them wink in the darkness.

I stop at the gate. Something dashes through the brush, rustling the leaves before going still. I flinch and glance over my shoulder, certain I'm going to see Father Marcus step out of the trees, the word *expelled* already on his lips. But there's no one. Clouds drift over the moon, blocking the last tendrils of light.

Voices echo from inside the chapel. I shiver and slip through the gate, pushing it closed with a creak.

The chapel's back door opens into a narrow room. A small table leans against the wall to my left, holding a leather Bible and a heavy brass candleholder. I brush my fingertips lightly over the candleholder, looking around the space. The room feels familiar. I frown, studying the shadows gathering in the corners, the stained glass window, the paintings staring down from the walls—

I feel the hot splash of blood hitting my cheek. I hear the sound of leather slapping against skin. *Thwap!*

I jerk my hand away from the table, horror rushing over me. This room seems familiar to me because I've seen it before. Jude knelt naked on the floor just feet from where I'm standing, cringing as Father Marcus whipped him.

I hold my breath and hurry through the heavy velvet curtains hanging open on the far wall. I don't inhale again until I reach the main altar. The air in that tiny room felt *wrong*, somehow. Spoiled.

Prayer candles flicker from the altar, casting a dull golden glow over the rows of wooden pews. I spot Sutton sitting on a windowsill near the front entrance. Dean hovers over her, his mouth buried in her neck. She wraps her legs around his waist, pulling him closer. I blush and avert my eyes. A boy I don't recognize hunches down in the front pew a few feet away, holding a Budweiser bottle and studying something on his cell phone.

A shape separates from the shadows to my left. I stumble away from it, smacking my hip into the altar. The candles wobble, wicks flaring.

"Leena?" I groan, a dull pain spreading through my side. "Is that you?"

Leena is still wearing her stage makeup. Dark circles of blush cover her cheeks, and she's smudged her lipstick. Sweaty strands of black hair fall loose from her braid and stick to her neck and forehead. She's changed out of her costume, though. A thick sweater hangs from her shoulders, half covering a pair of ripped jeans. She had to cut one of the legs short to fit it over her chunky white cast.

"You came." Booze makes her voice thick and sloppy. She hobbles toward me, balancing on just one crutch. A bottle of coconut rum dangles from her free hand. "I didn't know if you would."

I stare at the bottle. "Are you drunk?"

Leena wrinkles her nose. Her breath smells sickly sweet. "Brian bet me I couldn't drink the whole bottle," she says. "If I win, he's going to show me his car."

"Brian?" I glance at the boy sitting in the front pew. He's older than Dean. Greasy black hair falls over his forehead, and the corner of a tattoo peeks out from beneath his T-shirt. It looks like a woman's leg.

"You're not going anywhere with that guy." I shoot a glance at Sutton, but she's too distracted by Dean to catch my dirty look. I can't believe she left Leena alone with some creep. I take a step away from the altar and Leena stumbles backward, swaying. I grab her crutch to steady her before she falls. "Maybe you should sit down. I can find you some water."

"Don't do that." Leena's words slur. "Don't pretend to be nice."

She pulls her crutch away from me and rocks back on her feet, nearly stumbling over own her cast. We're standing near the edge of the pulpit, just inches from the stairs leading down to the pews. There isn't far to fall, but if Leena hit the ground at the right angle, she could reinjure her leg.

She lifts the rum to her mouth and tips it back, leaving her lips wet and sticky. I need to take the bottle away from her. I edge forward, like she's an animal I don't want to spook.

"Why don't you give me that?" I say, reaching for the rum. "You're going to hurt yourself."

"You don't care if I get hurt." Leena hugs the bottle to her chest. A tear spills onto her cheek and she wipes it away angrily with the back of her hand. "You *want* me to get hurt."

She rocks backward another step, sliding the

rubber-tipped foot of her crutch an inch closer to the edge of the pulpit. I cringe. "Leena, come on, you're really close to the stairs—"

"All this time I thought you were my *friend*. And then, when I saw you with Jude, I realized you were just playing me." Leena motions to me with her arm, sending an arc of coconut rum splattering across the floor. "You want me to get hurt so you can have him all to yourself. That's why you left the trapdoor unlocked, and that's why . . ."

Leena blinks, and it takes a long moment for her eyes to flutter open again. Another tear runs down her face, tracing a pink line in her makeup.

"I know you did something to Heathcliff," she says, her voice cracking. I swallow. My mouth feels dry.

"I didn't, Leena. I swear."

"You didn't like him." Leena leans into her crutch. The wood creaks beneath her weight. "And then, all of a sudden, he was *gone*."

My skin pricks with nerves. "What are you talking about?"

"You do terrible things. If you want something, you just take it, even if someone else gets hurt. You're . . . you're evil."

Heat spreads through my chest. I stare into Leena's unfocused eyes and, for a second, I want to push her.

She doesn't deserve her perfect life any more than I deserve my shitty one. I can practically feel her body tipping backward beneath my hands. If she weren't here, Jude and I could be together, and I wouldn't have to feel guilty about that damn bunny or the trapdoor. I could wipe the past clean and start over.

"You should be careful what you wish for, Sofia," Leena says in a small, trembling voice. "Jude may have chosen you, but God punishes sinners. You'll see."

Candlelight wavers behind me, casting our shadows across the floor. I study Leena. She's drunk. I could make it to the back door before she does, easy. And then, *oops*, all I'd have to do is slam the door and twist the dead bolt. I could stand back and watch this place burn.

I hear Brooklyn's voice whispering in my ear: *The evil lives inside of you already . . .*

Shame washes over me, and I stumble away from the altar. What the hell is wrong with me? I would never think those things. *Never.*

The sound of metal clicking against metal cuts through the chapel. I flinch, and jerk my head toward the front entrance. *Keys.*

"Shit! Someone's here!" Sutton hisses. She grabs Dean by the collar of his shirt and drags him behind a pew.

"Come on." I take Leena's arm and pull her toward the back room. She murmurs something and tries to push me away, but I dig my fingers into her wrist, holding tight. She stumbles forward on her crutch.

The keys jangle, then go still. We don't have time to make it to the back room now. I pull Leena's crutch out from under her arm, and help her crouch down behind the altar. Someone swears, and I see movement from the corner of my eye as Brian ducks behind the pew with Sutton and Dean. Dean knocks over an empty beer can with his foot, but Brian grabs it before it rolls into the aisle.

A creak echoes through the chapel. Someone releases a deep, phlegmy cough.

"Who's there?" he asks. Cold fingers walk down my spine. It's Father Marcus.

"Dammit," Leena whispers, huddling closer to me. Her ragged breath hits the back of my neck. I motion for her to keep quiet.

Footsteps make their way down the aisle.

I hold my breath and edge forward. Leena digs her fingers into my shoulders and I freeze, my heart thudding.

Father Marcus stops walking. "I heard voices. I know someone's here."

I glance over my shoulder. Leena stares back at me, her eyes rimmed with red. Sweat glistens on her forehead. I lift a finger to my mouth, then turn back around. Slowly, I lean past the edge of the altar and peer into the darkness.

Father Marcus stands near the center of the chapel, head cocked—listening. Shadows obscure his face, but moonlight glints in from the stained glass windows, painting the top of his head silver. He drifts forward, the hem of his black robes dragging along the floor.

Three shadows rise, silently, from the pews behind him. Sutton, Dean, and Brian hurry for the front door, their footsteps soundless on the tile. Sutton stays behind for a second, looking for me and Leena. She raises her shoulders in a desperate shrug—*there's nothing I can do*—before hurrying after the boys.

I hold my breath as she eases the door open and slips outside. The door clicks shut and Father Marcus whirls around. But Sutton's gone.

Leena's fingernails pinch the skin on my shoulders. "We're going to be expelled," she whispers.

Quiet. I mouth the word rather than say it out loud. Leena presses her lips together. Nods.

There's about three feet of open space between the altar and the velvet curtains that lead to the back room. If Leena and I can make it through there, we can get to the door without Father Marcus seeing us. I shift my weight to my front leg, poised to run.

"I know there's someone here," Father Marcus calls. "Best to just come out from where you're hiding."

Three feet. Maybe less. I could be out the door before Father Marcus made it to the pulpit. Leena would never make it with her cast, but Father Marcus would probably follow me outside, giving her a chance to get away.

The legs in my muscles tighten, itching to move. I lean forward.

A spray of pebbles hits the window, rattling the glass in the pane. I hear laughter outside, then running. Father Marcus whirls around.

"Little punks," he mutters, sweeping back to the front door. I shoot forward, dragging Leena behind me. The booze has made her slow and clumsy. She stumbles, banging a shoulder into the altar and nearly fumbling her crutch. A candle topples off the side of the altar and smashes into the floor. A hairline crack shoots across the candleholder. The flame flickers and sparks, but stays lit.

I shoot a nervous glance at the front entrance, but Father Marcus has already left to chase down whoever threw the stones. We're alone. The candle rolls across the floor, coming to rest next to a curtain. The flame grows and leaps onto the fabric. Leena blinks at it, her eyes not quite focusing.

"Just *go*," I tell her.

Leena looks at me, then lurches through the curtains. The flame gently licks the edge of the velvet. Something dark and hungry rises in my chest. I could just let it burn. Leena stumbles into something in the back room and swears loudly. It would be so easy to push past her on that stupid crutch. I could lock the door behind me. No one would ever know.

My fingers fumble for the cross at my neck. Jude's cross. I stomp out the flame, disgusted with myself. I hurry through the small room. It's empty—Leena must've made a break for the woods. I push the door open and hurry outside, letting it slam shut behind me.

"Come on!" Sutton calls from the woods. I catch a glimpse of her blonde hair and tanned legs before she disappears into the gloom.

It's too dark to see where I'm going, so I rely on muscle memory to carry me across the grounds. Muffled sounds reach me: footsteps crashing through the brush, heavy breathing, Sutton shouting *Hurry!* They seem far away, as if I'm hearing them underwater. I want to call out to the others, but I'm afraid Father Marcus is hiding in the shadows. Waiting to catch me.

I'm relieved when the trees part, revealing redbrick walls and my room's familiar window. Wind moves the curtain—the window's still open.

"Sutton?" I whisper.

A slim hand pushes the curtain aside and Sutton's blonde head appears in the window.

"Did it work?" She reaches for me and her fingers close around my wrist. "The pebbles? It was Dean's idea. He said we had to distract Father Marcus so you guys could get out."

"It worked." I wedge a foot against the wall, grabbing the windowsill with my other hand. Sutton grunts, half dragging me into the room as I struggle to pull my weight through the window. I lose my balance and wobble forward, but Sutton catches me before I crash into anything.

"Thanks," I say, brushing the dirt off the back of my jeans. A muscle in my shoulder twinges. I grimace and try to stretch it out.

Sutton leans past me. "Where's Leena?"

"She left before I did." I glance around the room, half expecting Leena to materialize from the shadows in the corners. "She isn't back yet?"

"No." Sutton frowns. "I didn't see her in the woods, either. You're sure Father Marcus didn't—"

"He didn't catch her," I say before she can finish. "But, Sutton, she was so drunk. I don't know how she's going to make it back here on her own." I think of Leena stumbling around on her crutch, her eyes blurry, and feel a sliver of guilt. "You think she'd get lost? Or something happened with her leg?"

"Leena's been going to this school for three years. She's not lost."

A floorboard creaks in the hall just outside our door. Sutton swears. She quickly pulls the window closed.

"Bed," she whispers, pushing me across the room. "Pretend you're sleeping."

"What about Leena?"

"We can't risk looking for her now." Sutton peels off her jeans and digs her polka-dot pajama pants out of her dresser. She yanks them on and climbs into bed, tugging her comforter up to her chin. "She'll have to find her own way back."

CHAPTER SIXTEEN

"**D**id you hear that?"

Sutton's voice jars me awake. I blink, slowly letting my eyes adjust to the darkness of our room. Sutton lies on her side in the bed next to mine. The whites of her eyes flash in the shadows.

"Hear what?" I murmur, my brain thick and heavy. Sleep pulls at me, dragging me down. My eyes flicker closed.

Wind howls through the trees. Only it's not wind. I ease my eyes back open, frowning.

"*That*." Sutton sits up, her shoulders rigid with fear. The sound loops back on itself, growing distant at first, and then louder. Closer. Recognition flutters through me.

"Is that a siren?" I ask.

Sutton kicks off her comforter and climbs out of bed. I sit up, but I can't quite remember how to make my legs work. It can't be a siren. We didn't do anything wrong. And, besides, Father Marcus didn't even see us. I stare, frozen, as Sutton crosses the room and throws back the curtains covering our windows. The muscles in her jaw go slack and her mouth falls open. She lifts a trembling finger.

"Fire," she whispers.

Nausea floods my stomach. "No," I say, climbing out of bed. I cross the room and crowd next to Sutton at the window.

Smoke hangs above the woods, dark and thick, like someone spilled oil across the sky. Red lights flash in the trees. Sirens howl.

"Oh God." Sutton bunches a hand near her mouth. "It's coming from the chapel."

A dark thought wraps around my brain. I glance at Leena's empty bed.

The blood drains from Sutton's face, leaving her skin ashen. "Sofia," she breathes. "What if . . ."

Doubt seeps through me. Leena never came home, and now there's a fire . . . "Leena left the chapel before I did," I say, trying to convince myself as much as Sutton. "I *heard* her."

But I didn't actually hear Leena get out. She was just gone.

"She could have circled back to the chapel after you left." Sutton lifts a hand to her mouth, lightly touching a finger to her lips. "She was so drunk. If she couldn't figure out how to get home, and it was too cold . . ."

"I locked the door." At least, I think I did. I close my eyes, rubbing my eyelids. I think of the moments right before I ran through the back door, trying to remember twisting the lock. I come up blank.

Static fills my ears, blocking out the sirens and Sutton's voice. I think of the candle toppling from the altar and rolling across the floor. The white flame leaping onto the curtain. Leena's expression as she watched it catch, light dancing in her unfocused eyes.

But I stomped the fire out. I stopped it. Didn't I?

A sharp knock raps on our door. "Roll call! Five minutes!" Sister Lauren shouts. There's an edge of panic in her tone.

Sutton grabs my arm and drags me into the hallway. Dazed students stumble past us. Winter coats cover their lacy nightgowns and striped pajamas, and they've shoved their feet into Converse sneakers and UGGs. A girl I recognize from geometry—Erika—wears reindeer slippers with tiny bells on the toes. They jingle as she shuffles toward the stairs.

"Single file," Sister Lauren calls. She stands at the other end of the hall, a rumpled pair of St. Mary's sweatpants hanging from her hips, her hair piled in a messy topknot. Short, spiky pieces stick out of the elastic and fall around her face. "Stay calm, everyone."

Her eyes flicker over to Sutton and me, and something in her expression sharpens. "Put your shoes on," she says to us. "We need everyone outside for roll call."

"Did someone get hurt?" Sutton asks. Her voice has a little-girl quality to it that I've never heard before.

"That's what we're trying to figure out," Sister Lauren says, counting off the other girls. "We all need to gather outside."

I grab my coat while Sutton yanks a pair of cowboy boots over her pajama pants. We hurry down the front stairs, taking the steps two at a time. I pause at the main doors, hit with a sudden memory of the first time I walked through them. I was on my way to meet my new roommates, feeling anxious and hopeful as I climbed the stairs behind Father Marcus.

It hasn't even been a month and already, everything's different. One of those girls might be—

I shudder and push through the doors. I can't even think it.

Cold hits me in the face. It snakes around my bare ankles and blows straight through my flannel pajama pants. We make our way over to the crowd of nuns and students already gathered on the lawn.

Two fire trucks race down the narrow, twisted road leading to the chapel, sirens blaring. Sutton huddles close to me, her icy fingers finding my hand.

"Oh God," she whispers. I barely hear her. I tug my hand away and turn, searching the faces of the girls around us. Leena has to be here. She *has* to be.

"Do you see her?" A note of panic has crept into Sutton's voice. I don't answer. My eyes dart over face after face, until I find every single girl who lives on our floor, and everyone I know from classes and play practice. Everyone except Leena.

Sutton seems to realize this at the same moment I do. "She isn't here. Oh God, Sofia . . ."

My mouth feels dry. "She . . . she must've passed out in the woods," I say. Fear leaves my voice high-pitched and weak. "That's why she's not back yet."

Sutton nods, but she doesn't seem to hear me. She stares at the smoke staining the sky, frowning. I spot a shadow moving through the trees and my heart leaps into my throat. I grab Sutton's arm, my knees buckling in relief.

"There!" I say, pointing. "That's her!"

The figure walks closer. My heart seems to go still inside of my chest and every muscle in my body tightens. Leena's coming. Leena's okay. I'm so busy searching for black hair and dark jeans that it takes a long moment for my brain to recognize Father Marcus's bald head and long black robes. Familiar panic fills my body. I twist my hands together, squeezing so hard the blood drains from my fingers.

"It's not her," Sutton whispers.

"Maybe he's coming to tell us he found her in the woods," I say, but a horrible thought creeps through my mind.

Leena's dead, just like you wanted. You killed her.

Father Marcus stops in front of Sister Lauren. He runs a hand over his head and says something in a low voice. I move to Sutton's other side, sliding an arm over her shoulders so it looks like I'm comforting her. Sutton flashes me a confused look. I lift a finger to my lips and flick my eyes toward Father Marcus. Sutton nods.

"Everyone's here except for Leena," Sister Lauren is saying. She tucks a strand of hair behind her ear and glances back at the burning chapel. "She must've snuck out."

"Are you sure the rest of your girls have been in their rooms all night?" Father Marcus asks. Sister Lauren turns, catching my eye. I quickly look down at my sneakers, pretending to study the pattern of dirt on my toe. The top of my head itches and I know, without looking up, that Sister Lauren's still watching me.

She knows, I realize. She knows we're listening. She knows we snuck out. It's like she can see through the layers of hair and skin and bone, down to all of the terrible things I'm hiding. I squeeze Sutton's shoulder, bracing myself.

"I checked the rest of the girls personally," Sister Lauren says. "They were in their beds all night. Father, did someone—"

Father Marcus lifts a hand. "Not here. Why don't you lead your girls back up to their dorms. I don't want them to see—"

A siren blares to life and, seconds later, an ambulance explodes from the trees. It zips down the road, red lights flashing in the darkness.

My heart slows until it feels as if I can count every beat. Shadows move in the ambulance's back windows. EMTs crouch over something. Someone.

That moment in the chapel plays on a loop in my mind. The candle lighting the curtain on fire. Leena staring down at the flames, then stumbling through the back room toward the door.

"Who's in there?" Sutton turns to Sister Lauren. "Is it Leena? Is it *her*?"

"Sutton . . ." Sister Lauren reaches for Sutton's arm,

but Sutton drops to her knees, lowering her face to her hands. A sob erupts from her lips, shaking her entire body.

I stand completely still. This isn't happening. But even as the words enter my head, I feel something stirring deep within my chest. *I wanted this.* I wanted Leena gone. I wanted her life. And, one way or another, I get what I want.

"No," I whisper, pushing the thoughts away. That's the jealousy talking. I will not be weak. I will not let the Devil in. Tears run down my cheeks, tracing cold lines on my face. I wipe them away with the sleeve of my jacket—then freeze.

The smell of smoke hangs in the air but it's faint. We're not downwind of the chapel, and the trees block most of the smoky haze from reaching the lawn. I see the smoke lifting high above the chapel, but I don't smell it. Not really. Except when I lift the sleeve of my coat to my nose.

My coat *reeks* of smoke.

CHAPTER SEVENTEEN

Father Marcus stands on the stage in front of the velvet curtains, flanked by two altar boys dressed all in white and gold. Lilies and tulips and roses crowd the stage around him, their ivory petals fading to brown around the edges. They'd be lovely, except for the stiff black ribbons tied to their vases. Reminders of why we're here.

Father Marcus clears his throat. The thick, phlegmy sound echoes off the walls. He leans over his Bible, bald head gleaming under the hot overhead lights. "We have come together," he says, "to remember before God the life of Leena Paeng."

It's two days before Christmas break, three since Leena died in the fire that burned down the chapel. I sit in the aisle seat nearest the back wall, wearing the same scratchy dress I wore the day of my mother's funeral.

I took the first seat I could find, not even bothering to see if Sutton saved me a spot. I'm not sure I could face her. Sniffling students and crying teachers fill the auditorium. They pass boxes of Kleenex down the aisles. Some hold skinny plastic candles with electric wicks. We're not allowed to have open flames in the school anymore.

Dried mud clings to the hem of my dress. I pick at it with my fingernail.

That's graveyard mud, I think. *It's mud from the ground where my mother was buried.*

"God alone is holy and just and good," Father Marcus continues. His voice is stiff and cold, like he's speaking about someone he's never met and not a student at his own school. "In that confidence, then, we commend young Leena to God's healing and mercy."

I pick and pick, until a crust of dirt lodges itself beneath my fingernail and a thread unravels from the black fabric, leaving a tiny hole at the edge of my dress. A girl in the seat in front of me reaches for a tissue and blows her nose. The sound rattles something deep within my chest. I'm not even crying. Leena was my roommate, and I can't muster a single tear.

Father Marcus clears his throat again. The sound is thicker this time. Wetter. "Leena was a child of God and, like all children, she stumbled . . ."

Stumbled. That one word sends me back to the chapel on the night of the fire. I see Leena struggling with her crutches, her eyes glassy with booze. I smell burning hair. Burning *skin.*

I shift in my uncomfortable dress. I shouldn't be here. I inhale, but my lungs feel like paper bags, like someone's blowing air into them, and then squeezing until they're small and crumpled and empty. The room tilts.

I stand and race for the door. People whisper and stare, but it doesn't matter. I have to get out of here. I can't *breathe.* I push the door open as quietly as I can, and then ease it closed behind me.

The air in the hallway tastes different. Fresher. I lean against the wall, sucking it into my lungs. The room stops spinning, but my legs still feel shaky. I sink to the floor, pulling my knees to my chest. I inhale, and then let it all out. I lower my forehead to my knees. A thin layer of sweat coats my face, making my skin feel clammy.

Just breathe, I tell myself. Don't worry about anything else.

I've seen a dead body before. I didn't stick around after the train accident to see Karen broken on the ground, but there have been others. Alexis was the worst. She'd been burned, just like Leena, and then arranged like a doll in Riley's bed. I'd pulled back the covers and there she was—wispy strands of hair trailing away from her bloody skull, blackened skin peeling off her cheeks. Fire ate her lips, leaving her mouth in a permanent snarl.

A strangled sob bubbles up my throat, breaking the silence of the hallway. My chest feels tight and I can't quite manage to catch my breath. Alexis's death was my fault, just like Leena's death, and Leena's accident, and Leena's bunny. Everything's always my fault.

I tug Jude's wooden cross out from under my shirt. I haven't had a chance to return it to him. Classes were canceled after Leena died, and we've been told to stay in our dormitories unless there's an emergency. I tell myself I'm only wearing it now so I can give it back when I see him, but if that were true, I probably wouldn't keep it hidden beneath my clothes. I press it between my hands and close my eyes.

"Please, God," I whisper. The idea of praying still feels strange, but at this point, I don't know who else to turn to. Jealousy has made my soul a weak, easy target for Brooklyn, and Sister Lauren said the only way to strengthen your soul is through a relationship with the Lord. I close my eyes, focusing all of my attention on God.

"Please," I whisper, my voice trembling. I picture a demon clinging to my back, digging long, pointed talons into my shoulders. Its horrible smile looks just like Brooklyn's.

"I'm begging you," I continue. "Help me get rid of this . . . *thing.* Help me be good—"

The door creaks open. "Sofia?"

Jude's voice makes me start. I drop the cross and wipe the tears from my cheeks with the back of my hand. He's in his altar boy outfit again, same as when I first met him. Between the white robes and the black curls, he looks almost angelic.

"You're missing the service." He sinks to the floor, robes pooling around him. He's shaved since the night of the play. His cheeks look smooth, and there's a tiny nick just below his chin. His skin smells like aftershave. Pine, and something else. Cloves, maybe.

I tear my eyes away from him and focus instead on a thin crack in the wall across from us. It stretches all the way from the floor to the ceiling. I try to keep my voice steady. "Believe me, Leena wouldn't want me in there."

Jude tips his head to the side. "You were one of her best friends," he says. "Of course she'd want you there."

The students inside the auditorium start to sing. I don't recognize the song, but the melody is low and lilting. Something sad. Jude and I listen for a moment in silence. I wipe my nose on the sleeve of my dress.

"You're wrong," I say once the singing stops. "She was mad at me. After she saw us . . ." My voice cracks. I swallow and try again, but a fresh sob lodges itself in my throat. I curl my hand into a fist and ball it next to my mouth to muffle the sound of my crying.

Jude squeezes my shoulder, as if he can read my mind. "Yeah. She seemed pretty upset."

"She *hated* me," I choke out. "And if we hadn't been in a fight, she never would have been drinking that night. She wouldn't have gone to the chapel, and she'd still be . . ."

"I know it feels that way, but it's not true. You can't know what would have happened that night if you weren't fighting, or if you didn't go out, or if you'd said the right thing, or done the right thing."

Jude's eyes lose focus. He swallows—hard—his Adam's apple jerking up and down in his throat. *"Believe me.* I know what it's like to relive one horrible moment over and over. I get it."

I stare at his face, wondering what memory tortures him. "How?"

He absently touches a spot on his arm. "It's complicated."

I'm suddenly aware of how close we're sitting. I think of Leena, and shrug his hand off my shoulder, my skin burning. This is why I didn't want to talk to him. I can't stand within five feet of Jude without completely losing track of what I'm doing. The unfocused, dreamy quality leaves Jude's face. He looks at me, eyes narrowing.

"Is that why you're avoiding me?" he asks. "Because you think it's your fault that Leena died?"

"I'm not avoiding you," I say. Jude lifts an eyebrow.

"Maybe a little," I admit.

"Leena was the friend you were talking about?" Jude asks. "The one you didn't want to hurt?"

I nod.

Jude exhales. "I'm really sorry she died. But I need you to know—I never had feelings for her. You didn't do anything wrong."

"She saw things differently," I say.

"She would have gotten over it after a while. People change. I've changed. It used to be that all I could think about was God. And now . . ."

Jude's voice trails off. I stare at him. "And now?" I press.

"And now all I can think about is you."

I open my mouth, then close it again. My mind has gone blank. I've wished that Jude would say those words to me from the moment I saw him. Now that Leena's gone, there's no reason for me to stay away from him. Everything I wanted is within my grasp.

Be careful what you wish for, Leena said. Those were some of the last words she ever said to me.

"Just be honest with me, Sofia," Jude says. "Do you have any interest in me at all? Or is this thing between us in my head?"

"It's not that easy," I mumble. I picture the demon clinging to my back again, its talons digging deeper and deeper into my shoulders.

Jude furrows his eyebrows. "Why not?"

"I kind of need to work on myself right now," I say, "but you make it so . . ."

I hesitate, struggling for the right word. Jude shifts closer. "I make it so what?"

"I can't think straight when you're around," I spit out.

Hurt flashes across Jude's face. I squeeze my eyes shut. Everything I say comes out wrong. "I didn't mean it like that," I say. "It's just . . . what if we're making a mistake? You said it yourself—you can't focus on your relationship with God when I'm around." Leena's unfocused eyes flash into my head. She whispers, her voice thick with booze. *God punishes sinners.* "What if what we're doing is a sin?"

"Do you really think that?" Jude asks, his voice quiet.

I stare down at my hands, unable to answer.

Jude stands and pushes the auditorium door open. Father Marcus is leading a prayer. His low, gravelly voice drifts into the hallway like smoke.

"At the moment of our death, make us ready to—"

The door swings shut behind Jude, cutting him off.

I sit in the hallway alone for a long moment, staring at the crack in the wall across from me, wondering if I made the right decision. The school loudspeaker crackles on, and then the sound of church bells fills the hall. They echo and clang, then fade to a soft rumble. I used to love the sound of church bells but there's something off about these. The real bells were destroyed when the chapel burned down. This recording is a pale imitation. Haunting and soulless.

I press my hands over my ears to block out the sound but, somehow, that just makes it worse. The bells blend together into one long, hollow ring. It doesn't sound like bells at all. It sounds like an engine. Like the blare of a horn.

Like a train racing toward me.

CHAPTER EIGHTEEN

I head to the dormitory kitchens as soon as I wake up on Christmas Eve. Students aren't technically allowed to cook here, but Sister Lauren snuck me the key so I could raid the pantry over the holiday break. I'm basically alone until after New Year's, but I didn't have anywhere else to go, so the school agreed to let me stay in the dorms. It's a relief to have the place to myself. There's no one around for me to hurt.

I dig through the cupboards until I find flour, baking chocolate, and a dusty bag of red-striped peppermint chips nearing their expiration date. My *abuelita* used to make the best cookies. On Christmas morning, she'd fill our kitchen with *biscochos* and *garabatos* and gingerbread men and—my favorite—double fudge cookies with peppermint chips. Mom and Grandmother didn't agree on a lot, but every year I'd find them standing shoulder to shoulder next to the oven, whipping up batter and dancing to old Christmas carols.

Mom and I started making the cookies together after Grandmother got sick. And now . . . my mother might be gone, but there's no way I'm giving up this tradition. It's part of my plan for redemption. I'm going to do exactly what Sister Lauren told me to—I've already freed myself of the distraction of Jude, and now I'm going to seek communion with other believers. My grandmother is the most religious person I've ever known. If she can't help me repair my relationship with God, no one can.

I gather my ingredients and pull up some of Grandmother's favorite Christmas carols on my phone. Then I get to work. I thought it would make me sad to do this alone, but instead it's the opposite. Music floats through the air around me, and it feels familiar to crack the eggs and stir up the batter. It's almost like being home.

Someone raps at the kitchen door after I've been working for an hour. I flinch, nearly knocking my mixing bowl off the counter.

"Sorry, Sofia." Sister Lauren steps into the kitchen,

holding both hands out in front of her. "I didn't mean to startle you."

"It's okay." I wipe my hands on my jeans without thinking, leaving two streaky white flour prints on the denim. "Crap," I mutter.

Sister Lauren grabs a towel off the counter, and tosses it to me. "Are you making Christmas cookies?"

"For my grandmother," I explain, wiping the flour from my jeans. "I'm going to go visit her at the retirement home today."

"That's so nice of you. Take a cab, though. There's a storm moving in—I don't want you on the roads when it starts to snow." Sister Lauren leans against the fridge, folding her arms across her chest. She's dressed in full habit, and her long black robes hide her feet.

"I thought you only wore your 'penguin suit' for Mass and class," I say. Sister Lauren grins.

"Father Marcus and I are visiting the children's hospital today," she explains. "We like to pray for the sick during the Christmas season. But we'll be back in time for Midnight Mass."

I wrinkle my nose. "Mass is at midnight? Why?"

"Tradition," Sister Lauren explains. "I wanted to invite you to attend. There aren't many students staying on campus over the holidays, but Father Marcus holds a full service, anyway. It's really quite beautiful. It'll be in the auditorium this year since the chapel's out of commission."

"Sure. I'll be there." I pull open the oven door to check my cookies, and a chocolatey, pepperminty smell wafts through the kitchen. Sister Lauren sighs.

"Those smell amazing. I'm sure your grandmother will love them." Sister Lauren starts back toward the door, then pauses, rapping her knuckles against the wooden frame. "And please be careful on the roads today. Mississippi never gets snow. They're closing half the town in preparation, so you should head back early."

"Thanks for the tip," I say.

"Have a good time. You deserve a merry Christmas."

"Thank you," I say.

Sister Lauren smiles and sweeps back out into the hall, her black robes billowing behind her.

* * *

It's raining and freezing cold when my cab arrives at Hope Springs Retirement Homes. I pay my driver, balancing the cookie plate in one hand as I push the door closed. Muddy water slushes around my heeled booties, making it difficult to walk without slipping. I teeter toward the front entrance. The automatic doors whoosh open, blasting me with hot, dry air.

Beige walls and thin, worn-down carpeting lead me through a narrow hall to an empty receptionist's desk.

Fluorescent lights flicker above me. I'm not really sure what the procedure is, so I poke my head down the hall twisting off to my left.

"Hello?" I call.

A beat of silence. Then a voice echoes back, "Hello?"

The voice wobbles, sounding weak and confused. I take a step back, suddenly uncomfortable. That clearly wasn't a receptionist. It sounded more like an old man who doesn't know where he is.

I swallow and try again. "Is anyone here?"

"Is anyone here?" the old man repeats back to me. The phone on the receptionist's desk starts to ring. The tinny sound echoes down the halls, but nobody comes to answer it. I shift my cookies from one hand to the other, and the cellophane crinkles beneath my fingers.

I play a quick game of eenie, meenie, miney, moe—landing on the hallway twisting off to my right. Framed pictures of leaves and flowers line the walls, all painted the same muted pinks and dull browns. I turn a corner and practically walk into a set of double doors. I think I hear voices coming from behind them. I lift a hand to knock, then change my mind and push the door open.

Little old ladies and tiny, wrinkled men crowd a large, L-shaped room. A group watches *Family Feud* from an ugly plaid sofa, while others slump around scattered folding tables covered in dominos and playing cards and puzzle pieces. They stare up at me with vacant, cloudy eyes. I step inside, letting the door swing shut behind me. A woman stands.

"Can I help you?" she asks, her voice tired. She's the only one under seventy-five in the entire room, so I assume she must be a nurse. She wears wrinkled khakis and a stained yellow polo that's several sizes too big.

"I'm here to see my grandmother," I say. "Roberta Flores?"

The nurse tilts her head, giving me a puzzled look. Deep wrinkles trace lines from the corners of her nose and down each side of her chin, making her jaw look hinged on—like a doll's. Her hair is exactly the color of used dishwater.

"I'm sorry," she says. "I didn't realize Roberta had any relatives."

I shift my weight from one foot to the other. "I've only been here once before, to help her get settled in. I wanted to come more often, but I have school . . ."

"Mmhmm," the nurse murmurs, pressing her thin lips together. "Well, come on. She's just over here."

I follow her through the folding tables, past the plaid sofa, and around the corner. Grandmother slouches in a faded green chair, the blanket my mother knit for her draped over her thin shoulders. She stares out the window, hypnotized by the water trickling down the glass. The familiar wooden rosary dangles from her trembling fingers.

"The rain has gotten them all worked up," the nurse explains. I frown and glance around the room. The man directly behind me has fallen asleep. A trail of drool stretches from his mouth to his chin. The woman across from him stares at her cupped hands, seemingly fascinated by the whirls and wrinkles on her palms. If this is what they look like worked up, I can't imagine how they act when they're bored.

"Roberta?" The nurse kneels next to my grandmother, gently touching her on the shoulder. "Your granddaughter is here to see you."

"It's Sofia." I take a tentative step forward. *"Hola, Abuela. Feliz Navidad."*

Grandmother turns to look at me. She moves in slow motion. It takes her ages to twist around in her chair, a century to lift her head. Her neck is no longer strong enough to hold her head steady, so her head rocks back and forth on her shoulders, looking as if it could tumble off her body and roll away. Loose skin hangs from her cheekbones, giving her face a sunken, hollow look. Her bloodshot eyes stare out from beneath paper-thin eyelids.

"I made cookies." I place the cookies on the table next to Grandmother's chair. "They're double fudge with peppermint chips. Our favorite, remember?"

Grandmother swallows and smacks her dry lips together. Tiny cracks split the corners of her mouth. I kneel on the floor next to her chair, folding my hands over her armrest. Rain slaps against the window and rattles the trees outside. Grandmother stares straight ahead, as if she doesn't know I'm here.

"*Abuela*," I say, again. "Grandmother, can you—"

Something dark appears in her left nostril. It seems almost solid, like something reaching out from the depths of her brain. It balloons just below her nose, then pops, sprinkling her wrinkled skin with blood. A thicker trail oozes from behind it. It winds down her face and seeps into the cracks in her lips.

I flail backward, catching myself just before I slam into the stained linoleum.

"Oh no." The nurse stands, looking around for a box of tissues. "This has never happened before."

Blood streams down Grandmother's face. It looks thicker than it should, and almost black. Like tar. I dig my fingers into the cracks in the floor and pull myself away from her. I feel responsible, but that's impossible. I didn't even touch her! My arms tremble, barely holding my weight.

The nurse swears and hurries away, muttering something about finding a towel. Grandmother's cloudy eyes search the room for a long moment before finally focusing on me.

"*Diablo*," she croaks.

A hollow space opens up in my chest. "Grandmother, no. It's Sofia. It's *me*."

Her lips start to move. They twitch at the corners, and curl up over her teeth. At first I think she's trying to smile. But then her mouth twists into a horrible, animal grimace. Blood drips from her lips in a solid sheet, staining her teeth red.

"*Diablo*." Grandmother's low, scratchy voice rips through the room. The drooling old man jerks awake, and the woman across from him looks up from her hands, startled. The nurse stops right behind me.

"Roberta's never spoken before," she says, twisting the towel between her fingers. She seems to have forgotten about wiping the blood from Grandmother's face.

"She's confused." I push myself back up to my knees, and reach for Grandmother's hand. She reels away from me. Her rosary clatters to the floor.

She lowers her hands to the sides of her chair and tightens them around the armrests. The wood creaks beneath her gnarled fingers. She pushes herself to her feet, swaying on her skinny legs. I can't remember the last time she stood on her own. It's been years.

"*Diablo. Diablo!*" Her voice is a creaky rasp. Blood cascades over her chin and splatters the knit blanket draped around her shoulders. She lurches forward, arms outstretched. She claws at the air in front of her, her curled yellow fingernails flashing under the fluorescent overhead lights.

Grandmother takes another shaky step forward, and her leg gives out beneath her. She drops to her knees.

"*Abuela!*" I move forward, but the nurse's hand shoots out in front of me, holding me back.

"You should go," she says. Whispers erupt around me, and I know without turning around that they're all watching me. Staring. Heat rises in my cheeks.

"But she might be hurt!"

"*Please.* Just go."

A part of me wants to yell. I listened to her favorite Christmas songs all morning. I made cookies from scratch. I wore the ugly velvet dress she bought me three Christmases ago, even though it's too tight across the chest and the sleeves don't even go to my wrists.

The nurse hurries to my grandmother's side, and helps her back into her chair. The nurse lifts the towel to Grandmother's face to stop the relentless flow of blood. I nod at the cookies on the side table.

"Those are for her," I say. "For Christmas."

The nurse glances at them, almost suspiciously. "Thanks."

I'm suddenly sure no one will eat them. The nurse will throw them away the second I'm out the door. Anger flares inside of me. I want to throw the cookies against the wall, just to hear the glass plate shatter. But I don't. I walk past the nurse, leaving the sad, beige-colored room without another word.

"Diablo!" my grandmother shouts after me. The other residents join in, their voices merging together in a single, horrible chorus. *"Diablo! Diablo!"*

CHAPTER NINETEEN

"Just drop me off here," I say.

My cab rolls to a stop in front of St. Mary's main entrance. I hand the driver a crumpled twenty-dollar bill and climb out. The rain has thickened into slushy snow during the ride. The cabbie's radio was tuned to news of the upcoming blizzard. It's going to be the biggest snowstorm in history, the newscasters say. Half the streets in Hope Springs have already been shut down— it took us twice as long as it should have to get back to St. Mary's.

Frozen grass crunches beneath my boots and wet flakes catch on my scarf. The cab peels away as soon as

I step onto the curb, its tires spitting up an icy spray of water behind it.

My grandmother's voice echoes in the back of my head. *Diablo.* I shiver, and hurry across the grounds without stopping to think about where I'm going. Wind gusts around me, rustling my hair and the hem of my velvet dress. Darkness seeps into the sky like spilled ink.

I walk past trees with bare branches frosted with a thin layer of snow. I don't stop until I reach the burnt husk of the chapel.

Only the skeleton of the building remains. Snow floats through the blackened beams of the ceiling, and broken windows reveal bits of gray sky instead of walls. Soot sweeps across the white siding. I step forward. The chapel calls to me, whispering my name. I'm the one who destroyed it, after all. A criminal always returns to the scene of their crime.

The front door swings open, and then bangs closed in the wind. I hear my grandmother's scratchy voice: *Diablo. Diablo.*

I tug at the front door, and it falls open with a crash, raining ashes down on my feet. I step inside.

Fire burned through the pews, leaving piles of blackened wood and singed Bibles in its wake. The massive wooden cross still stands near where the altar once was, blackened but still intact. The smell of smoke hangs in the air like a memory. Colored glass shines amid the piles of burnt wood, and an empty bottle of coconut rum lies beside what's left of the altar.

I stare at the bottle and an image flashes through my head: Leena's mouth wet with rum. Candlelight reflecting in her glazed eyes. I drop to my knees in the middle of the wreckage, ignoring the glass and wood digging into my shins. My chest tightens. I take fast, shallow breaths just to get the oxygen to circulate to my brain.

I did this. I destroyed the chapel. I killed Leena. Even my own grandmother thinks I'm evil. I push the words to the darkest corners of my mind and try to focus on other things. Like the cold air hitting the back of my neck, and the recorded church bells chiming in the distance. Smoke tickles my throat and I start to cough.

"*Please*, God," I choke out. I fold my hands together, squeezing so tightly that the tips of my fingers start to turn blue. The coughing subsides, but I can't catch my breath. It feels like someone's gripping my lungs and squeezing. Darkness creeps in from the walls. The floor seems to lurch beneath me.

"Please," I whisper. I squeeze my eyes shut. Tears sting the corners of my eyes. "Please . . . just take me. I can't do this anymore."

I hear Brooklyn's voice in the silence that follows my clumsy prayer.

We don't kill our own.

A cold hand touches the back of my arm.

I jerk forward, falling to my hands. A shard of glass jabs at my palm, but it doesn't break the skin. I hear a shuffle of movement and a shadow falls over the floor.

"Sofia? *Dammit*, are you okay?"

I recognize Jude's voice and push myself back up to my knees, my arms trembling so badly I can barely hold my own weight. "I'm sorry . . ." I say. "I . . . What are you doing here?"

"I stay for every holiday." Jude kneels next to me and wipes the tears from my cheeks with his thumb. "Save your breath, okay?"

I nod, and focus on breathing. *Just breathe.* I close my eyes. *Breathe.*

My chest loosens. Air comes easily now. Things stop spinning and the darkness fades. Jude draws me into his arms. I stiffen automatically, my heart racing. *I can't . . . Leena . . .*

But all I can think about are Jude's strong arms wrapped around me, his shoulder beneath my cheek. I relax, letting myself lean into him. He holds me tighter. For the first time since my mother died, I don't feel alone. I feel wanted. I feel safe.

Jude brushes my hair over my shoulder and kisses my temple. A shiver shoots down my spine.

"Is that okay?" he asks.

"Yes," I whisper. He curls his hand around the back of my neck and pulls my face to his. Our lips touch. He tastes like spearmint and there's a musky smell to his hair. I wrap my arms around his shoulders, pressing my body against his chest.

Jude shrugs out of his jacket and starts working on the buttons of mine. He unfastens them quickly, and I peel my coat off and toss it aside. I slide my hands beneath his thick sweater, running my fingers over the muscles in his stomach and chest. He moans and tilts me back, pressing me into the floor. I pull him down with me. His skin is hot.

"Sofia," he murmurs, his voice muffled by my hair. Something in the back of my head tells me I shouldn't do this. It's wrong. I think of Jude kneeling in the back of the chapel, the whip cracking against his back. I hear Leena's voice: *Be careful what you wish for . . . God punishes sinners.* I'm supposed to free myself of distractions. Rid myself of the Devil.

But then Jude moves his hand up my leg and over my waist, his fingers brushing against the edges of my bra. My dress rides up around my hips. His kisses get harder. Hotter. Hungrier. My doubts fade. I wrap my legs around his legs and move my hands down to the button on his jeans. I feel the cool metal edges against my fingers. *This can't be wrong.* I don't want to be alone, and Jude cares about me. He might be the only person in the world who still does.

"Are you sure?" he asks, and I nod without thinking. I unhook the button and unzip his jeans. Jude kisses my cheeks and my neck and my shoulders.

Steel-gray ash separates from the burnt ceiling beams and flutters toward me, landing on my wrist. I jerk back as if I've been burned.

Jude stops kissing me. "Are you okay?"

"Of course." I pull away from him, and prop myself up with one elbow, brushing the ash away with my hand. It leaves a streaky black line across my skin. I lick my thumb and rub, but the mark only seems to seep deeper into my skin.

Fear lodges itself in my throat. I've read stories like this in English class. About birthmarks that symbolize mortality, skin deformities that mark someone as evil. I press my thumb into my hand and rub so hard that my skin burns. But the black mark doesn't go away.

Leena's doing this, I think. She's warning me. *God punishes sinners.*

"Sofia?" Jude touches my arm and I flinch.

"Sorry," I say in a voice that sounds nothing like my own. "I just . . . maybe we shouldn't." I move my hand to my side so I don't have to look at the ashes on my skin.

"We don't have to do anything you don't want to." Jude rolls off me, and pushes himself to his knees. He buttons his jeans. "Are you okay? Did I do something wrong?"

Jude lowers his hand to my back. The second he touches me, something inside snaps clean in half. Tears form at the corners of my eyes. I blink them away.

"Sofia, tell me."

"I *can't*," I whisper, and my voice cracks. I shudder so deeply that Jude has to wrap his arms around me to keep me from shaking. I can't stop replaying what happened with my grandmother, what happened with Leena.

Jude kisses the top of my head. "Hey, you're okay," he whispers. "Tell me what's wrong. You can tell me anything."

"Not this. It's too terrible. You'd . . ." *hate me*, I think. I press my lips together before I can say the words out loud.

"Anything you've done, I've done worse," Jude whispers into my ear. He strokes my arm until I stop shaking. "We're the *same*. God forgave me. He'll forgive you, too." I shift in Jude's arms, finally looking up at his face. A lock of dark hair falls over his forehead, and wrinkles the skin between his eyebrows. He looks so concerned. It loosens something inside me. I stop thinking about Leena and think, instead, of him. Us. I want to rub the lines from his face and make his worry disappear. I want to trust him.

"Bad things keep happening," I whisper. "I think there's something . . . *wrong* with me."

"Wrong how?"

"*Evil.*"

Jude squeezes my arm, pulling me closer. "I know what evil looks like. You're not evil."

"You don't understand." I shift my eyes to my lap. I can't look at Jude as I say this next part. I don't want to see his face twist in disgust when he realizes how awful I truly am. "I was talking to Sister Lauren and she said she thinks that demons can . . . attach themselves to people who've done something terrible. It's like being possessed."

Jude's arm stiffens, but he doesn't pull away. "But you haven't done something terrible."

"Yes. I have," I say in a quiet voice. Then, before I lose my nerve, I tell Jude what happened with Brooklyn and my friends last summer. I tell him about Leena and the bunny and the night the chapel burned down. I even admit what I did to Karen. How I lured her onto the train tracks. How I let her die.

"Brooklyn said I was like her," I finish, my voice shaking. "She said I was . . . *evil*. And then, today, my grandmother said the same thing." A sob escapes my lips. I curl my hand into a fist, bunching it next to my mouth. "What if they're right?"

Jude is quiet for a long moment. Shadows hide his face, making it impossible to see his expression. He suddenly seems very far away. Fear curdles in my gut. I feel as if the floor could crumble out from under me at any moment. This was a mistake. I shouldn't have told him any of this.

"I was lost when I came to St. Mary's, but Father Marcus saved me," Jude says, almost to himself. "I felt unredeemable, like you, but I was wrong. No one is ever lost to the Lord. There's hope for all of us."

"You think I'm redeemable?" I whisper.

"Of course I do." Jude brings my hand to his mouth and kisses my palm. Heat floods through me, erasing my fears. I squeeze his fingers.

"I . . . I think I love you, Sofia."

A smile spreads across my face, so wide it makes my cheeks hurt.

"And that's why I have to do this."

My smile freezes. "Do what?"

Jude doesn't answer. My chest feels weird. My heart's beating too fast, and my lungs seem tight, as though they're straining against the air inside of them. The skin along the back of my knees prickles.

"Jude . . ." A sour taste hits the back of my tongue.

I push myself to my knees. "What are you going to—"

Jude pulls his hand back and whips it across my face. His knuckles slam into my cheekbone. I fly backward, crashing into the floor. My head spins, pain blossoming just below my skin. I swallow, tasting blood and soot at the back of my throat, and try to force my eyes back open.

Jude stares down at me, a lock of dark hair falling across his forehead. He leans forward and touches my face.

"Don't be afraid," he whispers, stroking my cheek. Darkness flickers at the corners of my eyes. I start to lose consciousness.

"I'm going to get the evil out of you," Jude says before everything goes black.

CHAPTER TWENTY

I feel the ropes first. Their rough texture against my skin. The slick of sweat between my wrists, and the thick knots. I'm curled on my side, and the ropes bind my hands behind me, pinching my shoulders together and jerking my arms back at uncomfortable angles. I groan, and pain blisters through my chin and jawbone.

"Are you awake?" Jude asks. I open my eyes. Candlelight moves across the blackened walls like a predator, hiding blurry shapes in the darkness. I watch the shapes for a moment, dazed, trying to remember what they are. Where I am.

"Jude?" I croak.

"You passed out. Do you remember?" His voice is sweet, like he's telling me I fell asleep while watching a movie. But that's not what happened. I fight against the pain pounding at my skull, trying to remember.

I see Jude standing over me, a strange look on his face. He pulls his hand back, and then—I close my eyes against the memory. A tear drops down my cheek and rolls over my mouth, leaving a film of salt on my lips.

"I had to run out to grab some supplies, but I won't leave you again. Promise." Jude hauls something off the floor with a grunt. At first, I see a backpack. The same black backpack Alexis had with her that weekend in the abandoned house. But then he drops it on the pew and it transforms into a green army duffel bag smeared with dirt and ashes.

"I'm going to help you, Sofia. You won't have to do this alone."

"What's that?" I ask, my voice cracking. The bag is big and lumpy. I stare at the shapes beneath the green fabric, my mind turning them into tools. Duct tape. A butcher knife.

A nail gun.

Jude crouches beside me. "Don't worry about that yet."

"You . . . you *hit* me." I still can't believe the words. Jude brings his hand to my chin. His touch sends shivers through my skin.

"Sofia, I didn't hit *you*. I would never hit you. I hit the demon inside of you." Jude's voice is barely a whisper. "I'm doing it because I love you," he says. "You know that, right? This is for us. I'm going to get that evil thing out of you."

A sob rises in my throat. "Jude," I whisper, leaning into his hand. This has to be a mistake. Jude wouldn't hurt me. "Don't do this. Untie me."

Something flicks to life inside of Jude's eyes and, for a moment, I see a shadow of the boy I thought I loved. The creases around his mouth soften. The tension leaves his shoulders. "Think about it, Sofia," he says. "You said yourself that you've been asking the Lord for salvation, but He hasn't answered. Remember?"

I think of all the times I've knelt on the floor in this chapel, my hands clenched together, trying to reach God. My voice cracks. "I remember."

"I'm here to give it to you. We can't wait for God to make you clean. *We* have to do it. Like this. Together."

I think of all the terrible things that have happened this year—things I've caused, even if I didn't mean to. I see candlelight reflected in Leena's dazed eyes. I see the horror on Karen's face when I tightened my fingers around her wrist and dragged her onto the tracks.

There *is* something evil inside of me. But Jude thinks I can be redeemed.

"Is it going to hurt?" I ask. Jude smiles, almost sadly.

"I'd never hurt you, Sofia," he says. He unzips the bag, and stares down at what's inside. He swipes a hand over his forehead and wipes the sweat on the back of his jeans.

He pulls something out of the bag and places it on the pew beside him. It looks like a set of handcuffs, except they're not normal—the cuffs themselves are vises attached to a thin metal lever. I picture how they work in my head. Someone twists the lever and the vises slowly crush the bones in your wrists.

The fear I'd been fighting hits me in a wave. I try to breathe, but my throat closes up and the oxygen leaves my head, making me dizzy. I start to cry.

Jude's at my side again in an instant. "Shh, Sofia, it's okay. Those aren't for you." He pushes the hair back from my forehead, his hand cool against my skin. "Father Marcus collects tools like this for *his* exorcisms. But I'm not going to use any of it on you, okay?"

Tears cloud my eyes. Jude's holding something, but my eyes are too blurry and I can't see it. I blink, trying to focus on his hands.

It's a Bible. Just a normal black Bible.

He presses his hand against the cover. "I'm going to pray for you," he says. "That's it. Is that okay?"

I nod. "Okay."

Jude flips the Bible open and clears his throat.

"*Credo in Deum Patrem omnipotentem,*" The words flow from his tongue. I remember what it was like to watch him perform, his velvety voice filling every inch of the auditorium.

"*Creatorem caeli et terrae. Et in Iesum Christum, Filium eius unicum, Dominum nostrum, qui conceptus est de Spiritu Sancto, natus ex Maria Virgine, passus sub Pontio Pilato . . .*"

My breathing steadies. I need to forget about the handcuffs and whatever else Jude might have in that bag. Prayer and Bibles are okay. And I wanted this—I begged the Lord to save me from myself. Maybe this is His way of answering my prayer.

Be careful what you wish for. Leena's words make a lump form in my throat. It's like she knew.

Jude paces the length of the chapel while he reads, his footsteps crunching over broken glass and ashes. I study the swirls of soot staining the walls, losing track of time. The ropes that bind my hands behind my back are too tight. The arm I'm lying on falls asleep and a dull headache pounds at the back of my head. Pins and needles prickle down the length of my arm, and spread through my hips. I stare into the shadowy corners of the chapel until the darkness seems to pulse. A cockroach darts across the floor, antennae twitching, and disappears into a pile of rubble.

Jude's Latin blends together until I can't tell where one word ends and another begins. Darkness crowds in from the corners of my eyes, and the floor seems to tilt and sway. My eyes droop.

Something wet hits my cheek—my eyes fly open, and I reel backward, wrenching at the ropes binding my arms.

Jude kneels in front of me, holding a tiny glass bottle. "Holy water," he explains. He smiles sheepishly. "Sorry. I didn't mean to surprise you."

I blink, shaking the water from my eyelashes. "Are we done?" I whisper.

Jude stands and slides the bottle of holy water into his jeans pocket. "Soon, my love," he says. He walks to the pew and leans over the duffel bag. "But I have to follow protocol. It's the only way to drive out the demons. Prayer and holy water are just the first step."

A shiver shoots up my spine. "First step?" I ask. "What does that mean? What's next?"

The muscles in the back of Jude's neck tighten.

"What are you going to do next?" A tremor has crept into my voice. I sound unhinged—hysterical. *"Tell me."*

Jude turns, a leather whip curled around his fingers. It's the whip Father Marcus used on him that morning in the chapel. The leather is frayed and stained red with blood—Jude's blood.

Panic claws at my throat. "I don't want to do this anymore." I yank at the ropes binding my arms, fear making my movements jerky. I picture the whip slicing through my dress, biting into my skin. Bile rises in my throat. The bruise where Jude hit me suddenly feels like nothing. A bump. "Let me go."

"I've been through it, too, Sofia," Jude says. But he doesn't look at me, and his hands tremble. "I know you're scared, but you don't have to be. I'm going to be right here the entire time. I love you."

His words prick into me like thorns. "This isn't love," I say. I swallow, trying to stay strong. "Jude, please. You have to let me go."

"That's the demon talking." Jude holds up his fist, and the leather creaks beneath his tightening fingers. "And *this* is how we overcome demons."

Jude loosens his hand and the whip unfurls. The leather tip brushes against the floor, making tiny patterns in the layers of ash. Jude slips a hand beneath one arm and hauls me to my knees. I inhale, and my breath shudders down my throat like a sob. I wonder if I could pull my hands loose if I caught him off guard, if I jerked my body away fast enough. I twist, trying to jerk my wrists out of his sweaty grip. But Jude holds tight.

"Take it easy," he says, kissing the top of my head. "I don't want you to fall. You could hurt yourself."

"Don't do this," I say again. But Jude doesn't respond. Fear rises in my chest, making my hands and legs stiff. I can't feel my toes or my fingers, can't feel anything other than my own rapidly beating heart. "Jude, stop," I beg. "Think about this. You love me, remember? You don't want to hurt me."

Jude circles me, stopping when he's directly behind my back. A sob bubbles up my throat.

"Jude, *plea*—"

The whip cracks against the arcs of my bare feet. Pain zips up my legs. I gasp and bite down on my tongue. Blood fills my mouth and trickles out around my lips.

"Stop," I say, squeezing my eyes shut. "Please stop."

The whip slaps into my back without warning, ripping through the thin velvet of my dress. The leather tears into my skin like some wild animal's fangs. Vomit spills onto my tongue.

I double over, heaving and coughing. Something thick and brown spews from my mouth and splatters across the dirty chapel floor. It's swirled with red. *Blood,* I think. I cringe, imagining Jude's whip cutting deep under my skin, leaving welts inside my body. I feel the vomit rising in my throat and I try to choke it back down.

I arch forward, pulling against the ropes binding my hands. I retch until my stomach feels raw, and a veil of sweat clings to my forehead. I stare at the brown-and-red puke, my eyes blurry and bloodshot. I swallow, tasting mint.

It's not blood, I realize, panting. *It's peppermint.*

Jude kneels beside me and takes my face in his hands. "It's working, Sofia. See? Your body is rejecting the demon. You're fighting it off."

I release a choked whimper. My eyes feel wet, but I don't remember when I started crying. *It's not a demon,* I want to tell him. It's the peppermint cookies I made for my grandmother. This isn't working.

Every muscle in my body aches. Every inch of my flesh burns. I want to tell Jude that we've failed, that I can't be redeemed. But maybe he'll finish sooner if he thinks this is working. And then he'll let me go.

Jude whips me again. And again. My back screams, and pain like fire shoots through my feet. My head lolls forward. For a long moment, I can't tell if my eyes are open or closed.

And then all I see is black.

CHAPTER TWENTY-ONE

I open my eyes. It's either been hours or minutes since I passed out, but I'm not sure which. Pain zigzags up my spine. Blood and sweat pool between my cheek and the floor.

"Water." I swallow, and taste the sharp mint and acid bite of vomit on my tongue. I blink my eyes open, and the chapel shifts and moves around me. The walls keep switching places.

I can't see Jude from my angle on the floor. Hope blossoms in my chest and, for a second, I think he's left. He's given up on my soul and abandoned me to die.

Then the shadows move and Jude steps out of the

darkness. Flecks of blood glisten along the line of his jaw and sweat clings to his hair. He digs through the duffel bag and produces a plastic water bottle. He kneels in front of me and carefully lifts my head. I whimper. The blood on my cheek has grown sticky, and my skin stings as he unpeels my face from the floor.

"Easy," he says, tilting the bottle toward my mouth. The water is so cold it makes me shiver, but I suck it down, feverish with thirst. "There you go," he murmurs, stroking my hair. I close my eyes and drink. The layer of vomit leaves my tongue. The room stops spinning.

Too soon Jude pulls the bottle from my lips. "Feel better?" he asks. I open my mouth to answer and a sob escapes instead. The muscles in my face spasm. I can't get my mouth to work.

"*Cold,*" I choke out. I press my lips together to stop their trembling. The cold stabs into my skin and my bones. I feel it like a dull ache in my muscles. Goose bumps crawl over my arms and legs.

Jude frowns and presses the back of his hand to my forehead. "You feel a little warm, actually."

"Something's wrong," I whisper. My throat feels dry again, despite all the water I just drank. I can't stop shivering. Chills jolt through me, making me twitch. "Jude . . . please. I think I have a fever."

"No, this is just your body rejecting the Devil," he

says, moving his hand to my cheek. His skin feels hot against my face. It practically burns. "It's a good thing, Sofia. It means we're making progress."

"I think I need to go to the hospital."

"You don't know what you're saying."

"This isn't working." I curl into a fetal position, bringing my knees to my chest. "You have to let me go."

"That's the Devil talking," he says. The heavy cross looms over him, its wood charred and blackened.

"This is almost over." Jude reaches forward and brushes the hair off my forehead, his fingers skimming my face. "And then we can be together."

I stare into the shadows, trying to separate Jude's eyes from the darkness. I don't know what to believe anymore. Jude said he'd never hurt me, but then he whipped me until I passed out.

"Don't touch me," I say, my voice low and angry. Jude pulls his hand away.

"I love you, Sofia," he says. "But you're evil."

He's not going to let me go, I realize. He doesn't care that I'm sick and hurt. It doesn't matter what he says. You don't do this to someone you love.

"You don't love me," I whimper. "You're *a liar.* Don't you *ever* touch me again."

I spit in Jude's face. He reels backward, saliva running down his cheek. His hand comes down hard and fast against my cheek, and my head snaps against the floor. The pain is like slamming into a wall. I release a choked gasp, lights dancing before my eyes.

"Dammit!" Jude stands and takes two quick steps away from me. I can barely see him through the fog covering my eyes. The room gets hazy.

"I shouldn't have lost my temper." Jude's voice draws me out of the fog. I open my eyes, then squeeze them shut again. The whole world is light and pain. I moan, wishing for unconsciousness. Every muscle in my body aches. Every inch of my flesh burns.

"Sofia? Did you hear me? I said I'm sorry. I know it's not you saying those things. It's the demon. I shouldn't listen."

I feel Jude's hand on my cheek, and a tear slips down my face. "The Devil inside of you is strong," he says. "We need to be stronger."

Jude pulls his sweater over his head and tosses it to the chapel floor. His bare skin gleams gold in the near darkness, muscles rippling across his chest and stomach. Pain twists through me. I just ran my hands over his warm body. I kissed his lips.

Jude leans over the duffel bag. Moonlight streams in through a broken window, and catches one of the scars twisting over his shoulder. The gnarled tissue glints, almost silver. I stare at it, and a sound like a scream fills my head. Jude didn't get those scars from a single morning of being whipped by Father Marcus. Scars like that could've only come from being whipped over and over again. I imagine the scars that will soon snake up my own back. I'll be marked, just like Jude.

"I was hoping we wouldn't have to use any of this," Jude mutters, sorting through the bag. I hear the metal clink of chains against something heavy and solid. I think of the handcuffs he dug out of that bag a few hours ago.

Father Marcus collects tools like this for his exorcisms.

I thought I'd reached my capacity for fear, but then I think of those cuffs clamped around my wrists, digging into my skin, crushing my bones. My insides feel loose all of a sudden. If I wasn't so dehydrated, I'd probably piss myself.

"Jude," I breathe, my voice shaking. "Please, I'll be good, I promise."

"That's the demon talking again. You don't know how hard this is for me, Sofia. You look like you, and you sound like you, but you're possessed by something terrible. I need to find a way to keep it quiet while I do my work." Jude kneels in front of me, holding a pear-shaped device attached to what looks like a long metal screw. "I'm afraid this is going to hurt," he says.

I arch away, but Jude clamps a hand against the side

of my face, pressing me against the floor. He forces my mouth open, and shoves the pear inside. I try to scream, but then Jude turns the screw, and the pear opens in my mouth like a flower. Metal blades crush my tongue and dig into the roof of my mouth. Their edges split my gums, and stretch the sides of my lips. Tears form in the corners of my eyes.

"We can't take the pear out of your mouth until you're ready to praise the name of the Lord," Jude says.

He grabs me by the shoulder and hauls me to my knees. I gather my breath and try to scream. Blades cut into my gums, and blood oozes down the back of my throat. I inhale—coughing on blood—and try again. The pear muffles my voice, making it impossible.

"You're only making it worse, Sofia," Jude says. He tips my body over his shoulder and stands, lifting me as easily as if I were a bag of flour.

Oh God. I picture Jude hauling me outside and dumping me, covering me with dirt, the horrible metal pear making it impossible for me to scream as I'm buried alive. Fear drops through me like a stone. I try to speak, but the pear keeps me from moving my tongue. Blood leaks from the corners of my mouth.

"Don't try to talk," Jude warns, carrying me across the chapel. "You'll hurt yourself."

I twist my rope-bound arms, wondering how difficult

it would be to pull my wrists free. The rough fibers chafe my skin like sandpaper. I tug—hard—on my wrists, and the ropes binding me roll down to my knuckles.

"Stop squirming," Jude mutters. "I'm going to drop you."

I tug again. The rope scoots down my fingers a little farther.

Jude stops in front of the huge wooden cross. He adjusts my body and his shoulder digs into my gut, making it hard to breathe. I twist my hands, and my thumb slips free. I close my eyes and pull—ignoring the pain blistering through my hand, and the blood leaking from my skin. With a sudden jolt, I pull one hand loose of the bindings.

"Hey—" Jude starts. I grab for his face and claw into the fleshiest part of his cheek. He screams and jerks, but I just dig my fingernails deeper into his skin. I feel blood pooling below my fingers and seeping into the cracks around my nails. Jude grabs my wrist, and yanks my hand back, losing his grip on my body. I pitch backward.

Jude releases an angry, animalistic yell. He shoves me into the wooden base of the cross to keep me from falling to the ground. I squirm, but he leans against me, pinning my wrist beneath his shoulder. He's taller than I am. I stretch out my toes to try and touch the floor, but I'm too high up. Jude grabs my other hand and presses it to one of the cross's short arms. I release a choked, desperate cry.

"Hold still," he whispers, grunting. He takes the rope still dangling from my wrist, and twists it around the cross, tying my arm in place. I scream and kick, but Jude doesn't seem to notice my struggles. He pulls my other arm straight and holds it in place against the cross. His broad hand is like a vise against my wrist. I grit my teeth against the cold metal pear, and try to push him away. But he's too damn strong. He leans down and pulls at the ropes binding my ankles with his free hand.

"Almost there," he mutters, tugging the knot free. My legs dangle below me, untied.

I kick at him, but he dodges to the side, easily. He uses the length of rope that had been binding my ankles to tie my other arm to the cross. When he finishes, he steps back, admiring his handiwork.

My head falls forward, sobs shaking my shoulders. Pain arcs up my back, holding me upright. I pull at my arms, and ropes dig into my wrists. I lift my head.

He's tied me to the cross in a perverse imitation of Christ's crucifixion. My arms stretch out to either side of my body, my wrists tightly knotted to the splintery wood. I'm dragged down by own weight, my body pulling at the bindings until my arms feel as if they're going to rip from their sockets. It takes all my strength to hold my head upright. I try, again, to scream, but the metal pear steals my voice.

CHAPTER TWENTY-TWO

"I'm doing this to help you," Jude says, but his voice is hollow. His eyes dart to the bindings around my wrists before moving back to my face. "Please, stop fighting. You'll be grateful when it's over. You'll *thank* me."

I nod, even though I can barely make sense of his words. Pain bites into every inch of my skin. It takes all of my energy not to scream or cry or throw up. It's all I can think about.

Jude digs something out of his jeans pocket. A blue plastic lighter.

The muscles in my shoulders tense. I shake my head, and the metal pear rattles against my teeth. Jude studies the lighter. He rolls his thumb over the switch and a red-orange flame dances to life between his fingers.

I imagine that flame licking my toes. My *fingers*. I can practically feel my skin growing red and itchy, my nerves flaring as the pain sears hotter. My breath comes hard and fast, and my skin suddenly feels too tight. I shrink back against the cross, trembling. Jude moves his finger from the lighter. The flame vanishes.

"Anything you've done, I've done worse," he whispers. "That's what I need you to understand, Sofia. We're the *same*. We belong together. God forgave me. He'll forgive you, too."

I want to tell him to stop. Don't do this. I'll be good, I swear. But the pear presses down against my tongue, making it impossible to speak. I plead with my eyes.

Stop, please, I can't take any more, I can't. Jude doesn't look at me. He flicks the lighter on. And then off again.

"Did I tell you my parents sent me here when I was thirteen? Technically, I was a year too young to start as a freshman, but Father Marcus made an exception. He's a great man, Father Marcus."

Flick. The flame jumps to life. *Flick.* It disappears.

"I'd been having a hard time at home since my sister, Chloe, died. She was only seven years old. We were out skating and I was supposed to be watching her, but my friends were hanging around in the woods, drinking and getting high." Jude swallows hard and closes his hand around the lighter. He finally meets my eyes. "I was stoned when Chloe fell through some thin ice.

"I was too high to save her, too high to run for help. *I'm* the reason she died. So, yeah, I understand what it's like to do something evil. I was just like you, Sofia. I didn't believe in God when I came here. Didn't think I could be saved. But Father Marcus wouldn't give up on me. Look."

Jude stretches out his arm, showing me the thick red burn in the crook of his elbow. It's the mark I noticed that morning in the chapel. I thought it was weird that he refused to tell me about it, but I was too distracted by his hair and his smile. *Stupid.*

Staring at it now, I see the faint outline of a shield emblazoned with a cross seared into his skin. Like a brand.

"It comes from this," Jude explains, curling his hand into a fist. He's wearing a thick silver ring. It's familiar, but I can't place why until he turns the ring so that I can see the design on the front—a silver cross, a shield. All at once, I remember where I've seen it before. It glittered from Father Marcus's hand the day I caught him whipping Jude.

Jude twists the ring around his finger absently. "Father Marcus knows true evil. He was a missionary for years and years. A *real* one. He didn't just go to the places everyone goes, like China and Haiti. He traveled to tiny little villages no one's ever even heard of. We're talking places with no electricity or running water. He's stayed in the jungle, living with the locals to better understand their customs."

Jude swallows. He twists the ring faster.

"Father Marcus has witnessed some of the most depraved demonic possessions imaginable. Things the Vatican would've scoffed at," Jude says, shaking his head. He sounds as if he's reading a script, as if he's memorized everything Father Marcus ever told him. "But that's only because they haven't seen what he's seen. There are children out there who cry tears of blood. Some of them even *levitate*, and their eyes roll back in their heads. He's seen grown men and women who speak in tongues and crave human flesh.

"In the face of evil like that, Father Marcus was forced to resort to more archaic forms of exorcism," Jude continues. He touches the burn on his skin with one finger, tracing the gruesome scar almost lovingly. "The day he branded this image into my flesh, he told me he claimed my body in the name of the Lord. After that, things were different for me. I started to grow closer to God. I started to *heal*."

Jude uncurls his fist and stares down at the plastic lighter on his palm. "You want to heal, don't you?"

I look from the lighter to Jude's twisted scar and, all at once, I smell burning skin, burning hair. He's going to brand me. He's going to light that ring on fire and press it into my skin. I shrink away from him, pressing my shredded back against the wood of the cross. I pull myself up by the bindings at my wrists, ignoring how my spine aches and my joints howl with pain. A scream wells inside of my chest. I choke it back, forcing myself to focus on the metal blades cutting into the insides of my cheeks. A scream will only hurt.

"Let me get that," Jude murmurs. He twists the lever attached the metal pear, and the blades peel away from the sides of my mouth. I inhale, and fresh, stinging air brushes up against the open wounds. The sharp, metallic taste of blood clings to my gums. Jude pulls the pear from my lips, and tosses it back into the duffel bag.

I blink, my eyelashes wet and heavy. Am I crying? Or is it sweat? Blood? I can't tell, can't feel anything but pain and fear. "Please," I beg. "Please don't do that."

"I don't want to hurt you," Jude whispers. His voice sounds so sincere. Like he really believes what he's saying. He flicks the lighter and fire appears, like magic.

"Then don't do this," I choke out. "Please stop. *Please.*"

Jude stares down at the flickering fire. The flame reflects in his dark eyes. "I begged Father Marcus to stop, too," he says. "But now I'm grateful for what he did. I was just like you, Sofia. I'd done an unforgiveable thing and I thought there was no hope for me, no chance of salvation."

Jude reaches out and strokes my arm. The feel of his skin against mine is somehow both comforting and disturbing.

"You said you felt possessed, like you had a demon clinging to your back. I've felt that way, too, Sofia. But Father Marcus saved me from the sins of the flesh. He made me clean."

Jude moves his finger in small circles over my skin, raising the hair on my arms. For a second, I want to trust him. Maybe this *is* the way to salvation, and all I have to do is survive the pain to be rid of the evil inside of me. It would be so easy to just . . . give up.

Then I hear my mother's voice in my ear. *Be strong, Sofia.* A single tear leaks out from the corner of my eye. Sergeant Nina Flores didn't teach her only daughter to trust lying boys with pretty smiles. She didn't teach me to give up.

My voice cracks in my throat. "Father Marcus was wrong, Jude. He didn't save you—he *tortured* you."

"He made me *whole*," Jude spits. He looks up at me and, for the first time, I see real anger in his eyes. "He exorcised the demons from my soul, and he presented my flesh to God for salvation. I'm free because of the things he did."

I swallow, disgust twisting my stomach.

"Father Marcus is a hero," Jude says, almost to himself. He lowers his ring to the flame. Fire curls around the silver shield. "People don't understand, but that's just because they haven't seen real evil. They don't know. Everything he's done, he's done for the Lord."

"Jude—"

Jude's arm shoots out so quickly that I don't have time to jerk away. He catches my chin in his hand and yanks my face forward roughly.

"I'm doing this for *us*, Sofia," he says. "I love you."

He presses the ring into my neck.

Blistering pain explodes through my head. Red and orange lights dance before my eyes and nausea floods my stomach. I feel the skin on my neck bubble and melt, and I thrash wildly against the cross. I don't care about the cuts on my back and my feet, or the welts inside my mouth, and the dull bruises on my cheeks. All I can think about is my neck, the burning ache searing through my body.

The entire room seems tinged with red, like my eyes themselves are bleeding. I don't realize I'm screaming until Jude covers my mouth with his hand. His fingers are chapped, and his skin smells like blood. I try to catch my breath, but sobs clog my throat. The pain is too much. I can't hold myself up anymore—the muscles in my arms go slack, and my body drops like a stone, yanking at the ropes twisted around my arms. My shoulders scream with pain and I wonder, dimly, if I pulled my arm from its socket.

Something tickles my neck and I flinch before realizing that it must be blood. The blood trickles down my skin and gathers in the space just above my collarbone, quickly soaking the fabric of my dress. I choke down another, shaking breath. I must look crazy, shaking and sobbing like this. I must look possessed.

Jude leans his forehead against mine.

"Shhh," he whispers into my hair. I choke my voice back, whimpering. All I can think about is pain and fear and heat.

"I claim this body in the name of the Lord," Jude says. He lowers his face to my forehead and presses his lips into my skin.

"Get off me." I moan, pulling my face away from him. The burn on my neck flares. "Don't touch me!"

"Sofia—"

The sound of church bells drifts in from outside, cutting Jude off. They're the same tinny, recorded church bells they played during Leena's funeral. Jude turns and stares at the chapel door.

"Christmas Mass," he murmurs. He runs a hand back through his hair. "Dammit."

I swallow and pain blisters through my neck. Jude rises up to his tiptoes and kisses my cheek.

"I've got to go, but I swear I'll be back soon," he says. His lips feel cold and clammy against my skin. Like something dead. I cringe.

He hurries to the front door. I let my head fall back against the cross. The door opens, and then thuds shut again, and I exhale, relieved.

The burnt wreckage of the roof stretches above me. I can see the night sky through the blackened ceiling beams, stars winking down from the dark, endless sky.

"God," I whisper. "*Help*."

The word gets stuck in my throat. I squeeze my eyes shut. Tears stream down my cheeks. I can't think of anything to say to him, anything to ask. He won't answer anyway. He never does.

He's forsaken me.

CHAPTER TWENTY-THREE

A gust of wind blows in through the tattered walls of the chapel, bringing my mother's voice with it.

Go, Sofia. Go now.

I stare at the tightly knotted robes binding my wrists to the cross. It's impossible. There's not enough time.

In my head, I see Jude racing across the grounds, his boots kicking up fresh snow. He didn't say where he was going, but I bet he's headed to the auditorium to tell Father Marcus he won't be staying for Mass. It isn't far through the woods, but the snow's falling heavily now. It could slow him down. Still, it'll only take a couple of minutes to get to the auditorium. Five, if I'm lucky. Then, maybe, another five minutes to talk to Father Marcus. And five minutes to get back.

That's just fifteen minutes. Maybe ten. And then Jude will come back and finish what he started.

For the first time, it occurs to me that I might die tonight. I could see my mother again in just a few hours. How will I face her, knowing I didn't fight for my life? That I didn't even try?

I grit my teeth and tug at my wrist. The rope feels coarse against my skin, and slick with sweat and blood. The cross groans, and the rope creaks, but the knot stays tight.

I cry out in frustration, my ragged voice echoing off the blackened chapel walls. I yank my fist down, and then up again to loosen the binding. I twist my arm. It feels like rubbing gravel into an open wound, like scrubbing my bare skin with sandpaper. Fresh blood oozes from my reddened skin. I press my teeth into my lower lip and pull. But the knot doesn't budge.

"*Come on!*" I shout. I collapse against the cross, cringing as my back presses into the wood. The ropes have cut off circulation to my hand. There's no loosening them. It takes all my energy just to wiggle my fingers. I stretch my feet, but my toes barely brush against the cross's heavy wooden base.

"*Fuck!*" I scream. I jerk both hands at once, thrashing,

my head swinging wildly back and forth. I curl my knees toward my chest and hurl them backward, slamming my bare feet into the wood. Pain licks at the ragged skin peeling away from the soles of my feet, but I don't care. I kick the cross again and again and—

I freeze, gasping. The cross *moved*. It shifted backward. Like it was tilting.

I suck down a breath, my chest rising and falling rapidly beneath my ruined dress. My head feels dizzy, a low thud at the back of my skull telling me I must've slammed it against the wood. I thought the cross was affixed directly to the floor. It's huge, much larger than a person. It never occurred to me that you could shift it.

If you can shift it, you can get it to fall.

I rock against the cross, testing. The cuts along my back flare. But the cross doesn't move.

I squeeze my eyes shut, forcing myself to breathe. How much time has passed now? Three minutes? Four? I imagine Jude racing up the stairs to St. Mary's, taking the steps two at a time, maybe double-checking his appearance in the glass door to make sure my blood isn't smeared across his face. There isn't a clock in the chapel, but I swear I can hear the *tick tick tick* of a second hand.

I lean forward, my wrists pulling against the ropes binding me to the cross. The knots scrape against my skin. Fresh blood rolls down my arms and drips from my elbows. My feet fumble along the bottom of the cross. The ruined skin along my soles flares and spits, but I just press them harder into the wood, gritting my teeth against the pain. Spots of light flicker across my eyes. The world around me tilts.

"This is going to hurt," I whisper. My voice doesn't tremble this time. It sounds steady—strong, even. I focus on each individual word so I don't have to think about what I'm going to do. "Are you ready for that? This is going to really, really—"

I hurl my weight against the cross. My back crashes into the wood and every single cut the whip slashed into my skin turns bright-white and screams. It feels like electricity ripping through my body, like nails driving deep into my muscles. My teeth slam together and my head snaps to the side.

The cross scoots across the floor, and then rocks back on its base. I open my mouth in a silent scream. My head lolls forward and a choked whimper crawls from my lips. The room flickers, like a candle sputtering. I don't have time to pass out. If I pass out, I'm dead.

"Five minutes," I say. "You only have five minutes left. Come on."

I wrench my body up by the wrists—and then I slam myself against the cross again. This time, it tilts on the edge of its base before crashing back in place. I sway from my ropes like a rag doll. Pain howls through me. It wraps around my spine and makes my toes curl.

I want to give up. I'm not strong like my mother. She would never give up.

Vomit rises in my throat and I swallow it down. It takes all the strength I have left to drag my body up by the wrists, to press my feet into the cross, and fling my body backward.

And then—

The cross rocks, then tilts. The air around me shifts as I plummet toward the floor. I have only a second to feel the sudden whoosh of triumph before the cross crashes into the tile, snapping clear of its base. I barely notice the ache spreading through my body. I gasp, staring up through the blackened ceiling beams. The moon hangs in the darkened night sky, shining down on me like a quarter. A laugh bubbles up from my throat.

I did it. I'm free.

I try to roll over but the cross is too heavy, and the ropes still knotted around my wrists pull me down. I drag my feet across the floor and push. I rock to the side, catching myself with one hand before the cross's weight shifts to my shoulders. I inch my knee up to help deal with the bulk and ease my body forward in a half crawl. If I move too far to the left or the right, I'll slam back to the ground and have to start again. There's no time for that. I swallow, and then slowly rise to my knees. The cross shifts. I sway backward, but maintain my balance. I grit my teeth together and slide one knee forward—then totter onto my foot. I drag the other knee forward and attempt to stand, the bottoms of my feet flaring with pain. But it's nothing compared to the pain in my back. The cross digs into my body, chaffing against my tattered skin. Blood sticks to my shredded dress, plastering it to the blackened wood.

I lurch forward. The cross is larger than I am, and it drags on the floor behind me. Each step is punishment. The wood is too heavy for me to lift and I'm doubled over, my knees practically buckling from the weight. I want to stop and try to catch my breath, but I worry that I'll collapse if I don't keep moving. I focus, instead, on my legs. I lift one, inch forward, and lower it back to the ground. My footsteps are short, my feet barely shuffling off the ground with each step. But still. I'm moving.

I have no idea how much time has passed. I picture Jude standing with Father Marcus in the auditorium, smiling that charismatic smile of his as he explains why he can't stay. Maybe the priest won't believe him. Maybe he'll hand him a Bible and tell him to find a seat. But I doubt it. I'm not that lucky.

Jude's probably already on his way back.

I stumble and stagger, my eyes glued to the velvet

curtains blocking off the back room. They're only three feet away . . .

Now two . . .

One . . .

I pitch forward, slamming into the wall. My foot slips out from beneath me and I crash down to one knee, groaning in pain. I press my lips together and pull myself back to both feet, gasping. I made it. I stand as best I can, and push through the curtains. I start to move through the opening, when something thumps against the wall. Pain shudders through me, and my body jerks backward.

I shift my head to the side to see what's keeping me from moving forward. It's the cross—it's too wide to fit through the door. The heavy wood clanks against the frame, my hand dangling.

"Shit," I whisper. I try to force the cross through the door, but I'm bent too far over, and I can't get it to tilt at the right angle. Either the top of the cross or one of the sides keeps thudding against the blackened frame. I'm stuck.

Blood drips from my body and pools on the floor beneath my toes, mixing with the ash to form a dull gray paste. The only way through the door is to break the cross. Which wouldn't be a problem, except that my *arms* are tied to the cross.

"Broken bones heal," I whisper meekly.

The front door creaks. I freeze, waiting for the sound of footsteps or a groan as Jude pushes the door open. I can't look over my shoulder, not with the cross tied to my back. I listen for a long moment, but I hear nothing over my own ragged breath. He isn't here.

Yet. He isn't here *yet.* I swallow, and the acid taste of vomit hits the back of my throat. The chapel door could fly open any second now. And if Jude sees me here, like this . . .

I slam one arm against the doorframe, hoping the wood's been burnt enough that it'll just give way. The door holds, but the cross splinters, and thin shards of wood jam into my skin. Pain spreads through my wrist and up into my shoulder. It feels dull compared to the sharp jabs along my back, but deeper. The kind of pain that won't fade after a few hours. Sweat coats my forehead, and nausea swirls through my stomach. The room around me spins.

I throw myself into the doorframe again and this time the wood cracks beneath it. One side of the cross stays attached to my back while the other—the one bound to my wrist—breaks free. I sigh, relieved, and then get to work on the knot. My blood has slicked the ropes enough that they slide easily off the broken edge of the cross, finally releasing my hand. I pull myself loose and my arm flops to my side.

It looks wrong, like there are too many bones rattling around below the skin. I try to move it, and pain shoots through my muscles. It's broken.

I release a scream that's half sob and collapse onto the ground, the cross settling heavily against my shoulders. I reach for my opposite wrist with my broken arm. Pain knifes through me as my fingers slip over the bloody knot, struggling to grip it. I dig and pull but the knot holds tight.

"Come *on!*" I scream as finally my fingers sink into the knot. I grit my teeth and pull, and the bindings unravel. The rope falls to the floor.

I hear something just outside. A crunch, like boots on snow.

Time's up.

CHAPTER TWENTY-FOUR

He's coming.

I stumble into the narrow room beyond. I prop my uninjured hand against the wall and kneel, my broken arm still cradled at my chest. The soles of my feet sting and ache.

I try the back door first—locked, of course. There's a window next to the door, one of the few in the chapel with the glass still intact. I briefly consider going back through the chapel and climbing through an already broken window, but they're all much higher off the ground. I could break my leg or twist an ankle if I jumped from that height. I shift my weight away from the wall—biting my lip through the pain—and fumble for a brass candleholder sitting on the table. Sweat coats my palms and my fingers slip over the heavy metal.

I groan, lifting the candleholder in my uninjured hand. It's heavier than I thought it would be. Or maybe my arm is weaker, tired from bearing the weight of my body on the cross. I aim the candleholder at a crack cutting down the center of the stained glass window, narrow my eyes—and throw.

Glass shatters outward, raining red, green, and blue shards across the snow. Cold gusts in through the opening, making me shiver. I rip a silky cloth off the table, wrap it around my fist, my broken arm still clutched to my chest, and knock the remaining glass from the window frame. I think, briefly, of trying to find my shoes. But there isn't time. And I'll run faster barefoot than in heels, anyway.

The window isn't far from the ground. I wedge one hand against the frame, hug my broken arm close to my body, and shimmy through the opening. Broken glass dusts the ground below me. I grit my teeth together and pull my body outside.

The ground rushes toward me. I swing my uninjured arm around to brace for the impact. Pain slams into my palm and shudders through my elbow. Glass bites into my skin. I roll away from it, my chest heaving.

I'm free.

A dozen tiny cuts tingle across my face, and my broken arm is useless. I clutch it with my opposite hand and make myself stand, my legs wobbly beneath me. The snow soothes my shredded feet, numbing the pain enough that I can stagger forward without gasping.

"Okay, Mom," I whisper, my voice trembling. "What now?"

Find a phone. Call the police.

The answer comes to me instantly, like my mother really is standing beside me, guiding me to safety. I take one step, and then another, until I'm sure I won't collapse under my own weight. I think of the cell phone hidden under Sutton's mattress and lurch into an unsteady run. *Please let it still be there,* I pray to God or my mom or the Universe—anyone who might be listening.

My body isn't well enough to move quickly. My muscles and skin and bones scream with pain, and it takes all the strength I have to keep my bare feet moving over the icy ground. The bones in my broken arm jostle against one another with every step I take forward, sending waves of nausea rolling over me. Snow flurries through the air, covering the trees and bushes, crunching beneath my toes. It glows white in the darkness, transforming the grounds into someplace unfamiliar and strange. Cold ripples through my bare feet and up my legs, coaxing goose bumps from my skin. I tighten my jaw and focus only on putting one foot in front of the other, on moving faster, faster . . .

A voice weaves through the trees.

". . . please . . . Sofia . . . come back."

I freeze, horror wrapping around my chest. My breath claws out of my lungs and up my throat, upsetting the silence around me with deep, ragged gasps. I press a fist to my mouth to hold it back. I duck behind a tree and sink into the snow, trembling.

Cold hugs my body. It's moved past soothing and onto brutal. Icy wind snakes up my velvet skirt and down the back of collar. It freezes the tears leaking from my eyes. I curl my arms and knees close to my body.

I grit my teeth together to keep myself from shivering. Wind blows in my ears, making it impossible for me to hear anything else. But the noise means Jude can't hear me, either.

Footsteps crunch in the snow. Then the wind shifts, carrying the sound away. I press my lips together, breathing through my nose. Tiny silver clouds hover in the air before my face. Darkness around me. I listen so hard that my head aches and my ears buzz. I strain my eyes staring into the darkness, but I see only ice-coated trees, their bare branches clawing at the sky.

I exhale, and my muscles start to relax. He must have

passed me. The tension leaves my neck and shoulders. I stretch my legs out to keep them from cramping.

The wind shifts again. It tickles my arms and creeps into my ears. Then—

"I know you're out here."

The voice sounds close, maybe a yard or two away from where I'm hiding. A scream bubbles up my throat—I bunch my fist in front of my mouth to keep from letting it out.

A tiny, dancing flame appears in the darkness—Jude's lighter. He'll see me if he keeps moving forward.

"I'm sorry," Jude calls. His voice makes my stomach turn. I press my back against the icy bark behind me, holding my breath. "I didn't mean to scare you."

I hold my breath. My heart thuds in my chest, so loud that I'm certain Jude will hear it, even with the wind blowing in his ears. Jude walks behind a tree, his lighter flickering out as he disappears from view. My leg muscles contract, tensing to run. It takes me another moment to spot the tiny orange flame again and, when I do, it's smaller. Like a firefly in the darkness.

My muscles relax—he's walking away from me. Silently, I pull my legs closer to my body. Something catches my eye. I turn—then press my lips together to keep from gasping out loud.

A single, bloody footprint mars the virgin snow. I

shift my gaze farther down the path and there's another one. And another. They glare up at me, such a bright red against the white. I stare at them in horror, willing them to disappear.

They lead right to me.

Jude heads farther into the trees, the darkness swallowing his tiny lighter flame. I exhale, my heart still hammering in my chest. But he'll circle back this way eventually, and then he'll see the bloody footsteps and follow them to me. I can't just run. I need a plan.

I hear my mom's voice. *If you can't walk, then crawl.* It's something she used to tell me when I was frustrated. *Keep going,* it meant. Never give up.

I ease down onto my knees and one hand, still clutching my useless broken arm to my chest. Even though I'm not putting any pressure on it, my arm still feels numb and unsteady and *wrong.* I dig my teeth into my lower lip and force myself forward. *It's no worse than the cuts on my feet,* I tell myself. But that's not true. It feels like something isn't lining up right, like all my nerve endings are grinding against one another. I cringe against the pain and do an awkward three-legged crawl through the snow. After a few feet, I glance over my shoulder to see whether I'm trailing blood.

Nothing but pure, white snow stretches behind me. I exhale, relieved. My hands and knees leave pockmarks in the path, but the snow's still coming down hard. Soon, even that trail will be hidden.

I groan and stagger forward. A shallow creek runs through the woods ahead. I can't hear the sound of water but I know it's close; I can practically picture it weaving through the trees. It cuts across the grounds and flows up past the dormitories. I'll be able to run in the water without worrying about trailing blood. Then I'll get to the dormitories, to Sutton's phone under the mattress in our room. Maybe Sister Lauren's there, too—her room is on the ground floor. She'll help me.

I move my hand over the ground as I crawl, preparing for the earth to transform into wet, slimy rocks. Darkness presses in, thick and ominous. Even the moon has ducked behind a cloud. I watch for Jude's lighter, but see nothing. Snowflakes kiss the back of my neck. I shiver as the cold melts into my skin.

I crawl onward, dragging my knees through the snow, ignoring the pain stabbing into the bones of my injured arm. Cold air numbs my shins and nose and mouth. I lower my hand to the ground—

—and pitch forward. Hard. My palm slams into ice and slides out from beneath me.

"Dammit." I breathe, pushing myself back up. I run my hand over the water's frozen surface. It's solid, but thin. I lean forward and jam my elbow into the ice. It cracks beneath me, soaking my arm with freezing water. I push myself up to my feet and step in.

Cold like I've never felt before envelops my feet. I swear under my breath, and hug my broken arm closer to my chest. It's so cold it burns, so cold that the bottoms of my legs disappear. It feels like my body ends at my knees, like I'm tottering forward on bloody stumps. I force myself to move. To walk. Then run. I can barely feel the sharp rock bed beneath my feet, digging into my ragged skin. The icy fire licks at my legs, creeping up past my thighs. Broken ice floats through the water around me.

Jude's voice echoes through the woods. He must've realized he went the wrong way. He's circling back now. I release a choked sob, fear curling around my spine. I push my legs against the current. Faster, *faster*. A dim light flickers through the trees. I glance over my shoulder. Looks like his lighter, but I can't be sure. I turn back around and press onward.

The girls' dormitories materialize from the darkness, the moss-covered brick barely more than a shadow in the trees. I stumble out of the creek, my legs so numb they give way beneath me. I slam into the ground, ice tearing the skin along my knees. I gasp and shove myself back to my feet. My toes curl into the snow as I pitch forward. I sprint to the first-floor entrance, my fingers fumbling for the doorknob. For one horrible second I worry it'll be locked. But it turns, easily, beneath my hand.

"Sister Lauren!" I throw the door open and hurry inside. My voice echoes off the walls. I push the door closed behind me, taking a second to slide the dead bolt shut. There are at least three other entrances into the dorms, but the lock could hold Jude off for a few precious minutes.

"Sister Lauren!" I call again. Her room is at the end of the hall. I stagger forward, collapsing against her door. I beat my fists against the wood. *"Please,"* I whisper, closing my eyes. I lift my hand to knock again and that's when I remember—Midnight Mass. Sister Lauren isn't here. Nobody is.

I wipe a tear off my cheek and try the doorknob—locked. My heartbeat speeds up. I force myself to breathe. *In, and then out.* The auditorium is back toward the chapel—too far to run without Jude catching me. So what's next?

"Phone," I whisper out loud. Sutton's phone is one floor up, but I remember seeing a landline in the kitchen on this floor. I push myself off Sister Lauren's door and lurch down the hall.

My bare feet slap against the floor. The icy water numbed my wounds, and I barely even feel the sting of pain through my skin as I run. I glance behind me to see if I'm leaving behind bloody prints. The cold must've done something to the cuts because I spot only a few drops of blood glistening from the tile.

I push through the kitchen door, pausing for a moment to catch my breath. The phone hangs on the far wall, next to the fridge. It looks like something from the '70s—avocado green, with a curly cord dangling from one end. I dart toward it without bothering to turn on the lights, yanking the receiver from its cradle. I lift the phone to my ear and poise my finger to dial.

No dial tone.

"Shit!" I jab the dial pad with my finger, but nothing happens. The storm must've knocked out the phone lines. I push down the hook, then release. Silence.

A door creaks open. I freeze, the phone still at my ear. The door swings shut with a soft thud.

"It's Sister Lauren," I whisper to myself. Footsteps move down the hallway. Creaking. I sink back against the wall. The footsteps don't sound like Sister Lauren's. They're heavier. A boy's.

Fear creeps down through my arms and legs. I hug my broken arm to my body and curl my toes into the linoleum. My fingers dig into the sides of the phone so hard that the plastic creaks.

I place the phone back on the cradle. An axe hangs on the wall behind a pane of glass that reads BREAK IN

CASE OF FIRE. My eyes linger on the case, but I don't have time to break the glass—and, besides, Jude would hear it shatter. I lower my hand to the drawer nearest to me and pull it open gently. A two-pronged carving fork lies inside. I curl my fingers around the wooden handle. It feels good in my hand.

Someone moves down the hallway, his footsteps almost silent. I swallow, staring hard at the kitchen door. I won't be able to leave this room without him seeing me. I need to hide.

I sink down to the floor, carefully opening a cupboard door. There's a lot of space below the sink, as if it was made for trash cans and recycling containers. It's empty now, so I climb inside, leaving the cupboard door open a crack so I can see out into the kitchen. My broken arm screams with pain as I squeeze into the tight space, but I grit my teeth together, refusing to make a sound.

I watch the door, the carving fork clutched tightly in one hand. And wait.

CHAPTER TWENTY-FIVE

The kitchen door creaks open, and a shadow spills across the floor. I stare at the dark shape, willing it to go away.

"Sofia?" Jude steps into the kitchen, letting the door swing shut behind him. He flips the light switch, but nothing happens. The storm must've knocked out the electricity, too. Jude swears under his breath and rakes a hand back through his hair.

"I saw the blood in the hallway," he says. "I know you're in here."

Blood. My eyes dart across the kitchen floor. It's hard to make out anything in the dark, but the more I search, the more I see. There's a bloody toe print next to the phone, barely visible in the shadows, and a smudge across the drawer where I grabbed the carving fork. Tiny red drops glisten on the linoleum, stopping directly in front of the cupboard where I'm hiding.

I tighten my grip on the carving fork. Sweat gathers between my fingers and the wooden handle. It's only a matter of time before he sees all that blood. And then he'll know exactly where I am.

"I love you, Sofia," Jude says in a low voice. "Everything I did was for us."

His footsteps are silent, his movements careful, like a predator. He reminds me of videos I've seen online: jungle cats hiding in tall grass, coyotes stalking their prey.

I lean as close to the crack in the cupboard doors as I dare, wincing as I shift my broken arm to the side. Jude stops in front of the pantry, then leans close to press his ear to the door. He lowers his hand to the doorknob and turns it, slowly, so the latch doesn't click.

He waits a beat—then rips the pantry door open.

I feel a little flicker of triumph. *Not there, asshole.*

Jude pushes the door closed and lowers his forehead to the wood. "Please, Sofia. I only wanted to help you."

His voice sounds soft, almost sweet. But I see how the muscles in his shoulders have tightened, and how he's curled his hand into a fist. I'm not fooled. I squeeze the carving fork tighter.

"I was just trying to take care of you." He pulls the door to the walk-in freezer open, then swears under his breath when he finds it empty. He shakes his head, pushing the door shut again. "I want us to be *together*."

He practically spits the word *together*, giving it sharp edges. He's getting frustrated. He runs a hand through his hair again, and this time he leaves it mussed. It sticks out on his head in odd angles. He's running out of places to look. My eyes shift to the blood spots on the floor. In the darkness, they look black. Like drops of oil.

"It'll be better this time. I promise."

I curl my toes into the splintery cupboard floor. Blood pools beneath them. The skin along the bottoms of my feet stings.

I barely notice. I have a plan.

Jude moves away from the freezer. He takes a step closer to the sink. I can't see his face from this angle anymore, so I study the soles of his heavy leather boots. They're all water-stained and flecked with ashes and blood. My blood.

Something sour hits the back of my throat. I imagine jamming the carving fork through the leather, and down into his toenails. I imagine driving the forked prongs deep enough to pierce flesh. I tighten my grip on the weapon. It feels good. *Right*. As though the wood was designed to fit against my palm.

Jude steps closer. The glistening drops of blood I trailed along the linoleum are less than a foot away from his shoes. All he has to do is glance down at the floor and he'll see them. I swallow. My chest feels tight, my throat dry. It's now or never.

"Sofia—"

I push the cupboard door open. Jude takes a quick step backward, eyes going wide.

"Wait," I say. I'm kneeling on the kitchen floor, my broken arm curled against my chest like an injured bird. I use the cupboard door to help push myself to my feet, careful to keep my uninjured arm hidden in the folds of my dress. I lean against the door and wince at the sudden flare of pain through my broken arm. "I'm sorry. I shouldn't have hidden from you."

The surprise drains from Jude's face. He presses his lips together and the muscle in his jaw tightens. He's all control again.

"I was worried," he says. I tilt my head down, looking up at him through my eyelashes. Concern creases the skin between his eyebrows.

"Are you hurt?" he asks. "I know I went pretty hard on you."

"Nothing more than I deserved." I take a step toward

him, my uninjured arm still pressed to my side, hiding the carving fork in the tattered folds of my dress. Jude looks down at my feet, at the blood pooling on the linoleum beneath my dirty toes.

"The Lord will make you clean," he murmurs, almost to himself. He reaches for my shoulder, and it takes all of my willpower not to cringe away from his touch. He pulls me toward him, wrapping one arm around my back to hold me to his chest. My broken arm is pressed between us.

"I knew you'd understand," he whispers into my hair. "I'm doing this for you. For us—"

I whip my arm out from behind my skirt and drive the carving fork deep into his shoulder.

Jude's face crumples. His eyes lose focus. I wait until they flicker back to mine, until I'm certain he can see my face. I twist the fork. Jude opens his mouth to scream, but no sound comes out.

"Go to hell," I say.

Jude stumbles backward, smacking his hip against the side of the fridge. I shove past him, and scramble onto the counter. Pain flares through my broken arm and licks at my shredded feet. I barely notice. I reach for the window above the sink, grunting as I shove it open one-handed. Cold air gusts in, wrapping around my body and making my skirt flap up around my legs. I climb out, holding tight to the window ledge as I lower myself to the ground. Snow crunches beneath my bare feet.

Jude grabs my wrist before I let go of the window. He digs his fingers deep into my skin, cutting off the circulation to my fingers.

"*Devil,*" he chokes out. I try to yank my arm away from him, but he holds tight. My other arm is useless— there's no way I'll be able to push him off me.

"Let me *go!*" I snarl. Jude cocks an eyebrow. He reaches for the carving fork still jutting out of his shoulder.

Brooklyn's voice echoes through my head.

You'll have to use your teeth.

I sink my teeth into Jude's hand, biting down until I taste blood. He screams and reels away from me. I can't seem to unclench my jaw. I dig into his skin until something tears, and flesh comes loose in my mouth. My weight shifts backward. I'm falling.

I slam into the frozen ground shoulder first. Pain rips through my broken arm. Everything feels white-hot and dazzlingly bright. Stars explode in front of my eyes. I clutch my arm, groaning. Blood coats my lips and teeth, filling my mouth with the taste of salt and pennies.

Jude's blood. That thought makes me grin. The pain in my arm doesn't seem so bad all of a sudden. It's just a dull, throbbing ache, like a muscle cramp. I push myself to my feet and stumble toward the driveway twisting past the dormitory. If I follow it for long enough, it'll lead to the main road, which runs all the way to Hope Springs. Someone there will help me.

Snow swirls around me, thick and cold. I can't hear Jude, but I know he's coming. I picture him pulling the carving fork out of his shoulder, climbing through the window after me. I shuffle through the snow, willing my legs to move faster. The pain is back. It doesn't feel dull anymore. It's bright and sharp. It burns through me like a fire. It's so all-consuming that I can't tell whether it's coming from my broken arm or my shredded feet or the whip marks across my back. My knees buckle. I stumble, and then collapse onto my knees.

Something moves through the trees. I stiffen and squint into the swirling snow. It's too big to be an animal, and it can't be Jude—Jude's still behind me.

"Help." I try to shout, but my voice is too weak. I crawl forward, every movement agony. I'm in the middle of the driveway, I think. I feel concrete beneath my knees.

"Help!" I call again, louder this time. The figure pauses, and then, slowly, turns toward me. I think I see a white coat. Dark hair.

Mom, I think, desperately. Tears clog my eyes. It can't be my mom. She's dead.

"Help," I call again. And then my arm trembles and gives out.

CHAPTER TWENTY-SIX

"Sofia? Oh my God." Rapid footsteps pound against the driveway. Sister Lauren kneels next to me. She touches my cheek, her hand warm against my skin. "What happened? Are you okay?"

I try to lift myself off the ground but my arm wobbles beneath my weight. "We have to get out of here," I say. "He's *coming.*"

Sister Lauren frowns. "Who's coming? Who did this to you?"

"Jude! He's right—" I turn and look back at the dormitories.

The kitchen window is empty.

"No," I whisper. Cold sweat breaks out on the back of my neck. My eyes dart, wildly, around the grounds, but I can't see farther than three feet in any direction. Snow gusts around me, turning everything white. He could be here now, watching us. I picture him standing in the shadows between the trees, smiling that manic smile, the carving fork sticking out of his bloody shoulder. I have to choke back a scream.

He could be *anywhere*.

Sister Lauren pulls a cell phone out of her pocket and dials. "We have an emergency at St. Mary's," I hear her say into the receiver. "I have a student badly injured . . ."

She pauses, a frustrated look on her face. "Fine," she says after a moment. "Just please send someone as soon as you can.

"Come on." Sister Lauren tucks the phone back into her pocket and slides my arm around her shoulder to lift me up. I stand, gasping as the tattered soles of my feet press into the ground. Blood gathers between my toes.

"You need a hospital." Sister Lauren eases me forward, one arm wrapped tight around my waist. "But the roads are a mess because of the blizzard. The police are on their way, but we'll have to make do with what we have in the infirmary until an ambulance can get through."

"The infirmary?" I freeze. The thought of heading

back to the dark, empty dormitory fills me with dread. "No, we can't go back there—"

"You're losing too much blood, Sofia. You need a sling for your arm, and there's dirt in your wounds. You're going to get an infection if we don't clean you up."

"But—"

"There's a lock on the door. No one's going to hurt you."

Sister Lauren coaxes me forward, her forehead creased in concern. I take one step, and then another. The dormitory looms over us, windows dark and empty. I picture Jude hiding in the shadows beyond the glass. Waiting. Watching. Goose bumps climb my arms.

Something rustles through the bushes behind me. I flinch out of Sister Lauren's grip, stumbling backward. A scream claws at my throat. I whirl around.

Nothing there.

"It's okay," Sister Lauren says, her voice calm, like she's talking to a spooked animal. She approaches me slowly, her hands held in front of her. "The infirmary is right inside. You'll be safe."

"Yeah," I breathe. "Okay."

I let her lead me into the dormitory. I can barely feel my broken arm. I wonder if I'll ever be able to move it again. The door slams shut behind us. I jump, muscles going suddenly tense. But no one leaps out of the shadows. The hallway stretches before us, silent and empty. The infirmary is only three doors down. I spot the familiar sign, its black letters so badly peeled that they read FI MA Y instead of INFIRMARY. Sister Lauren fumbles for the right key and fits it into the lock. The door clicks open.

"Come on," she says. She ushers me inside and I collapse facedown onto the narrow hospital bed, my chest heaving with ragged, shallow breaths. Sister Lauren closes the door behind her and flips the dead bolt. It slides into place with a heavy thud.

We did it. We're safe.

It's dark in the infirmary. I can just make out a short row of carefully made beds, each separated by a thin, threadbare curtain. I lift my head and spot a metal cart next to the door, covered in rust stains that look almost like blood. A skeleton stands in the corner behind it, positioned with one arm lifted above its head. Like it's waving.

Sister Lauren hurries over to the sink on the far wall. She fumbles with a drawer, and then a match sparks to life, filling the tiny room with a warm orange glow. The flame illuminates a row of cupboards just above the sink. Dusty blue and green bottles wink from their shelves. Sister Lauren lights a candle and sets it on the counter.

"Emergency candles," she explains, shaking out the

match. "We have them in every room in case of a power outage."

She cringes, looking over my shoulder at my tattered, bloody back. "I'm going to see if I can find any bandages. And maybe a needle. You might need stitches."

I nod, barely lifting my head. The bed feels warm and soft beneath my cheek. I hear drawers slide open and closed. Cupboard doors creak.

Sister Lauren rushes back to my side, her arms filled with ointments and bandages. She drops them on the metal cart. Jars and bottles roll everywhere. A tube of Neosporin hits the floor.

"Sorry." Sister Lauren jerks a hand back through her hair and I realize, for the first time, that she's scared. "I didn't know what you'd need, so I figured I should just grab it all."

She deals with my broken arm first, disinfecting and bandaging the cuts, before carefully looping a sling around my shoulder. Then she takes a deep breath and picks up a bottle of disinfectant and a bag of cotton balls. She seems a little calmer now, her movements less erratic.

"I'm going to lift up the back of your dress so I can take a closer look at your injuries," she says. "Is that okay?"

I nod. A second later, I feel Sister Lauren's cool hands

on my back, peeling away the tattered remains of my dress. She lowers a cotton ball to my skin. I expect the disinfectant to sting, but it feels cool. Nice. My eyes flicker closed.

"Why don't you tell me what happened?" Sister Lauren says, dabbing my back with the cotton. "Start from the beginning."

"It was Jude," I say quietly. Sister Lauren spreads some disinfectant over one of my cuts, and I cringe. "He said he wanted to save me."

The rest of the story comes in a rush. I tell Sister Lauren about how Father Marcus performed an exorcism on Jude when he first came here. I tell her about the morning I saw him being whipped in the chapel, the horrible scars on his back, and how he tied me up. How he beat me. By the time I'm done talking, Sister Lauren has finished disinfecting my back and started on the cuts covering the bottoms of my feet. She wraps the wounds in thick cotton bandages.

"We need to get the police here," Sister Lauren says. She shuffles through the closet and the cupboards until she finds an old St. Mary's sweatshirt and a pair of scrubs. Her fingers tremble as she helps me slide my broken arm through a sleeve, and then gingerly places it back inside its sling. "*Immediately*. I don't care if there's a storm. That boy needs to be locked up."

Something bangs into the door, making the wood shudder and creak. I flinch.

Sister Lauren stiffens. "What was that?"

I curl my fingers into the stiff mattress, my heart beating so hard I'm worried it's going to rip out of my chest. Every nerve in my body flares to life. Every muscle tenses. I picture the axe in the kitchen, hidden beneath a layer of thin glass.

BREAK IN CASE OF FIRE.

The infirmary door groans and shudders. A blade slams through the wood, its edge sharp. Glinting.

CHAPTER TWENTY-SEVEN

"It's him." I try to stand, but my legs are numb. I stumble backward, whacking my ankle against the cot leg.

"Sofia, calm down." Sister Lauren lowers a hand to my shoulder, her other hand fumbling for the silver cross hanging from her neck. "We must have faith."

I want to shake her. Doesn't she understand how serious this is? How dangerous?

The axe crashes into the door. The wall shudders. A long, narrow sliver separates from the wood with a crack and flutters to the floor. Jude wrestles the axe back. I catch a glimpse of his dark eyes through the hole in the door. They focus on me.

"Sofia, please. Just open the door," he says.

I shake my head, and he slams the axe into the door again. The blade tears into the narrow opening, widening it into a large hole. Jude lowers the axe, gasping, and reaches through the hole. His hand slides through easily, but he can't get his arm past the jagged wooden edges. He swears and pulls his arm back.

"The Lord will not forsake us," Sister Lauren says, her voice trembling. "The Lord will not forsake us. The Lord will not . . ."

She sounds as if she's in shock. Her hand tightens around my shoulder, and I think of Jude's thick fingers circling my wrists, holding me in place. Her fingers seem small and fragile in comparison.

I catch sight of Jude through the hole in the door. He hoists the axe back over one shoulder, preparing to swing. I glance around the small room, looking for a weapon. Bandages and bottles of ointment crowd the metal cart, and dusty bottles glint from the shelves above the sink, but there's nothing sharp. Nothing heavy. There isn't even a window in here. We're trapped.

Sister Lauren bows her head. "Pray with me, Sofia," she says, fumbling for my hand. "We will be saved if we pray."

Jude slams his axe into the door again. Splinters fly into my legs, wood pricks through the thin fabric of the scrubs and nips at my ankles. Sister Lauren weaves her fingers through mine, and pulls me down to the floor beside her. Fear makes me clumsy. My knees slam hard into the tile, and I wince at the sudden pain. Sister Lauren folds her hands around my trembling fist, and presses her forehead to mine, my slinged arm wedged between us. Sweat breaks out on my palms. The Lord has never listened to my prayers before. Why would He start now?

"Our Father, who art in heaven," she whispers urgently, "hallowed be thy name . . ."

It's a prayer I've heard before, but I still don't know all the words. I listen to Sister Lauren recite it once all the way through. Her voice steadies as she speaks.

"Thy kingdom come, thy will be done, on earth as it is in heaven." She sounds strong now. Brave. It gives me courage.

"Our Father, who art in heaven," I recite, joining in as Sister Lauren starts the prayer over. My voice shakes and I stutter once or twice, but I manage to follow along. My fear dulls, just a little, as the prayer flows through me. I feel like someone's lit a fire just below my collarbone. I'm speaking to God at last. He's actually listening—I know it. He hears me in my time of need.

The axe crashes into the door. Wood cracks, and then something heavy thuds to the floor. The sound raises the hair on the back of my neck. I clench my hands together, my fingernails digging into my skin. My arms shake so badly that I can barely hold them steady.

"Thy kingdom come . . ." I pray. "Thy will be done . . ."

There's a beat of quiet. Then a lock clicks. Fear rips through my body.

He's in.

"On earth as it is in heaven . . ."

The door creaks open. Jude steps into the room. Cold seeps up through the tile, chilling my knees. But I'm not trembling anymore. The prayer has done what I always wanted it to do. I feel like God is with me, like He's protecting me. I glance up, still whispering the prayer under my breath.

Jude stands in the hallway, the axe hanging at his side. Crusty brown blood stains his shoulder, and a bite mark mangles the back of his hand. The skin around it has swollen and turned a deep, ugly red.

Good, I think. Jude grunts, heaving the axe up so that he's holding it with two hands.

I sneak a look at Sister Lauren. Her head is still bowed, her lips moving silently. She looks . . . serene. Peaceful. Maybe it's my imagination, or maybe there's some light slanting in through the open door, but I swear I see a halo of white illuminating her body, turning her into something holy.

"Our Father, who art in heaven," she starts again. She squeezes my fist, and I whisper the next part along with her. Our voices weave together, sounding like one. "Hallowed be thy name . . ."

Jude steps toward us, lifting the axe above his head. He releases a deep, animalistic cry that echoes off the walls of the tiny infirmary. My voice falters. I let go of Sister Lauren and throw my arm over my head.

Sister Lauren lifts her head and raises one hand. "Stop," she says.

I expect Jude to drive the axe through her face. I brace myself to feel the warm spray of blood across my cheeks, to hear the wet thud of her body hitting the floor. I cover my mouth with one hand.

But Jude lurches to a stop, looking almost confused. His fingers spring open, and the axe crashes to the ground. Jude looks down at his hands and then back up at Sister Lauren.

"I told you to *stop*," she says. Her voice sounds different this time, like it's layered with the sounds of dozens of other voices. I turn to her, amazed. Her eyes have taken on a golden cast. She looks like she's glowing from within.

The confusion drains from Jude's face. His skin looks pallid. Sickly. Desperation fills his eyes.

"What are you?" he asks. Sister Lauren stands and

moves toward him, her hand still raised in front of her. Her skin seems to radiate some unearthly light. Jude flinches and stumbles backward, smacking his leg against the ruined door. It swings open, slapping against the wall.

Jude turns and tears down the hall.

Sister Lauren lowers her hand. She strolls into the hallway after Jude without another word.

I push myself off the floor with one hand, knees shaking. My chest heaves. I feel light-headed, as if everything inside my skull has been scooped out and replaced with helium. I allow myself one second to calm down. Then I stand and race into the hallway after them, my sling slapping against my chest as I run.

The dormitory is empty. I don't hear footsteps or voices. I jog down the hall and throw open the door to the quad. Icy wind and snow whirls around me, pushing me back inside. I lean forward, against the wind, and force my way out.

Jude kneels in the middle of the snowy field, head bowed, almost as if he's praying. I step outside, letting the dormitory door swing shut behind me. Snow soaks through the bandages covering my feet. Snowflakes kiss the tip of my nose.

Sister Lauren stands over him. She's saying something, but the wind carries her voice in the other direction. She lifts a hand and Jude's shoulders begin to shake.

He's not praying. He's sobbing.

I hobble toward them as fast as I can. The light that seemed to radiate from Sister Lauren's skin grows brighter. I stare, stunned. This isn't sunlight or a trick of my eyes. Sister Lauren is actually glowing. I stop in my tracks. I no longer feel the wind whipping at my back, or the icy snowflakes landing on my nose and forehead. I feel warm.

God hasn't forsaken me—he's been here all along.

Sister Lauren clenches her hand into a fist. Jude's face swells like a balloon. He lifts his hands to his throat and claws at his own skin, leaving deep red gashes on his neck. I watch, horrified, as blood seeps into his eyes and trickles from his nose. His cheeks grow redder and redder. Purple and blue veins stand out against his skin.

Jude's eyelids stop flickering. His pupils roll back in their sockets. He pitches forward and lands in the snow. Dead.

"He saved us," I murmur, dropping to my knees. A giddy laugh bubbles up from my throat. "God saved us."

Slushy snow wets the knees of my scrubs. It seems to be coming down faster now. Icy shards prick my hands and the back of my neck. Wind howls through the naked trees, making the branches tremble.

None of it bothers me. I press my uninjured hand to my chest above the sling, a smile spreading across my face. God didn't forsake me. Tears pool in my eyes, freezing before they can slide down my cheeks.

Footsteps crunch through the snow. Sister Lauren lowers her hand to my head, her palm warm on my cold skin.

"Why are you crying?" she asks, brushing a lock of hair away from my forehead.

"Because God answered our prayers." I wipe the icy tears from my cheeks. "I'm not evil. This proves I can be good. That God loves me."

Sister Lauren throws her head back and releases a deep, strange laugh that sounds nothing like her normal voice. There's an edge to it. It could cut you.

"What's funny?" I ask. Sister Lauren stops laughing.

"*You* are," she says, touching her hand to my cheek. "You're one of us, Sofia. God didn't save you."

A chill that has nothing to do with the weather sweeps through my body. I picture it like frost spreading across a lake in winter. It freezes my lungs and chest, then crawls up my throat, turning my breath to ice.

"What are you talking about?" I want to look up, to prove to myself that this isn't really happening. But the cold holds me in place.

Sister Lauren kneels in front of me. I know it's Sister Lauren because she's wearing Sister Lauren's clothes. She has Sister Lauren's short brown hair, pulled back in a messy ponytail. Sister Lauren's silver necklace glints from her collarbone.

But something isn't right. I watch, horrified, as the skin on Sister Lauren's forehead and around her eyes smoothens. Her cheeks grow fuller and her pupils darken. Her mouth looks too big, too full of teeth. She shakes her head and Sister Lauren's hair falls loose of its ponytail. It shortens before my eyes, transforming into Brooklyn's familiar spiky pixie cut. The color fades into an orangey bleached blonde.

"Hello, Sofia," Brooklyn says. Her smile widens and, all at once, I realize why it seemed familiar that day in the van. It's Brooklyn's smile staring out at me from a stranger's face. "Did you miss me?"

CHAPTER TWENTY-EIGHT

I fall back on my heels, my hand propped against the ground behind me. This can't be real. It's a dream. I dig my fingers into the icy dirt.

"You aren't here," I say.

"I've been here the whole time," Brooklyn says.

"You're not here." I close my eyes. *Wake up,* I tell myself. *Wake the fuck up!*

Brooklyn stands, brushing the snow off her jeans.

"I told you I was coming for you, Sofia." She takes a step toward me, and I shift back onto my hand and knees in an awkward, one-armed, crablike crawl. Brooklyn's smile sharpens, amused. "You shouldn't be so surprised."

I think of my computer freezing, horrible pictures flashing across the screen. And then Brooklyn's voice whispering through the speakers: *I'm coming for you.* I crawl backward clumsily. Dull pain thumps through the soles of my feet, but all I can think of is getting away. Brooklyn takes a slow step toward me.

"It took a lot of work to get you in here. You should be grateful that I was willing to go through the trouble. Do you have any idea how hard I had to work to get your mom to crash her car?"

I close my eyes, a tear sliding over my cheeks. "You killed my mother?"

"Not just her. I had to take care of Abby Owens, too. And she *scratches*."

I think of the gauges on the windowsill back in my dorm, and understanding washes over me. Leena and Sutton's old roommate didn't get pregnant and run away like they thought. Brooklyn murdered her. A sob claws at my throat.

"Why are you doing this to me?" I choke out.

"Have you forgotten about our little talk in Leena's hospital room? *When someone does something unforgiveable, a demon attaches itself to them.* You did something unforgiveable, Sofia. You pulled a girl in front of a train and watched her die. And more than that, you want, you lust, you covet. You're weak. And I'm the price you have to pay for your sins."

I crawl farther backward, my broken arm swaying in the sling at my chest. "But *why*? Why bring me here?"

"You kept fighting your true nature, and I needed you alone and isolated. I needed to show you how good it feels to let the evil in. Admit it, Sofia. You've done some pretty twisted things but didn't you like it? Didn't it feel good?"

"No, it didn't." My voice cracks. Rocks and ice dig into my palm. "It felt terrible."

"Don't lie, Sofia. That's another sin." Brooklyn crouches in front of me. "You can't get away from me. You're mine. Pure *evil*. Like me."

"I'm not evil," I whisper. I keep crawling backward, the muscles in my arm and legs burning from the weight of my body. I should stand, *run*.

Brooklyn touches my chin with one finger. "And then you went and hooked up with the only guy on campus even more depraved than you are."

Brooklyn glances over her shoulder. Jude's body is still slumped in the snow a few yards away from us. "He had bad boy written all over him," she says. "I get why you liked him, though. You really are just like me."

A tree trunk slams into my back and I groan. I move my hand behind me, dragging my fingers over the cold bark. I'm blocked in. The only way out is through Brooklyn.

Brooklyn cocks her head. "Do you recognize where we are?"

I take in my surroundings, but I don't see anything familiar. Everything is white. The snow has become an icy sleet. It comes down at an angle, biting into my face and hands. Ice clings to my cheeks and eyelashes and hair.

"Let me help you remember," Brooklyn says. She stares at a spot in the snow, and the ground begins to tremble, as if there's something drilling up from below the earth. I push back up against the tree, hugging my knees to my chest.

"What is that?" I ask, staring hard at the snow. It shudders and tumbles away to reveal frozen dirt. A memory surfaces in my brain:

I'm crouching in the mud, digging a shallow hole while rain falls all around me. I clutch a bloody pillowcase in one hand.

"No," I breathe as it dawns on me that I'm sitting at the exact same spot where I buried Leena's bunny.

My pillowcase lurches out of the ground, crusty brown blood blossoming across the fabric like an ugly flower. It hovers in the air two feet above the snow, turning in a slow circle. Something inside it wriggles.

I swallow, tasting vomit on my tongue. "Don't," I say. "Please."

The pillowcase falls away, revealing Heathcliff's

frozen, bloody body. Skinny pink maggots burrow into his fur and writhe from his nose. They crowd around his eye sockets, eating the last of his rotten, bloodshot eyes.

"Do you know how good it feels to snap a bunny's neck?" Brooklyn asks, staring at the dead animal. She flicks her hand, and his body jerks violently, sending a few maggots flying to the snow. I scream, then curl my hand into a fist in front of my mouth. The bunny drops to the ground just inches from my foot. His back leg twitches, then goes still.

"It's like breaking a stick in half," Brooklyn says. "And then all the light drains out of the little fucker's eyes just like"—she snaps her fingers—"*that*. I think you'd enjoy it, Sofia. It makes you feel powerful. Like God."

"You're *sick*," I whisper, tearing my eyes away from the maggots eating Heathcliff's face.

"The trapdoor was trickier," Brooklyn says, her face twisting. "I thought I was going to have to make up some excuse to get Leena to walk across it at just the right moment, but I lucked out. She's clumsier than I expected."

Leena's scream echoes through my head. I shudder and squeeze my eyes shut. "Stop it," I say. "I don't want to hear any more."

"And then there was the night of the fire. Do you know Leena passed out in the trees just a few feet away from the chapel? You ran right past her, Sofia. You almost tripped on her crutch. If you had thought of someone other than yourself for a single second, you would have found her. If you'd have looked down even once, you would have seen her lying on the ground and she never would have had to die."

"You killed her, too," I say. A tear oozes out of the corner of my eye.

"I might have set the pieces, but it was the evil inside of you that sealed her fate. You coveted her life. You let your jealousy consume you. Leena was drunk, and she had a broken leg, and you left her alone in the woods. A good person wouldn't do that. A *good* person would have tried to help her. I dragged her back to the chapel, dumped her body, and knocked over a candle. But you watched the place burn." Brooklyn's smile quirks. "It was a beautiful fire, don't you think?"

Brooklyn's words wash over me. I don't want her to be right. I don't want to have evil inside of me. I feel my body shutting down, ready to give up.

"I tried to be good," I choke out. "I prayed. I asked God to help me."

"But he didn't come for you, did he? I did." Brooklyn says. "I did all of this for you, because you wanted it. You say you wanted to be a good girl, but that's not how you felt in your soul. You liked how it felt to hurt other people. *You are evil.* Admit it. I may have broken that bunny's neck and locked the chapel door, but you were the one who *liked* it."

Something inside of me releases. I didn't murder Heathcliff or Leena. Brooklyn set me up. She preyed on my jealousy and weakness.

I push myself away from the tree. All along I thought I was making these things happen myself. But it was just Brooklyn trying to break me. I feel stronger all of a sudden. As though the exhaustion and pain from this night has drained out of my body, leaving me whole again.

I'm not evil. Not yet, at least.

I push myself into a crouch, the muscles in my leg tingling. Brooklyn turns back around, frowning.

"What are you—"

I slap her across the face, relishing the sharp tingle of pain that shoots through my palm. "You're wrong," I spit. "I'm *nothing* like you."

And then I leap to my feet and run.

CHAPTER TWENTY-NINE

Icy grass crunches beneath my feet. My pant legs bunch around my ankles, the soggy fabric dragging in the snow. I tear across the quad, heading for the boys' dorms. Or where I think the dorms should be. Sister Lauren said a couple of other students stayed behind over the holidays—the girls' dorms were empty, but maybe one of the boys can help me.

Snow swirls around me. Frozen curls hang over my forehead, making it impossible for me to see even two feet in front of me. I brush them back but they just fall forward, blocking my vision again. Bandages peel away from the bottoms of my feet, and I feel a sharp sting of pain as my cuts burst open.

The dorms can't be far now. I take another step and my foot hits a patch of ice. It slides out from under me and I fall—*hard*—on my back. My head whacks against the frozen ground. A deep ache spreads across my shoulders and down my spine.

I lie there, watching the ice and snow swirl through the velvety black sky. Cold seeps through my sweatshirt and the seat of my pants. Misty gray puffs of breath hover above my mouth, and my heart beats against my ribs like an animal. The world around me seems to spin. I close my eyes, waiting for it to stop.

I could stay here, I think. I could just let her catch me.

But I open my eyes and drag myself up to my hands and feet, pausing to catch my breath before I stand. I take a tentative step to my left. I can't remember which direction I was running away from, or where I was headed. The snow is too thick. Everything looks the same.

I barely make it two steps into the blizzard before slamming into something solid. A *wall*. I slide my hand over icy brick, so relieved I could cry. I did it. I found the dorm. I follow the wall until the bricks give way to a door, and then I run my fingers along the wood, silently cheering when they brush against the cold brass doorknob. I twist, but the knob won't turn.

"Help me!" I curl my uninjured hand into a fist and beat against the door. The wood trembles and shakes in its frame. "Help me! Somebody! Help me, please!"

Nobody answers. I beat at the door until the skin peels away from my knuckles, and my voice goes hoarse from screaming. My broken arm lies limp and unresponsive in its sling. Tears leak from my eyes. I glance behind me, expecting to see Brooklyn barreling through the snow, her lips spread in a manic smile, fingers curled toward me like claws.

But there's no one. Only ice and trees and swirling darkness.

Two hands clamp down on my shoulders and spin me back around. I try to scream, but my voice gets lodged in my chest and I only manage a whimper. It takes me a long moment to recognize Father Marcus's icy blue eyes and the white tufts of hair sticking out from his balding head. He stands at the door I was just pounding against, squinting into the snowy darkness, a threadbare robe hanging from his shoulders.

"*You,*" I breathe. I don't know whether to be relieved or terrified. Father Marcus beat Jude. He made him into the monster that tied me up in the chapel and tortured me.

But there's no one else.

"Miss Flores?" Father Marcus's voice sounds thin and scratchy, like he just woke up. He swallows, his Adam's apple bobbing up and down in his throat. "You shouldn't be out of your dormitory. There's a storm—"

"*Please*," I cut in, gasping. "You have to help me. I'm being chased by the Devil."

The word *Devil* falls from my mouth unplanned. I cringe, certain I've lost my chance at getting help. He'll think I'm crazy.

But Father Marcus steps outside, his bare feet crunching in the snow. He crosses himself and something desperate flashes across his face. Something frightened.

"Where?" he asks.

"I don't know." I wipe the sopping, wet hair from my eyes and look back over my shoulder. "Close, I think. She was right behind—"

Brooklyn emerges from the darkness, smiling. Her skin looks almost blue, but she doesn't shiver. I shrink away from her, and Father Marcus moves in front of me, pushing me behind him with a sweep of his arm.

"I see you've gone for help," Brooklyn says, her smile twisting into something cruel and ugly. She hoists Jude's axe onto her shoulder. She must've stopped to collect it before coming after me. "Does this make you nervous?" she asks. She strokes the wooden handle, almost lovingly.

I swallow, tasting something sour and thick at the back of my throat. I stare at the axe's sharp blade, my stomach turning. I can practically feel it cutting open my skin, cracking my head like an egg.

I glance at Father Marcus's face. In the darkness, it's hard to see the lines on his skin, or the thin red cuts along his lips. He looks younger. He fumbles for something below his robe and brings out a heavy golden cross inlaid with red and green jewels. Brooklyn stares at the cross, her eyes narrowing into catlike slits.

"This one is beyond salvation, Father," she says, taking another slow step forward. "Her soul is weak. One more sin and she's ours forever."

"Back, demon!" Father Marcus holds the cross before him like a weapon.

Brooklyn stops walking. "You can't save her," she says.

"*Credo in Deum Patrem omnipotentem.*" It's the same prayer Jude recited while I lay crying on the floor, my wrists tied behind my back. But coming from Father Marcus, it sounds different. Stronger. He moves closer to Brooklyn. "*Creatorem caeli et terrae. Et in Iesum Christum, Filium eius unicum . . .*"

The smile fades from Brooklyn's lips. She stumbles backward.

"*Dominum nostrum, qui conceptus est de Spiritu Sancto, natus ex Maria Virgine . . .*"

The axe slips from Brooklyn's hand. She swears.

"*Passus sub Pontio Pilato, crucifixus, mortuus, et sepultus,*"

Father Marcus shouts. A zealous light fills his eyes. He grins wildly. It's pure, unfiltered joy—the kind of smile you see only on little kids and the mentally unstable. "Tremble before me, demon! You are nothing compared to the glory of God."

I turn back to Brooklyn. I want to see the look of fear in her eyes when she realizes she's lost. I want to see her desperate and trembling and afraid.

But Brooklyn isn't there anymore. All I see is swirling snow and the dark shadows of trees.

Cold fear seeps into my chest. "Where'd she go?"

"We've defeated her, child." Father Marcus's smile widens. He lifts his arms toward the sky in triumph. "Blessed be the name of the Lord," he booms.

I look around, but Brooklyn really is gone. I smile, tentatively, then wince as Father Marcus grabs me by the shoulder and pulls me into an awkward half hug, jostling my broken arm.

"You really think she's—" I stare at Farther Marcus, instantly forgetting the end of my sentence. His smile seems wrong, somehow. His mouth looks strained. Like the skin could rip apart.

Two tiny cuts slash past the corners of his lips. They're thin, almost like paper cuts.

"Father . . ." I whisper. The cuts lengthen, traveling up the sides of Father Marcus's cheeks. He makes a kind of gurgling, coughing sound deep in his throat. He drops his cross, and both of his hands reach for his face. His fingers tremble.

I should run, but I can't drag my eyes away from Father Marcus's grotesque face. The cuts grow deeper, wider. It looks as if someone is carving through the skin and muscle on his cheeks with a sharp, invisible knife. They reach past his cheekbones and up to the corners of his eyes. Blood trickles from his warped smile. It runs down his cheeks in a smooth red sheet, coating first his lips, and then his chin and neck. It stains his undershirt, and trickles from his shoulders and arms, sprinkling the snowy ground. It doesn't look red anymore. Now it's black and lumpy. Like tar.

Father Marcus tries to scream, but his mouth stays frozen in that horrible, morbid smile. The sound gets mangled in his throat, becoming something guttural and animalistic. He drops to his knees in the snow, still clawing at his face like he might, somehow, be able to push his skin back together. The manic gleam fades from his eyes. His pupils grow dull.

He falls over backward.

I stare at his limp body, frozen in horror. Memories play on a loop in my mind. I hear the echo of Riley's voice, screaming for me to help her, and then Brooklyn's hammer driving into her chest, the wet slap of her heart hitting the ground. I did nothing then. I stood by and let it all happen. Now it's happening again.

Town isn't far from here. If I run, and I don't look back, I could still get away. I stumble around the priest's body, trying to remember how to get to the main road.

Brooklyn's axe whips up from the ground and flies past me, sweeping straight through Father Marcus's neck. His head jerks away from his body. It rolls through the snow, leaving a trail of blood behind it. I stagger backward, gripping my chest with one hand. I don't realize I'm falling until I feel my knees slam into the hard, frozen ground.

Father Marcus's head rolls to a stop just a foot away from me. His dull eyes stare out at me, wide-open and shocked. His cracked blue lips are slightly parted. Lumpy black blood oozes from the stump where his head separated from his body. It doesn't look real.

I spot a twitch of movement in the blood. It's thin and black. Like an eyelash. My stomach turns. Another twitch, and then something scurries away from Father Marcus's head. A spider. It darts through the pool of his blood and disappears into the snow, leaving a trail of black behind it.

I pull myself backward as another spider crawls out of the severed head, and then another, and another. They swarm over one another, crawling through the blood and out into the snow. A spider crawls out of Father Marcus's nose and hurries across his face, its legs leaving tiny dots of blood on his skin. Another sticks a thin, spindly leg straight through his eyeball. I hear a kind of gushing, popping sound when it appears, and yellowish puss slithers down his face. I look away before the rest of the spider can crawl out.

I push myself back up to my feet. I can't stay here. I have to get away. My legs feel distant and weak, and I'm almost surprised when I'm able to lurch forward unsteadily. I take a wobbly step away from Father Marcus's body.

The smell of smoke drifts through the air. I freeze.

A tiny orange flame unfurls from the ground directly in front of my big toe. It twists and dances into the night. Smoke stings my eyes, and the heat presses against me, coaxing sweat from my skin. I stumble backward, coughing, and waving a hand in front of my face. The fire roars and curls and spreads through the snow as if it's gasoline.

A circle of flames grows around me, trapping me.

Something moves in the darkness beyond the circle of fire. I stare into the shadows, orange and red light searing my eyes. Sweat gathers in the small of my back, and heat presses into my neck and legs and hands. The circle closes in around me, flames reaching for my body like hands.

I catch a flicker of movement to my left. I whirl around, heart pounding. But it's just the fire.

"Where are you?" I shout. I tighten my hands into fists and turn around slowly. I can feel Brooklyn watching me beyond the flames, circling me like a predator. Wind howls through the trees, making the branches shiver and quake.

The sound sharpens into a low, cackling laugh. Brooklyn's laugh. A space opens in the flames, and she steps into the circle with me.

"Why are you doing this?" I ask. "What do you want?"

Her grin widens. I can see all her teeth.

"I want you to kill me," she says. She tilts her head and folds her hands together, like she's about to pray. Everything about it looks perverse. The Devil playing at being innocent. "Isn't that what you want? To be rid of me at last?"

Brooklyn flicks her wrist and the flames slither closed behind her. They grow taller and brighter, clawing at the night sky like fingers. Fire licks at my back and ankles. I smell something burning and dance forward, yelping. Brooklyn laughs.

"Or you could try to run. But I'll find you. I'll always find you, Sofia."

Fury flares through me. I can see the rest of my life

play out like a movie. Every few months, I'll head to a new city and try to start over. Brooklyn will leave me alone long enough to make a few friends. To feel safe. And then she'll destroy everything. She'll snap her fingers and burn it to the ground.

I won't live like this. I take a step forward. Brooklyn cocks an eyebrow.

"Come on, Sofia. You know you want to. Get your revenge. Make me suffer."

I press my lips together, tasting blood at the corners of my mouth. Father Marcus's body lies in the snow a few feet away, his ruined smile still leaking thick, tar-like blood. Jude's axe sits on the ground next to his lifeless hand.

Brooklyn's grin quirks even wider.

I know this is a trick. I feel the wrongness rushing through my veins like blood. *One more sin,* Brooklyn said.

But deeper than that, I feel something else. *Want.* It hums through me, making my bones tremble. I'm tired of being everyone else's punching bag. I want to destroy something.

I kneel in the snow and wrap my fingers around the axe's thick wooden handle. It's heavy and hard to lift with just one hand. The want buzzes louder. It fills my ears with static. It makes my skin purr.

"Give it to me," Brooklyn says, and this time she

isn't smiling. Her mouth is a snarl. A dare. "You know I deserve it. Prove to me that you're not weak."

Something inside me snaps. I lift the axe, barely noticing the weight pulling at my muscles, or my broken arm burning with pain in its sling. I swing, and the blade sinks into Brooklyn's chest. It rips through cloth and skin; it cracks ribs and tears muscle. Blood sprays my face and neck and hands. It smells coppery, like pennies, but below that is something else. The smell of something going rotten.

I yank the axe out of Brooklyn's chest. The blade makes a slurping sound as it leaves her body. Brooklyn glances at the wound casually, like she's examining a new tattoo or piercing. She drags her fingers through the blood, staining them red.

"Sofia—" Blood bubbles from her mouth and streams over her chin. It coats her teeth and lips.

I swing the axe again and Brooklyn flies backward. Her body smacks into the icy ground, arms flailing above her head like a rag doll. I climb on top of her and I bring the axe down, over and over. Her blood feels tacky and warm against my skin. Almost like candlewax. I feel it in my nostrils and in my ears and in the corners of my eyes. It sinks between my fingers and crusts up under my fingernails.

Brooklyn laughs. The sound is deep and unnerving.

It echoes in my ears. I bring the axe down again. My muscles burn, and my broken arm has gone numb, but I keep swinging. It's as if I'm being controlled by something else, something much stronger than my weak, ruined body.

The flames around me flicker, and then die, until all that's left is a black circle of soot. I pull the axe out of Brooklyn's body and swing it again, almost enjoying the low, meaty sound of the blade sinking through her organs. Brooklyn's eyes have rolled back in her head. Her chest is shredded and bloody. But, *still*, she laughs. The sound echoes through the air. It's like an air siren. Like an emergency alert, warning people of a flood or a tornado. Doesn't anyone else hear it?

Lights flash from in the trees. I notice voices, too, but they don't seem real. They're like something out of a dream. I should look up, but all I can think about is Brooklyn. I have to destroy her. I have to—

"Put down your weapon!"

The command cuts through me. I freeze, finally lifting my head. The sun has started to rise, and a silvery-white glow paints the horizon. The scene around me slams into focus.

Two police cruisers have pulled onto the quad, their thick tires crushing the dry, icy grass. The cops Sister Lauren called. They've parked a few yards away, doors thrown open to act as barricades. Police officers duck behind the doors, aiming silver-and-black guns through the open windows. Red and blue lights flash from the tops of the cruisers, and a siren howls through the air.

I glance around the quad, dazed. Father Marcus lies crumpled in the snow a few feet away. He's not just dead, he's been completely torn apart. The police officer closest to me levels his gun at my head. His hands tremble.

"I said *put down your weapon!*"

"It's okay," I shout. I stand, my legs wobbling beneath me. "I already—"

A half-dozen hammers click into place.

"Drop your weapon and put your hands on your head!"

Weapon? I glance at my hand and see that I'm still clutching the bloody axe. I look down at Brooklyn's body.

Brooklyn's bleached pixie cut has grown back into Sister Lauren's shaggy brown bob. The wrinkles have slithered back across her forehead and crinkled the skin around her eyes. Her cheeks have hollowed, making her look older. Sister Lauren's eyes stare up at me, cloudy and still.

I've killed an innocent person. Brooklyn is gone.

"No," I whisper. I lower my arm to my side, and the axe slips from my fingers, hitting the ground with a hollow thwack. Dimly, I notice a couple of police officers leap out from behind the cruiser and race toward me. Someone jerks my arm behind my back, and slides a cold, metal handcuff over my wrist. My broken arm is still in its sling, so he lets the other cuff dangle from my wrist, useless. Another officer has his gun aimed at my head. He's saying something I don't quite hear.

"You have the right to remain silent. Anything you . . ."

But all of this seems far away. Like it's happening to someone else, or like it's a story I heard once, but forgot the end of. I stare at Sister Lauren's face and horror lodges itself deep inside my gut. It seeps into my organs and my bones and my skin. It becomes a part of me at a cellular level.

"That's not her," I say, more to myself than to the officers leading me back to the police car. "You don't understand. She was a demon, but I killed her. We're safe now. We're finally safe."

CHAPTER THIRTY

I've been a patient at the Mississippi Hospital for the Criminally Insane for a month and two days when Nurse Simmons tells me I have a visitor. I curl my fingers into the sleeves of my straitjacket, digging my stumpy nails into the canvas. I'm not sure who it could be. Everyone I know is dead.

The visitor's room looks almost exactly like a suburban living room, except that bars cover the windows and all the paintings and furniture are bolted into place. Two men wait inside. One wears a stiff blue policeman's uniform. The other is dressed in a suit and tie, a wool coat hanging from his shoulders. They sit shoulder to shoulder on the white sofa, a manila folder on the coffee table in front of them.

I stiffen and Nurse Simmons places a hand on my elbow, gently nudging me forward. "It's okay, Sofia. The nice officers here just have a few questions for you."

She moves her hand to my back to steady me as I slide onto the hard plastic chair bolted to the ground. She's still holding the restraint chain attached to my straitjacket. When I'm seated, she kneels and fastens it to a metal ring protruding from the chair, then slides a heavy padlock through the links. The chain gives me a one-foot circle of freedom.

I lift my head, studying the men through my greasy curls.

"Thank you for speaking with us, Sofia," the man in the suit says. He's short, with broad arms and shoulders and skinny legs. He reminds me of a bulldog.

"It's nice to see you again, Sofia," the man in the police uniform says. He flashes me a nervous smile. There's a gap between his two front teeth.

"I know you." I sit up straight, shaking the hair out of my eyes. "You came to my house the night my mother had her accident. You're the officer who told me she was dead."

The officer's smile vanishes. He licks his chapped lips.

"I'm Detective Ramirez, and this is Officer Schultz,"

the man in the suit says. "We were hoping we could ask you a few questions."

I catch a whiff of musky-scented cologne as he flips the folder open and slides it toward me. I wrinkle my nose and lean closer, metal chains clinking like bells against my chair.

A photograph of a teenage girl lies inside the folder. She stares up at me, only she's not really staring because she's dead. Choppy, bleached-blond hair frames her hollow cheeks and vacant eyes. Skinny blue veins spiderweb across her skin. She lies on a metal table, a white sheet pulled up to her neck.

"This girl was found in the woods surrounding Riley Howard's family lake house," Officer Ramirez explains. "Can you tell us whether you recognize her as the girl you knew as Brooklyn Stephens?"

"This is highly inappropriate!" Nurse Simmons snaps. "Sofia is a very sick young woman." She tries to close the folder so I won't see the photograph, but Officer Schultz blocks her hand.

"Miss Flores is a key witness in an ongoing murder investigation," he explains. "We need her to identify the body."

Detective Ramirez brushes a piece of lint from the front of his coat. "You're welcome to wait outside if it'll make you more comfortable," he adds.

Nurse Simmons presses her lips into a thin line. "Very well," she says. But she doesn't leave the room. She stands against the wall, crossing her arms over her chest.

Officer Schultz turns back to me. "Sofia? Can you identify this girl?"

I study the photograph. The dead girl has Brooklyn's hair and Brooklyn's face. Brooklyn's black liner is smudged around her eyes. I've seen her lips twist into Brooklyn's half-crazed smile.

"I don't know," I mumble.

Officer Schultz and Detective Ramirez share a look. Officer Schultz leans forward.

"Don't get too close," Nurse Simmons warns, but Officer Schultz doesn't seem to hear her. He slides his elbows onto the coffee table.

"Sofia," he asks. "Help us out here. Is this the monster who murdered your friends?"

I feel my lips curve into a smile. *Monster.* I guess you could call the thing that killed Riley a monster. I prefer to call it *Diablo*, like my grandmother does. I glance down at the photograph. Brooklyn lies on the metal table, but she's hollow—a shell. There's no monster inside of her anymore. It's moved on, leaving her dead body behind.

I murmur something below my breath and Officer Schultz frowns, leaning closer. The wooden coffee table groans beneath his weight. "What was that, Sofia?"

"Officer, *please*," Nurse Simmons says, taking a quick step away from the wall. "Don't get too—"

I lunge forward, catching the fleshiest part of Officer Schultz's earlobe between my teeth. He screams and jerks away from me but I clamp down—tight. The salty bite of blood hits my tongue. A bit of warm flesh comes loose in my mouth.

Nurse Simmons digs a needle out of her pocket. It flashes under the fluorescent lights. She jabs it into my neck, and something cool and tranquil spreads through my body.

I pull away from the police officer and spit his skin onto the coffee table. It slides across the wood, leaving a trail of blood behind it. A hot, hungry feeling stirs inside of me. It's even stronger than the drugs coursing through my veins.

"That isn't the monster," I say, grinning. I feel Officer Schultz's blood on my lips. "You've got the wrong girl."

The demon isn't inside Brooklyn anymore. It's inside me.

ACKNOWLEDGMENTS

As always, I have a mountain of people to thank for bringing this book to life. First of all, a huge thank you to editor extraordinaire Hayley Wagreich, for reading this book a million times and helping me find the story at the center of all the gore. Hopefully, those yoga bells won't sound so creepy anymore! I couldn't have done this without the rest of my Alloy family there to support me—particularly Josh Bank and Sara Shandler, who never cease to be absolutely brilliant. Thank you to Heather David, for all your help on the social media front (particularly those amazing Twitter banners) and Annie Stone for that first brainstorming session. Thanks, also, to Theodora Guliadis for letting me take over the PLL Twitter for a day. I can't believe this is my job sometimes.

The team at Razorbill is the best in the business and I am so lucky to have them behind me. I couldn't have written this book without Jessica Almon's brilliant, insightful notes, or the nonstop support I received from Casey McIntyre and Ben Schrank. Sometimes I just sit and stare at this book's perfect cover, and I have Kristin Smith to thank for the eye-stopping design. Felicia Frazier, Rachel Lodi, Venessa Carson, Alexis Watts, and the rest of Razorbill's sales, marketing, and publicity team all worked so hard to help people discover my books. You guys are wonderful! In addition to the people named here, there are so many others working behind the scenes to make this book happen. I am grateful to all of you. I couldn't have done it without your support.

And finally, thanks to my fabulous, supportive family and friends. I'm consistently blown away by all of you. I couldn't have asked for better people in my life.

And, of course, thank you to Ron, who hasn't read this book yet but will, even though it'll give him nightmares.

UNCOVER THE ORIGINS OF EVIL.

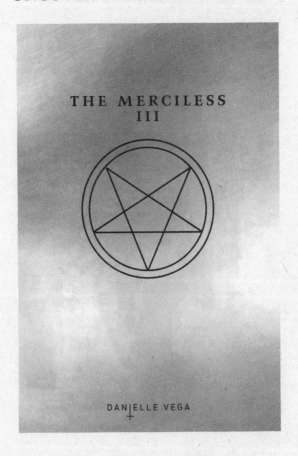

Turn the page for a sneak peek!
Reader discretion is advised

PROLOGUE

The blood feels warm beneath the cold metal. She shifts her body, trying to lessen the weight of the chains, but this only makes them dig deeper, bite harder, until her skin is raw. Shredded. A drop of blood winds around her wrist and splatters onto the floor next to her bare foot. It looks like a tiny flower. Red and perfect.

"Help," she whimpers, but the word sounds too small for what's happening to her.

A man laughs.

She jerks her head to the left, and then to the right, but she doesn't see him. The chair is stiff behind her back, and the chains hold her firmly in place. There are no windows in the small room, no overhead lights. It's very dark, lit only by flickering candle-light that glimmers over the objects hanging on the walls.

A blade. A spike. A chain with sharp, cutting edges.

She tries not to look at them.

A footstep sounds, and then a shadow falls over her. She hears him breathing. She presses her lips together, trying to be quiet, but a sob escapes, echoing off the wall.

"Shhh." His voice is barely a whisper. "God is listening. He wants you to be strong."

He steps away from her, and there's a sound like metal scratching on metal. He's taken something from the wall.

No. Not that. Not again. She throws her weight against the chains. She curls her toes into the floor. She twists and slides, but she can't get free. He's speaking again, telling her to be calm. To stay still. She doesn't want to stay still.

He lifts something over his head. It sounds big. Heavy.

"This will be over soon," he says.

But he's lying.

CHAPTER ONE

I stare at the phone for so long my eyesight blurs.

"Ring," I whisper. I rest my chin in my hands and wrap my fingers around my face, digging them through my tightly braided hair and directly into my scalp. "Come on. Ring."

The phone refuses. It's a useless hunk of white plastic that's so old it's almost yellow. I pick it up and the dial tone pierces my ears with a sharp beep. Not the shitty landline's fault, then. I drop the phone back onto the receiver with a little more force than necessary.

It's only the first night of the helpline, but so what? Why the hell isn't anyone calling? The people in this town need serious help, and I know everyone's heard about what I'm doing. Between weeks of Facebook posts and flyers and announcements over the school loud-speaker, there isn't a single person in this suburb who doesn't know about *Brooklyn's cute little project*. Or whatever they call it behind my back.

I even agreed to set up the helpline in the school basement, even though there are dozens of empty class-rooms right upstairs. It smells like a toilet down here, and there aren't enough overhead lights to illuminate the long, narrow room. And the walls are all plastered with freaky motivational posters. *You have potential! Reading is winning!*

I uncap a Sharpie and doodle tiny vampire kittens all over my last Teen Helpline flyer. I came up with the idea a month ago, when a story about a teen suicide in Southaven was all over the news. People kept saying this poor girl killed herself because she didn't have any-one to talk to, which I thought was bullshit. The only helpline around here is affiliated with the community center and run by this super-conservative moms group that won't mention the word *drugs* and doesn't believe in gay people.

I'm not even kidding. They *don't believe in them*. Like they're unicorns.

Anyway, the girl who killed herself needed someone real to talk to. Like me.

I wanted to call my project the Teen Hell Line (get it? Because being a teenager is hell?), but Ms. Carey vetoed the swearing. Now I'm stuck with Teen Helpline, which is so boring. No wonder nobody's calling. Or maybe the teens in this town want to stay screwed up.

I watch the clock tick toward 8:00 PM. I'm drawing a tiny set of fangs on another kitten when the phone rings.

Finally. I grab the receiver. "Teen Helpline, this is Brooklyn."

"Hello?" a girl asks. "Is this where you call to get advice about stuff?"

"That's right," I say. The helpline is supposed to be anonymous, but this girl's voice sounds familiar. "Did you have something you wanted to talk about?"

"You can't tell anyone what I say, right?"

She's definitely someone I know. I clear my throat. *Anonymous*, I remind myself. That's the whole point.

"I have to call the police if you tell me you're in danger, but otherwise that's right. This is completely anonymous."

Some of the tension leaves my chest. All those YouTube videos I watched to prepare must've helped, because my voice was calm and warm—totally professional.

"Okay." The girl pauses. Takes a deep breath. "Because I was wondering whether you knew if, um, I could get pregnant . . ."

I flip my notebook to the page where I jotted the

phone numbers to Planned Parenthood and a couple of counseling centers.

". . . from a toilet seat," the girl finishes.

My fingers go still. "Damn it. Deirdre, is that you?"

The girl on the other end of the line dissolves into a fit of laughter.

"You left one of your flyers at the shop," Deirdre explains. She works at Liquid Courage, this tiny tattoo parlor in downtown Friend. I can picture her there now, a couple of ballpoints sticking out of her frizzy hair, bare feet kicked up on the front desk. "Sorry, but I couldn't help myself. It's been slow as shit tonight."

She laughs again, releasing a snort that makes her sound like a donkey. Normally I'd give her shit about it, but right now I'm too pissed.

"You're tying up the line," I snap. "Someone with a real problem might be trying to call."

"Oh, please. Has anyone called? Like, at all?"

I grind my teeth together. "That doesn't mean nobody *will*. The whole point is to be here. It's not a popularity contest."

"Whatever. It's just a little advice line."

I bite back a bitchy comment. Deirdre and I are friends because we both understand that life is shit. The difference is that Deirdre thinks it's funny, and I want to fix it.

"Just because you'd see a house on fire and watch it burn doesn't mean some of us wouldn't try to help," I say.

"Don't start with me," Deirdre moans. "Ditch the holier-than-thou attitude and come have a drink at Liquid. Santos already left, so we'll have the place to ourselves."

Santos is a bad decision I made last summer. I cringe at the memory. "What about Ollie?" I ask. Ollie and Santos own the tattoo parlor together. "Ollie said he'd fire your ass if he caught you drinking at work again."

"*Please.* Ollie loves me. You still grounded?"

She says "grounded" like someone else might say "contagious." Deirdre graduated from high school last year, moved into her own place, and immediately forgot what it was like to have parents. She acts like being sixteen and living at home are rare, horrible diseases. School hasn't been the same without her, but we still hang out almost every day.

"Officially, I'm grounded until I learn that 'two wrongs don't make a right,'" I say, cradling the phone against my shoulder and making air quotes she can't see. "Unofficially, I'm betting they'll give in by tomorrow night. Dad's been complaining that I 'sigh too loudly' when he's grading papers, so I know he's ready to get rid of me."

"They didn't buy that stealing lipstick was a political statement?"

Last week, I got caught pocketing a tube of Rich Girl Red from Drugmart. It's bullshit, because the people who own Drugmart are sexist assholes who don't sell day-after contraceptives, and refuse to give their employees health insurance. They *deserve* to be stolen from. Unfortunately, my parents didn't see it that way. Neither did the Drugmart security guards. They tell me I'm lucky they let me off with just a warning.

"Look, Deirdre, I really gotta go. Someone—"

"Yeah, yeah," Deirdre says. "Call me when the wardens let you out of your cell, okay?"

"Will do."

I drop the phone onto its crusty receiver and lean back in my chair, sighing. The motivational poster directly in front of me shows a boy in a thick sweater running down the path toward a quaint-looking school building. He's holding a report card, and he has this wide, vacant smile plastered across his face. The slogan reads: *Always do your best!*

I slide my chair over, angling my body so I'm not facing him anymore. He seems smug.

The clock ticks from the wall. *Tick. Tick. Tick.* The helpline is open until eight. Someone still has thirteen minutes to call. I can handle thirteen more minutes.

A spider creeps across the floor, legs twitching. I lean over in my chair and crush him beneath the sole of my combat boot.

Tick. Tick. Tick.

Five minutes left. I color my nails in with my Sharpie. A phone beeps—I jump, drawing a thick line across my pinkie—but it's just my cell, not the helpline phone. I dig it out of my pocket and check the screen.

It's a text from my mom: Pick up milk on your way home?

OK, I type back. I shove the phone back into my pocket, and then lick my thumb and try to scrub the Sharpie line off my pinkie.

Tick. Tick. Tick.

Two minutes left. I stand, and start shoving my books and notes back into my backpack. It used to be my mom's, from when she was in high school, and it's falling apart. The only things holding the threadbare fabric together are the faded patches ironed onto it. There's an alien face with black, almond-shaped eyes, a rainbow-colored peace sign, and a logo for Pearl Jam.

I pull my jacket on, catching one last glance of the *Always do your best!* boy as I fumble with the buttons. The photograph looks like it was taken in the fifties. It's black-and-white, and the edges have all turned brown and gone dog-eared. I do the math in my head. If the boy had been fourteen when the photo was taken, and the photo is sixty-five years old, he'd be in his late seventies now. Or dead.

"See you later, dead boy," I say as I head for the door. I start up the creaky wooden stairs.

A high-pitched ringing sounds behind me.

I groan. It's probably Deirdre again, or another prank call. I drop my backpack on the floor and hurry back to the phone.

"Teen Helpline," I answer, balancing the receiver between my chin and shoulder. "This is Brooklyn."

Silence. I sink down into my chair. "Deirdre, come on, I have to—"

A ragged inhale interrupts me. I stop talking. That doesn't sound like Deirdre. I press my lips together, my heart thudding in my chest. It's a real caller. My *first* real caller.

I read online that you're supposed to be patient with the kids who call in. Not everyone wants to talk about what's bothering them right away. Sometimes people just want to hear another voice and know there's someone else out there.

"You don't have to say anything if you don't want to," I say, doing my best to keep my voice soft and soothing. "But I'm here to listen when you're ready. Do you think you can tell me your name?"

I wait for a beat, staring at the black smudge on the floor that used to be a spider. One of its legs twitches— then goes still. The caller doesn't answer me, but I hear slow, shallow breathing, so I know she's there.

"Okay, you don't have to tell me your name," I say. The breathing stops. "Can you—"

A loud, desperate sob echoes from the receiver. I'm stunned into silence, my heart beating so hard it makes my chest ache.

"Hello?" I try again. "Are you safe?"

The crying dies down a little. "Help," a girl's voice whispers. "He's . . . he's hurting me."

I grip the phone with both hands. "Who's hurting you? Where are you?"

There's a beat of silence. I press my ear hard into the receiver, listening for breath, crying, *anything*. There's a *click* and the dial tone blares.

She's gone.

I don't remember standing, but I'm on my feet and my chair has toppled to the floor. I'm still holding the phone. The dial tone echoes off the concrete walls of the basement.

Calm down, I tell myself, placing the phone back on its hook. This could still be another prank. I left flyers for the helpline all over Friend, and there are more assholes in this stupid suburb than anywhere else in Mississippi. I pick my chair up and sit down again, thinking.

She said someone was hurting her. It didn't sound like a prank. It sounded like a real girl in trouble.

I dial 911 with trembling fingers.

"Friend Police Department, what's your emergency?" The woman's voice is clipped and efficient, with a hint of the familiar Mississippi accent I've worked so hard to lose.

"I work at a teen helpline," I explain. "I just got a really weird call . . ."

I repeat what the girl said to the operator. For a second, I hear only the clacking of computer keys. Then, "Thanks for the information, miss. We've traced the call, and the address we're showing is 4723 North Maple Avenue. Does that sound right?"

Her voice has the rote tone of someone verifying information I already have. I clear my throat. "I . . . I don't know. It's anonymous."

There's a pause. "Of course. We'll dispatch an officer right away."

I wait for her to say more, but she doesn't. A second later, I'm greeted with another sharp dial tone.

I hang up the phone and drop my head into my hands, my palms slick with sweat. I feel like I could run ten miles. Like I could scale the side of a building. But all I can really do is sit here. It's up to the cops to help now.

I swallow, my heartbeat slowing. Friend isn't exactly known for its stellar police force. The cops here spend most of their time trying to catch underage kids sneaking into dive bars, and yelling at homeless people for loitering outside of gas stations. Friend is very safe. Which is just another way of saying boring.

I drum my fingers against the table. *4723 North Maple Avenue.* That's just a few blocks away from the school.

The police station is all the way across town. Friend isn't big, but it'll take them at least ten minutes to wind through the narrow, twisting streets.

I think about the fear in the girl's voice, her desperate sob. *He's hurting me.* She might not have ten minutes. I could hop on my bike and be there in two minutes, easy.

I grab my backpack and race up the stairs.